SENT
to the
DEVIL

ALSO BY LAURA LEBOW

The Figaro Murders

SENT
to the
DEVIL

LAURA LEBOW

MINOTAUR BOOKS
NEW YORK

www.minotaurbooks.com

Library of Congress Cataloging-in-Publication Data

Names: Lebow, Laura, author.
Title: Sent to the devil / Laura Lebow.
Description: First edition. | New York : Minotaur Books, 2016.
Identifiers: LCCN 2015045813| ISBN 9781250053565 (hardcover) | ISBN
    9781466856202 (e-book)
Subjects: LCSH: Da Ponte, Lorenzo, 1749–1838—Fiction. |
    Librettists—Fiction. | Murder—Investigation—Fiction. | BISAC: FICTION /
    Mystery & Detective / Historical. | GSAFD: Biographical fiction. |
    Historical fiction. | Mystery fiction.
Classification: LCC PS3612.E28 S46 2016 | DDC 813/.6—dc23
LC record available at http://lccn.loc.gov/2015045813

Our books may be purchased in bulk for promotional, educational, or business use. Please contact your local bookseller or the Macmillan Corporate and Premium Sales Department at 1-800-221-7945, extension 5442, or by e-mail at Macmillan SpecialMarkets@macmillan.com.

First Edition: April 2016

10 9 8 7 6 5 4 3 2 1

Prologue

Peter Albrechts's patience was running out.

Like most military men of high rank, he could easily wait weeks for an enemy under siege to surrender, but had little forbearance when subordinates were ill-prepared, inefficient, or tardy.

Where was the damned man? It was past one o'clock. He should be home in his bed, not standing in the middle of a dark, deserted city square. Strict adherence to a routine was important for a warrior. He must stay fit for battle, in case the emperor should call on him to lead the troops once again. True, he had been retired for many years, but he was still more capable than that fool Lacy the emperor had put in charge.

He walked over to the monument in the center of the plaza. He'd always liked the bronze column, dedicated to the Virgin Mary, although he scoffed at the legend that claimed that she had aided Vienna in its war with Sweden a hundred years ago. Victory was achieved through discipline and good planning, not through prayer and superstition.

A slight rustle sounded from behind the stone plinth of the monument.

"Who's there?" he called.

There was no answer. He shrugged. Probably just the breeze. It had been warm that day, unusual for Vienna in April. He had heard that summer weather had arrived in Semlin already. The troops camped there had better invade Belgrade soon, or men would begin to die in the swampy conditions caused by the heavy spring rains.

He glanced down at the paper in his hand. He had no time for such nonsense. Once his correspondent showed himself, he would quickly learn that he had chosen the wrong man to threaten. One did not insinuate such things about a war hero. How dare the scoundrel sully the Albrechts name!

The breeze whispered from behind the plinth once more.

He had waited long enough. He shoved the page into his coat pocket and turned away from the monument.

There was a stirring behind him, and then his body was jerked backward. A heavy arm circled his neck.

"Good evening, General," a voice hissed in his ear. "I knew you would come."

"Who are you?" the old man cried as he struggled to pull the arm away. "What is the meaning of this?"

His assailant twisted him around and shoved him onto the low stone steps of the monument. "Are you ready?" he asked. As he leaned over the general, he pulled a small dagger from his coat pocket.

"Ready for what? Who are you? What is it you want—money?" He tried to push himself up, but his aged arms betrayed him, and he fell back. He stared up at the man's face. "You! What do you want with me?"

"You know what I want you to do," the man hissed. He knelt, pushed the general's head against the cold stone, and brought the dagger to his wrinkled neck.

Rage surged through the old man's veins as the man continued to talk. Blood pounded in his ears, deafening him to the words. *How dare he! I am General Peter Albrechts!*

"No!" He tried to shout, but his voice was merely a croak. "No! I will not!"

His assailant grunted. He pulled back his arm. The old man saw a blurred motion, and then pain seared his neck.

An owl hooted in the distance as blood spattered over the stone steps.

"I am dying!" he cried. But he could not hear his own voice, only a loud gurgling, and after a few moments, nothing.

PART I

A Solemn Oath

One

The second message was waiting on my desk when I arrived at my office.

The cheap paper had been hastily folded, sealed with a messy blob of wax, and its front scrawled with the words "Lorenzo Da Ponte, Court Theater." I turned it over in my hands. There were no marks on the outside to show that the letter had traveled through the postal system, and no insignia pressed into the wax to identify the sender. I went to my cupboard, placed the note on a high shelf, returned to my desk, and pulled out the aria I had been writing. I had no time this morning for the game my mysterious correspondent insisted on playing.

I'd been working night and day for the last nine months. I am the poet of the Court Theater in Vienna, where I am responsible for editing all of the librettos—the texts—and coordinating the productions of operas performed there. I augment my salary by taking on commissions to write librettos myself, and last fall I had written three at the same time, one for each of the city's top composers. The opera I had written for my friend Wolfgang Mozart, *Don Giovanni*, had debuted in Prague six months ago, and had been a big hit there. There was no rest for us after our triumph, however, because soon after, Emperor Joseph II had ordered a performance of the opera here in Vienna. Mozart and I were busy adapting our work to the more sophisticated tastes of the imperial capital. And once *Don Giovanni* premiered in May, I had commissions for several more librettos. I was tired. Sometimes I wished that I'd been born a Viennese nobleman, instead of a leatherworker's son from the Veneto who had to work for a living.

But although I was overworked, I had to admit that I was happy with my life in Vienna. I loved my job, and had achieved professional recognition for my talents. I treasured my relationship with the emperor, who had supported me from the very first day he had appointed me to my post. I had a small circle of friends with whom I could discuss literature, art, and music. And lately, I had even returned to writing my own poetry, which was my first love.

When I had edited the aria to my satisfaction, I put it into my satchel. My stomach grumbled as I pulled my watch from my waistcoat pocket. Half past one already! I had an appointment for dinner at two. I closed my satchel and went to the cupboard, where I pulled on my cloak. My eyes went to the high shelf. I sighed, grabbed the message and shoved it into my cloak pocket.

. . .

Outside in the Michaelerplatz—the gateway to the Hofburg, the large complex of buildings that housed the imperial government and the emperor's personal apartments—small groups of newly inducted soldiers in crisp, shiny uniforms stood under the leaden sky laughing and teasing one another, their smooth faces flushed with excitement. In the Kohlmarkt, I stopped and peeled off my cloak. The spring weather had been unseasonably balmy for a week now.

At the end of the Kohlmarkt, a small crowd had gathered to watch two laborers bang a large board over the entrance of one of the city's most popular print shops. A large painted sign indicated that it had been closed by the Ministry of Police. The once-free presses of Vienna must now be cautious about what they printed, or suffer the fate of this one. I hurried by. I had had my own encounter with the Ministry of Police two years before, and now tried to avoid trouble whenever possible.

I turned into the Graben. As late as last autumn, the large plaza had been the place to see and be seen for Viennese society, but as the snows of winter melted and the emperor and his troops marched off to war, the large expanse had lost its frivolous air. Instead of promenading down the plaza and stopping to chat with friends, people now hurried to their destinations, greeting one another with nothing but a quick nod.

"We are the aggressors in this war, not the Turks!" Ahead of me, a young man stood on an upended crate at the base of the elaborate plague column that dominated the middle of the Graben. A few shoppers and workmen were gathered around one side of the monument's enormous plinth, which was decorated with sculptures symbolizing the triumph of faith over disease. I stopped at the back of the group, nodding at a square-jawed man in his early thirties who leaned on an ornate stick next to me.

"Our ally Russia is to blame!" the young man shouted. His features were handsome, but his long hair was tangled and his beard unkempt. He wore a threadbare coat over breeches that were torn at both knees.

"That's nonsense!"

I started as the man next to me called to the protester.

"Read the papers. The Turks have been stocking arms since the Crimean crisis. They are stirring up the peoples in the Caucasus against Russia."

"The Turks are just trying to defend themselves, sir," the orator replied. "Russia provoked them. The emperor was a fool to sign a treaty with—"

My neighbor snorted. "The Turks declared war first!" he shouted. "You are the fool! How can you believe they are an innocent party?"

A group of market women had stopped to watch the argument.

"They had to declare war. They had to defend themselves before Russia's army grouped along their borders—"

"If the Turks are just defending themselves, as you say, why did they refuse offers by France and Britain to mediate their dispute with Russia?" my neighbor asked.

The war protester turned to the newcomers in the crowd. "Friends, you look like solid citizens of the empire. Do you want your fathers, your sons, your brothers to give their lives for Catherine of Russia's expansionist policies?"

"No!" a middle-aged woman holding the hand of a young child shouted.

The man left my side and, using his stick for aid, pushed his way to the front of the crowd. His twisted right leg dragged behind him. "Russia is not our enemy," he shouted at the orator. "You are young and naïve. We need Catherine's help in keeping the Prussians away from our own borders!"

Two constables approached the assembly. "Everyone move along," one shouted. The market women turned away.

"We should also have France as an ally against Prussia." The orator looked down at the crippled man. "The French carry on a large trade with the Turks. By declaring war against the Ottoman Empire, Joseph has alienated the French."

As the constables continued to press, the group broke up. I lingered as the angry man moved close to the orator's box. The protester shouted to the backs of the dispersing crowd. "Think of the lives lost already! Our men sitting in that swamp in Semlin waiting for the Russians to distract the Turks in Galicia before we can invade their garrison in Belgrade. How many of our boys will die of disease as the weather gets hotter?"

"That's Turkish propaganda!" The crippled man shook his fist. "Joseph will be taking Belgrade any day now! The Turks will surrender. Everyone knows how bad morale is in their army. Our boys will be home before the end of summer."

"How many will never come home?" The young protester

looked the man up and down, taking in his dress suit and elegant stick. "It is easy for you to speak in favor of sending them to their deaths, while you sit at home, comfortable in your palace."

"You insolent swine! How dare you speak to me like that!"

I watched, astonished, as the man raised his stick and swung it at the orator. The young man ducked and fell off the crate. He sprawled on the ground against the low balustrade that surrounded the monument.

"Hey now, stop that, sir." One of the constables grabbed the assailant's arm.

"Let go of me!" the man said, his face red with anger. "I am Baron Walther Hennen. I'll report you to your superior officer."

The constable withdrew his hand.

Hennen glared at the orator. "As for you—you are one to speak about avoiding service in the war. I know who you are. You had better be careful, or you'll end up in Semlin before you know it." He turned and limped angrily in the direction of St. Peter's Church.

I continued on toward the Stephansplatz. I wasn't sure what to think about this war. I was not a native Austrian, so I had no emotional connection to the hostilities. But I worried that a prolonged war could affect my life here in Vienna, especially my position at the theater. When the emperor had left a few weeks ago to join the troops at Semlin, he had ordered the city theaters to remain open. If the war dragged on, though, that situation could change, and I might be out of a job. But I knew the emperor well, and

I respected his wisdom and trusted his judgment. If he felt it was necessary to support the empress of Russia in her war against the Turks, who was I to question him? I just hoped the Turks could be defeated quickly.

In the Stephansplatz, the buildings were draped in black bunting, as were the main doors of the great cathedral. A funeral mass had been held yesterday for General Peter Albrechts, a hero in the late empress's war thirty years ago. I had not attended, but I had heard that the crowd of mourners had spilled out of the cathedral.

I walked by the west portal of the cathedral and crossed the small side plaza to a nondescript office building. I climbed four flights of stairs, made my way down a small corridor to the office at its end, and poked my head in the open door.

"Alois?"

"Lorenzo!" Alois Bayer rose from his desk. "I was beginning to worry that I had my dates confused."

"I'm sorry. I was held up by a disturbance in the Graben," I explained as I gently returned his embrace. My elderly friend was growing more fragile every time I saw him. "That young man who is always protesting against the war—he and a bystander almost came to blows."

"Was anyone hurt?"

"No, some constables broke up the fight before any violence occurred," I said. I settled into the chair next to Alois's desk and looked around the familiar space. Books were piled on every free surface. I took a deep breath and inhaled one of my favorite smells—the scent of old books punctuated by a slight trace of the peppermint drops Alois ate constantly. A thin straw-filled pallet lay on the floor behind the desk. I frowned. "What is that? Are you sleeping here now? What happened to your room over in the Wollzeile?"

Alois shrugged. "The cathedral needed it for one of the new priests. I don't mind it here. It gives me more time to study."

I opened my mouth to object, but closed it as the red tinge of embarrassment spread over his papery cheeks. "Are you ready for dinner?" I asked. "I'd like to try that new catering shop over by the Greek church."

He hesitated. "I'm not that hungry, Lorenzo. The older I get, the less appetite I have. I have a nice bottle of Tokay. Why don't we stay here and drink it instead of going out for dinner? We haven't had a good talk in a long time."

I shook my head. I knew why he was protesting. Since he had retired from the active priesthood, he lived on a small stipend from the cathedral, and he spent most of his money on books. I worried that he seldom ate a hearty meal, which is why I had made a point of inviting him out today.

"Nonsense," I said. "We can discuss whatever you want at the catering shop." I put my hand up as he shook his head. "I invited you out to dinner, and out to dinner you will come."

"No, no, Lorenzo," Alois protested. "You have better things to do with your money."

"Better things to do than spend an afternoon with a good friend, enjoying a delicious meal?" I stood. "No more protests. You'll insult my Venetian honor if you don't come," I added, smiling.

"Well, since you put it that way—" He laughed. "Do you mind if we stop by the cathedral for a moment on the way out?" He took a book off his desk. "I want to return this to the archivist."

"As long as we're quick about it," I said. "I'm famished."

I helped him into his thin, worn cloak and followed him out of the office. We slowly made our way down the stairs. In the small lobby, I held the heavy door for him, and followed him out into the gray, warm afternoon.

The dark, bulky north tower of the cathedral hovered over the busy side plaza. The tower was much shorter than the ornate, elegant tower on the south side of the building. Legend had it that when the church decided to erect the second tower in the fifteenth century, the master builder had sold his soul to the devil to ensure the success of the project, and one day, while the man was high on the scaffolding, he uttered a holy name, angering his evil patron, who caused the scaffold to fall to the ground, taking the unfortunate builder with it. The tower had never been completed.

We waited as several carriages trundled by, and then crossed to the portico. To our left, several yards down the exterior wall of the cathedral, stood the old Capistran Chancel, a Gothic stone pulpit where Saint Johannes Capistrano, a Franciscan monk, had raised a crusade against the Turks in 1456. Fifty years ago, the Franciscans had erected a statue to commemorate the saint, who had died after defeating the Turks in Belgrade. The order's own founder, Saint Francis, stood beneath a richly wrought golden sunburst, his feet trampling the body of a dead Turk.

Two cathedral workmen stood atop rickety ladders, removing the black funeral bunting from the tall north doors.

Alois and I ducked around a long piece of swaying fabric and stepped into the vestibule. Felix Urbanek, one of the priests, came to greet us.

"Father Bayer, Signor Da Ponte. How good to see you both," he said. He turned to Alois. "Have you come for the meeting about funding the new parishes, Father?"

"No, we just stopped in so that I could return this book to the archives," Alois said.

"Careful, Fathers!" a workman shouted from behind us. His colleague had climbed to the very top of his ladder, which teetered precariously as he tried to reach the highest swath of bunting. We moved deeper into the vestibule.

Urbanek shook his head. He was a homely man, with froglike features and a sallow complexion. His bright, intelligent eyes seemed to belong to another face. "It's taking them all day to clean up after that funeral. Did either of you attend?"

Alois and I shook our heads.

"You missed quite a show. There was much beating of the breasts over the death of the great man."

"The general was a war hero," Alois said quietly. "The country owed him a debt."

"He was merely doing his duty, as we all are, Father," Urbanek said. "He was generously rewarded for his service—a title, several fine houses, a large pension. What about all of those who fought under him, the men who never came home from the wars?" He gestured toward the bunting. "Where is their glory? I'm not the only one in Vienna who feels—"

Alois opened his mouth to speak. "How did he die?" I

asked, hoping to head off an argument between the two priests.

"A seizure of some sort, I believe," Urbanek said. "It was sudden." He turned back to Alois. "I'm glad you are here, Father," he said. "I am starting a committee to help the poor children who have lost their fathers in the current siege." He sighed. "Already there have been too many deaths. It would be a great help to me if you would agree to chair the meetings. I'm busy with a lot of other things right now."

Alois hesitated, and shook his head. "That's a job for an active priest, someone younger and more energetic than I, I'm afraid," he said.

Urbanek pursed his lips. "You cannot find the energy to help war orphans?"

"No, you misunderstand me," Alois said. "It is just that I—"

Urbanek waved his hand. "Never mind, Father Bayer. I'll find someone else to do it. If you'll excuse me, I'll bid you good day." He nodded at me and turned away, heading toward the south transept.

Alois sighed. "He's always trying to recruit me for his latest committee," he said. "I've done my share here, Lorenzo. I'm tired. I just want to spend my last years with my books. Is that so bad?"

I shook my head. "No, my friend. In fact, I wish I were able to join you." We laughed. Alois excused himself and ascended the stairway that led to the upper offices and archive. I walked onto the main floor of the cathedral. To my left, past the expansive choir, lay the elaborate high altar with its marble statues of bishops and saints. I turned my back on it and wandered over to the Gothic sandstone pulpit sculpted by Anton Pilgram in the late fifteenth century. The pulpit resembled a giant wine cup set against a large pillar. The bowl of the cup was made of four blocks of sandstone carved to resemble oriel windows, from which figures of the four fathers of the church—Saint Ambrose, Saint Jerome, Saint Gregory, and Saint Augustine—presided over the nave of the cathedral. A stone stairway curved around the pillar, its banister strewn with intricate carvings of frogs, snakes, and lizards. I had heard that the sculptor had hidden a self-portrait beneath the stairway. I ducked my head and leaned in to find it.

"Lorenzo, is that you?" A voice sounded behind me. I turned to see a dark-haired priest with a wide, crooked smile extending his hand to me. A second cleric, whom I did not recognize, stood behind him.

"Maximilian," I said, shaking his hand. "It is good to see you. How is your work coming?" Maximilian Krause had been a lawyer before taking holy orders, and was an expert on the writings of Ludovico Muratori, a modern church reformer. I often ran into him in various bookshops in the city.

"Very well," he replied. He gestured to the man behind him, who stepped forward. "Father Dauer, have you met Lorenzo Da Ponte? He is the poet at the Court Theater. Lorenzo, this is Hieronymus Dauer. He's just joined the staff here."

As I shook hands with Dauer, I studied his face. He looked like no priest I had ever seen; instead, he resembled one of the heroes of the novels the ladies had taken to reading lately, with wavy chestnut hair; a long, aristocratic nose; and a heart-shaped mouth. His gold-green eyes considered me and dismissed me with a blink.

We strolled down the nave toward the great front portal.

"Father Dauer comes to us from the abbey at Melk," Krause said. "He was rising in the ranks there, but our provost stole him away to help manage the cathedral. Now that the state is so involved in church affairs, we needed someone with his political skills and talents."

Dauer gave a satisfied smile at his fellow priest's praise.

"You two have something in common," Krause continued.

Dauer arched a delicate brow.

"You both have lived in Venice."

"Were you born in Venice?" I asked Dauer.

He shook his head. "I was born here," he replied. "But I spent my childhood and teenage years there. My father was attached to the Austrian embassy."

"Lorenzo is a native," Krause explained. "We are lucky that he has chosen to live and work here."

Now it was my turn to look pleased at the compliment. I bit off the correction I wished to make to Krause's statement. I would much prefer to be back in Venice, my beloved home, instead of here in Vienna. But I was no longer welcome there.

"Excuse me, please, Fathers," a small voice said. A girl of about sixteen, dressed in an elegant satin dress festooned with bows, the neck cut low as was the latest fashion, was attempting to maneuver her way around the three of us. We moved to let her pass. She smiled gratefully and entered a small chapel to our right.

Dauer stared after her. "Look at her," he hissed. "Dressed like a common prostitute to light a holy candle. Why does her father let her out of the house wearing that dress?" He shook his head. "I must confess, my friends, that I am amazed at some of the behavior I've witnessed here in the city. The moral laxness—I've never seen anything like it." His eyes narrowed. "It's due to the emperor's reforms, I believe. There are no longer any rules about how to behave properly." He gestured toward the young woman, who had pushed aside her skirts and was kneeling before the altar in the chapel. "That is the result."

Although I never would criticize my Caesar aloud, I agreed with Dauer's assessment. Over the last seven years, the emperor had attempted to apply the modern ideas of the French *philosophes* to Viennese society. He had ordered equal treatment for all the social classes in matters of taxation and criminal punishment; had modernized medieval church practices; and had built new schools and hospitals. But instead of the society he had aimed to create—one based on freedom and reason—it seemed to me that the emperor's efforts had had the opposite effect. Instead of acting for the greater good, everyone these days did whatever they wanted, with no concern for the well-being of their neighbors, and no consideration of propriety.

"The result of what?" Alois joined us.

"Father Dauer was commenting on the young lady's attire," Krause explained, nodding toward the chapel, where the young woman had stood and was now lighting a candle.

"I'll speak to her," Dauer said, turning toward the chapel.

Alois placed his hand on the new priest's arm. "I would not advise it," he said gently. "You will not make friends that way, my son. Her father is the government minister who oversees the cathedral's treasury."

Dauer stiffened. "You are probably right, Father Bayer," he said. "I appreciate your guidance."

"Let me be, you cruel man!" a woman's voice cried from behind us. A tall, slender young woman, shrouded in black satin and velvet, her face covered by a dark veil, rushed out of the Chapel of the Cross. She was followed by a much shorter, thick-set man with light hair. He took her arm.

"My love, please. Listen to me," he said.

She shrugged off his hold. "I want to die too! Oh, my poor father! Can you really be dead? How could you have left me?"

All four of us gaped at her.

The young woman clutched her companion's arm. "Swear to me! Swear to me that you will do something! Promise me you will avenge his blood!"

Dauer turned to me. "I see my presence is required, gentlemen. Signor Da Ponte, it was a pleasure meeting you." He hurried over to the couple and murmured a few words to the young woman. She collapsed in his arms, sobbing. Dauer gently led her back into the chapel. The light-haired man followed.

"Christiane Albrechts," Alois said. "The late general's daughter. The man is her fiancé, Count Richard Benda. Father Dauer has just been appointed her confessor."

"You know everyone, Father Bayer," Krause said.

"I was her confessor years ago, when she was ten years old," Alois explained. "Her mother had just died. Of course, her father was often away. And like most men, he had wished for a son. She was a lonely child, perhaps too serious for her own good. When the general was home, he managed her education. I thought his choices inappropriate for a young lady. I approved of the books he encouraged her to read, but he also taught her to hunt and ride astride." He sighed. "It was a sad time. The two of them, alone in the palace on the Freyung, she pining for her mother, he for the son he never had. But she has grown to become a lovely woman. I was happy to hear of her engagement to Count Benda. He is a good man. He'll do his best to make her happy."

We stood quietly for a moment.

"While you are here, Father Bayer, I would like to ask a favor," Krause said. "I'd be honored if you would read my latest article and give me your thoughts."

"More of your natural religion ideas, Maximilian?" Alois asked, his eyes twinkling.

Krause laughed. "If you are referring to the idea that religious belief should be instilled in our flock through rational discourse rather than medieval mumbo jumbo, well then, I would say yes, that is my topic."

"I agree with you that many of the superstitious activities the church encouraged in the past should be abolished," Alois said. "Worshiping the icons, dressing the statues of the saints and parading them around the city—everyone knows those practices are ridiculous. But if you are arguing that we should not teach about the existence of Heaven and Hell, there is where we part ways."

"But surely you don't believe that we should lead people to God by using fear of retribution and threats of burning in Hell," Krause protested. "That flies in the face of all modern church philosophy."

I stifled a yawn.

"No, no. Not that," Alois replied. "I just worry where all this new thinking will lead, that is all. If we take your theories to their logical ends, the laity might question whether the church is necessary at all. That is my fear."

I coughed.

"Yet you support the emperor's reform of the church, Father Bayer, do you not?" Krause persisted. "You must admit, the cathedral has changed for the better since Joseph took away control of the church from Rome." He looked at me. "You're a priest, Lorenzo. What do you think?"

I smiled. "I think it's time for dinner."

The priests laughed. "Send your article over to my office, Maximilian," Alois said. "I'd be happy to read it." We said our good-byes to Krause and headed outside.

Dusk was falling as I made my way home after a pleasant afternoon. We had tried the new catering shop near the Greek church, and the food had been tasty and plentiful. After the waiter had cleared away the dishes, we directed our attention to finishing the bottle of wine I had ordered. Our wide-ranging discussion eventually turned to the cathedral.

"These new men!" Alois said. "Maximilian, spouting all

the new philosophies, and now Dauer, with his political acumen. I can no longer keep up with them. I'm happy to be retired."

"There are a lot of new ideas floating around this city," I agreed.

"But enough of that," Alois said. "Tell me. What are you working on now?"

"Mozart and I are modifying *Don Giovanni* for the premiere on May seventh," I told him.

"The old Don Juan farce." Alois laughed. "People never tire of that story." *Don Giovanni*, like many other operas and plays that had come before mine, was based on the Don Juan legend, the story of a noted libertine who is dragged to Hell by the ghost of a father whose daughter he had seduced.

"I hope the public here in Vienna is not tired of it," I said.

"I'm certain they won't be," Alois said. He reached over and patted my hand. "You told me it was a hit in Prague last fall. It will be successful here, you'll see. Tell me, what kind of changes are you making?"

"Well, it is always necessary to change some of the arias to suit the talents of the new cast. Sometimes a singer isn't comfortable with an aria that hasn't been tailored to his or her particular voice. Wolfgang prides himself on writing music to suit each performer. He calls it 'fitting the costume to the figure.'"

Alois smiled.

"And of course Vienna is a much more sophisticated city

than Prague," I continued. "So we might have to add some scenes to appeal to the tastes here."

"All that must take a long time," Alois said.

"We'll soon know how much work there'll be. We've been working through the Prague libretto and score with the cast here, and we'll finish that tomorrow."

"What else are you doing?" my friend asked.

"I'm setting aside time to write a bit of poetry," I answered. "I'm thinking of having a small collection published."

"That's wonderful, Lorenzo! I'd love to read some of them."

"I'd be honored if you did. I'll bring them by your office in a day or two." We chatted about books for a while, enjoying our comfortable companionship, and did not notice the hours passing until the owner of the catering shop finally shooed us away. As I paid the bill, I remembered the pallet on the floor of Alois's office, and considered offering to help him pay for a room at my own lodgings. But I bit my tongue for fear of embarrassing him.

Now I was heading to my lodging house, through the great Stuben gate cut into the medieval battlements of the city, and over the wide bridge that crossed the *glacis,* the sloped, grassy field designed to deny cover to an approaching enemy. Like most Viennese, I would prefer to live in the city, but lodgings are much less expensive out in the suburbs. My father still needed my help educating my stepbrothers back in Ceneda, so I tried to cut my expenses so that I could regularly send him funds. I have a long walk to and from my office every day, but I try to view my situation as an advantage. I've been so busy lately, my walk to and from work is all the fresh air I get.

The evening was as warm as the day had been, and I carried my cloak over my arm as I walked across the dusty, broad path that ran parallel to the city walls and made my way over another, smaller bridge that spanned the Vienna River. Moments later, I turned into my street. I had to admit that it was pleasant out here. Small, neat houses lined both sides of the street, and a strip of land planted with linden saplings ran down its center. Shrieks of girlish laughter greeted me as I approached the house of my landlady, Josepha Lamm. Ahead of me, a burly young man was maneuvering a cart laden with hay through the narrow opening into the house's courtyard.

"Good evening, Signor Da Ponte," he called.

"Good evening, Stefan." I gestured at the cart. "Are you giving up stonemasonry in favor of farming?" I asked.

He laughed. "No, sir. This is for Sophie's party. Come, you'll see." He rolled the cart into the courtyard. I followed.

My jaw dropped at the sight before me. Madame Lamm's normally neat courtyard was strewn with hay. Six young women, dressed in white gauze dresses tied at the waist with satin ribbons, had formed a circle and, holding hands, were attempting to dance around a small goat in the center of their ring. A blond, heavily pregnant girl sat forlornly on a bench to the side. The goat jumped up and put its hooves on one of the dancers.

"Stefan, help! Get it off me!" she cried, laughing. The young man pushed at the animal.

"Good evening, Signor Da Ponte," the girl said. "Would you happen to know anything about goats?"

"Hello, Sophie," I greeted my landlady's daughter. "What is the meaning of this bucolic display? Where did you get that poor animal?"

My landlady came out the door of the house, carrying a tray with a pitcher and several mugs. "The goat belongs to Hoffer down the street," she said. I put my satchel on the ground and took the tray from her. She pointed toward the small garden that lay beyond the courtyard, and I carried the tray over and placed it on a table next to the garden bench.

Sophie extricated herself from the embraces of the goat and came to me. "It's my sixteenth birthday, signore. We're having a country party, like the queen of France." The emperor's younger sister, Maria Antonia, had built a rustic hamlet on the grounds of the great palace of Versailles, where she and her lady's maids escaped from the boredom of court life and played at being shepherdesses.

"I think the royal farm animals are more obedient than this goat," Sophie added. I smiled at her. She never failed to charm me, with her pleasing features, shapely figure, laughing gray eyes, and friendly smile.

Stefan captured the goat and tied a length of rope around its neck. "I'll take him back to Hoffer," he said, dragging the animal out of the courtyard.

"Thank you, Stefan," my landlady called. "Would you like a punch, signore?"

"Oh no, thank you, Madame Lamm. I'll just go up to my room."

"There's a cold supper in the kitchen when you are ready," she said.

I thanked her and went into the house and up to my room on the second floor. I dropped my satchel on the floor, crossed to the cupboard and put my cloak on a hook, and then took off my coat and waistcoat and hung them next to the cloak. My eyes fell on the pocket of my cloak. I sighed, then pulled out the message I had received that morning. I had put off looking at it long enough. I broke the seal, unfolded the paper, and read the contents:

33   27   54   71   52   33   61   33   28   55
Verrò
21 aprile

"I am coming. April 21," the Italian read. I had no idea what the string of numbers meant.

I went to my desk and took a folded packet of paper from its small drawer. It was a duplicate of the newest one, again hastily addressed to me at the theater, with the same messy, unmarked seal. My hands shook as I unfolded it and placed it by the newest message. My eyes traveled between the two pages, comparing the contents. They were the same.

Loud laughter came from the street below my window as Sophie's party broke up. I studied the messages. What was the meaning of the numbers? Was someone toying with me for his own amusement, or did he have more sinister motives? What was going to happen on April 21, seven days from now?

As I stared at the notes, my mind full of worry, the happiness I had gained from an afternoon with an old friend completely unraveled.

Two

The next morning I worked for an hour in my office, then took my *Don Giovanni* libretto and went upstairs to the main hall of the theater. Workmen were arranging chairs on the stage, where Mozart and I would continue leading the cast through the libretto and score we had written for the performances in Prague. We had already worked through the first act and part of the second act of the opera last week. These preliminary rehearsals were very informal— Mozart would accompany the singers on a fortepiano as they tried out their arias. Later, once we had determined what changes must be made, we would begin rehearsing with the orchestra. I stood down in the parterre watching Thorwart, the assistant theater manager, directing the workers on the stage.

Most of the cast members had already arrived and sat chatting with one another in the seats behind me. The company had changed members since Mozart and I had last worked together on *The Marriage of Figaro* two years ago. Only three singers from that cast remained—the talented and handsome bass Francesco Benucci; the delicate soprano Luisa Laschi, now the prima donna of the company, heavy with child; and the scowling Francesco Bussani. New to the company were two men who had just arrived in Vienna a few weeks before: the baritone Francesco Albertarelli, who would sing the title role of Don Giovanni, and the highly touted tenor Francesco Morella.

Our cast also included two sopranos who had performed in Vienna for many years. Aloysia Lange was Mozart's sister-in-law, and had been a star in the recently closed German opera company. Caterina Cavalieri had been a star of the Italian opera company five years ago. But her voice was starting to fade, and her squat, bosomy figure was showing the effects of middle age and too much pastry. She was the longtime mistress of Antonio Salieri, music director of the company, however, so a role had been found for her. She would sing Donna Elvira, a woman used and abandoned by Don Giovanni, while Lange played Donna Anna, the daughter of the libertine's murder victim. I watched, amused, as the two sopranos exchanged cool nods.

"Good morning, everyone!" Mozart bustled into the hall. He placed his score on the bench of the fortepiano, nodded at me, and greeted the singers one by one, shaking hands with each of the men, kissing Laschi, and giving a hug to Lange.

"How do you feel?" he asked her. Like Laschi, Lange was in the advanced stages of pregnancy.

"I'm fine," she said. "A bit tired, but—"

"Wolfgang! My favorite composer!" Caterina Cavalieri swooped over and pulled Mozart away from his sister-in-law.

"Hello, Caterina." Mozart bowed with a flourish and kissed her hand. She giggled.

"I know I said this last week, but I wanted to say it once more. I am thrilled to be working with you again," she cooed. "I cannot wait to see what you are going to do with my role."

Thorwart climbed down from the stage and came over to me. "We'll be lucky if those two make it through the first three performances," he muttered, gesturing toward the two pregnant sopranos. "I don't welcome the expense of hiring replacement singers, but the emperor specifically requested this cast." He sighed. "I don't know why—he won't be here to see any of the performances, the way this war is going." He shook his head. "And he has no idea what it costs to put on these productions."

"Well, he did close the German company and transfer all its resources to us," I reminded him. "Surely that gives us a big enough budget to replace the ladies when the time comes?"

Thorwart laughed. "You are naïve, Da Ponte. Most of those savings went to the higher salary the emperor gave Salieri when he promoted him to music director. And now Mozart has a salary too, as court composer."

"I'm sure the emperor is aware of our costs," I said.

"Well, if I were you, I wouldn't be so certain. If this war drags on, we may be the next to close." He glanced over at the stage. "No! You over there! Put the singers' parts on their chairs!" He nodded at me and scurried off.

"Let's begin, everyone," Mozart called. I bounded up to the stage with my libretto as Mozart sat at the fortepiano. "I want to begin with the sextet," he said. In the libretto, Don Giovanni, the notorious seducer, seeking to escape the consequences of his actions, orders his manservant to pose as the master and woo one of the libertine's former lovers. In the dark streets of Seville, where the opera is set, the servant attempts to escape the woman and several neighbors who seek revenge for the evildoer's many crimes. The characters express their deepest emotions during a sextet. I was pleased with my work on the number, and Mozart had set my poetry to beautiful, evocative music.

I leaned back in my chair as the six singers worked through the piece. Occasionally Mozart would stop them to suggest a different way of singing a phrase, but overall, I was impressed by the way the singers took to the music so easily. When they had finished the ensemble, Benucci, who played the disguised servant, sang an aria in which he pleaded with the others to spare him from harm. With his inflections and gestures, the talented bass convinced me that he was indeed arguing for his life.

The aria came to a close, and Benucci feigned the servant's escape through a side door on the stage.

"Bravo, Signor Benucci!" Mozart cried as the rest of the cast applauded. "Please don't change a thing. That was perfect." He turned to the tenor, Morella. "You are next, signore. Remember, in this aria, you are telling us that your beloved is your treasure, your very reason for living. Please give me a signal when you are ready."

Morella stood and squirmed uncomfortably. He straightened his cravat, held the sheets of music at arm's length, and squinted to read them.

"Signor Morella? Are you ready?"

Morella coughed loudly. "One moment, maestro, if you please. I have something caught in my throat." He coughed again. "All right, maestro. I am ready."

Mozart played the first few bars of the aria. "'Meanwhile, go and console my treasure—'" Morella sang in a tight voice. He coughed again. His face reddened as he threw the music onto his chair. "I am sorry, maestro. My throat is very dry today." He waved a hand around the stage. "The air in here— if it would not be too much trouble, I would prefer to sing the aria another day."

Mozart glanced over at me and raised his eyebrow slightly. "Fine, Signor Morella. We'll work on it together, you and I, perhaps tomorrow." Morella heaved a loud sigh of relief, took up his music, and sat.

We rehearsed the rest of the act. At its end, Don Giovanni was taken to Hell. Francesco Albertarelli's performance was brilliant, as we had expected it would be. The emperor had paid dearly to lure him to Vienna, and would be pleased to hear that he had gotten his money's worth from the young baritone. The singers gathered their parts and left, Cavalieri sailing out accompanied by the young men. The workmen began to move the chairs off the stage and extinguish the lights.

I walked with Mozart to the lobby. "What do you suppose is wrong with Morella?" I asked.

Mozart shrugged. "Chances are there is a line in the aria he does not want to sing. I've seen that plenty of times before. I'll meet with him tomorrow and find out. Oh, and I've been thinking, Lorenzo. You've been saying we should add some physical comedy. What about some sort of burlesque scene after the sextet?"

"Good idea," I said. "I'll sketch out a few possibilities."

"Come for dinner on Sunday. Constanze has been asking after you. There won't be anyone else there, so we can work on the new scene afterward."

"I'd love to come," I said. We shook hands and Mozart left. I started downstairs to my office. In the narrow hallway, a tall ladder and a mandolin leaned on the wall outside my door. I shook my head. With a different production being performed every day, there was not enough space for all of the props in the small rooms behind the stage upstairs. I would have to take care that Thorwart and his workmen did not wall me into my office.

I felt a brief stab of worry as I opened the door, wondering if another mysterious message waited on my desk. But all that sat on my worktable was a stack of new librettos for my review. I pushed them aside, sat down, and pulled a fresh sheet of paper from my drawer. I started to toy with ideas for a burlesque scene, and after a few moments I was immersed in my work.

A few hours later, I put my scribbles and my *Don Giovanni* libretto into my satchel, took my cloak, and climbed the stairs to the lobby. The porter was about to lock the front door, as there was no performance scheduled for this evening.

"Oh, Signor Poet," he said. "I did not know you were still here." He held the door for me. "Have a good evening, signore."

I paused halfway through the door and looked back at him. "Did you leave a message in my office yesterday?" I asked.

"Let me think. Yes, one came for you, early in the morning. I put it on your desk." He frowned. "Was there a problem with it, signore?"

"No, it is nothing. Do you remember who brought it?"

He thought for a moment. "A boy. Yes. He was waiting at the door when I arrived to open up. It was early, about eight."

"A servant? What did he look like?"

"Hmmmm. Let me think. He wasn't wearing any uniform, signore. No livery. I remember that."

"Tall, short? Young, older?"

He closed his eyes. "An older boy, tall—no, no, that was the one who came later in the day."

"Dark hair, light?" I prompted.

He shook his head. "I am sorry, Signor Poet. I cannot remember. It was just a boy. I take so many messages every day, I cannot remember every boy."

"I understand," I said. "If I should receive another message, and I am here, would you please send the boy down to my office?"

"I will, signore. Good night."

I wished him good night and left.

Wednesday passed without the arrival of another mysterious message, so I breathed easier as I made my way to work on Thursday morning. The temperature was still warm, and I left my cloak in my room and carried only my satchel, into which I had tucked a few of my poems. I planned to drop them at Alois's office on my way to the theater.

Dark clouds lowered over the spires of the Stephansdom as I cut across the Strobelgasse to the plaza in front of my friend's office building. Ahead of me, a large crowd had gathered around the Capistran Chancel. Out of the corner of my eye I saw the ragged war protester near the entrance to the north tower. He placed his box at the edge of the crowd and climbed up on it.

I approached a young man dressed in a postal uniform who was standing at the back of the crowd.

"What is happening?" I asked.

"Good morning, sir. It's a body. Up there by the chancel."

"A drunk?" I asked.

"I don't know, sir. I cannot see from back here."

"Friends! Our men are dying from disease at the miserable camp in Semlin!" the protester shouted. The crowd, its attention focused on the old chancel, paid him no attention.

In front of us, a washerwoman balanced a large basket on her hip. She turned around. "It's an old man—a priest, by the looks of him. He's dead," she said, her cheeks ruddy with excitement.

A wave of icy cold washed over me. I pushed my way past the washerwoman and plunged into the crowd, straining to get to the front.

"Hey, watch where you are going," a merchant snarled at me.

"How many of our husbands and brothers must die to feed the empress of Russia's greed for land?" the protester shouted.

"Pardon me, I must get through." I propelled myself to the front of the crowd. My head felt light, as if I were floating. As I neared the wall of the cathedral, the throng of onlookers suddenly parted, revealing a horrible sight. An old man lay at the base of the chancel, his right arm draped over the sandstone plinth, his left hand cradled near his side. His eyes stared blankly at the sky. His mouth was frozen open in surprise, his forehead smeared with a thick reddish-brown paste. My stomach turned over as I breathed in a salty, metallic fetor. Below his head, at the collar of his cassock, snowy white tubes protruded from a mess of dark blood. I stared at them, my jaw slack with disbelief, and then my legs gave way.

Three

I squeezed my eyes shut, willing the awful sight to disappear. But when I opened them, Alois's body was still splayed on the sandstone. The stem of the chancel and the leftmost steps to a small portico that led into the cathedral were spattered with crimson.

"A robber," a man next to me said. "The stupid old man. He shouldn't have tried to fight."

My legs were numb. I could not get myself back on my feet.

"This is murder, you fool!" another man said. "No thief would slaughter a man like that."

"The Turks! It's the Turks!" a young servant girl wailed. "They must be here, hiding in the city."

A dull murmur rose from the crowd. Two constables appeared and pushed the crowd back with their sticks.

"Do you need help, sir?" A young man leaned over me.

"I cannot get up," I croaked.

"Let me help you." He put his hands under my arms and lifted me to my feet. "Did you know him?" he asked me, gesturing toward Alois.

I gulped. "Yes, he was my friend," I managed to respond. He handed my satchel to me.

"We must bring our men home right now! The emperor has made a huge mistake. It's not too late to fix it," the protester shouted.

"That one should watch his words," the young man said. I followed his eyes to the edge of the plaza, where a plain black carriage had just pulled up. The door opened, and a man climbed out. I shuddered as I recognized his sharp features.

"Everyone move back!" the constables shouted. They had been joined by three others. "Get about your business!" The crowd grumbled, and then began to disperse.

I took a step back as Georg Troger walked through the passage the constables had cleared. From my place at the front of the remaining spectators, I could see him stop at the chancel. His dark, cold eyes stared down at Alois. He turned, spoke briefly to one of the constables, and returned to the carriage. A moment later, it drove away.

"You must leave, sir." The constable pushed at me with his stick.

"Please, I knew this man," I cried. "He was my friend. What has happened? What did Captain Troger say?"

The constable looked at me with pity. "There's nothing you can do for your friend now, sir. Please move along. Inspector Troger's orders are to clear the area."

"But I must speak with someone. I must know what happened," I protested.

The constable's face softened. "I'm sorry, sir. There is nothing I can do for you. They've sent for the hearse. You have to go."

I forced myself to take one last look at my poor friend, and then walked toward the Stephansplatz. Before I turned around the corner of the cathedral, I looked back. Two priests, Krause and Urbanek, had come out the door of the small portico. Urbanek fell to his knees before the body and began to pray.

I stumbled through the Graben, my eyes clouded with tears. The pit of my stomach was empty and cold. What monster had done this to Alois? He had been the gentlest of souls. I could not picture him attempting to resist a robbery. The Alois I knew would have given his attacker his money willingly, even with a blessing.

In the Kohlmarkt, I let the mass of bureaucrats making their way to their offices at the Hofburg carry my numb legs down the street. When the mob debouched into the Michaelerplatz, I automatically headed toward the theater. But as I approached the building, I found that I could not control myself. I veered off to the right, walked down a quiet side street, and entered the courtyard where my ordeal with the Ministry of Police had begun two years before.

The small yard looked the same—rows of windows in tall buildings, no carriages or horses idling nearby. But where two years before the space had been deserted and dark, today it was bustling with bewigged bureaucrats chatting with one another before the workday began. I stood in the center of the court. Was I in the right place? Yes, there was the center door, ornamented with one simple lamp.

I went through the door and up a flight of stairs. Was this the floor? I peered down the long hallway, where clumps of workers stood outside office doors. No, it must be up another flight. I dragged myself up to the next floor and looked around. Ahead of me was the long hallway that occasionally still featured in my nightmares. But unlike that night two years ago, when the doors were all closed and nothing but sporadic pools of light lit the way, today the office doors all stood open.

A tall man in a gray woolen suit approached. "Can I help you, sir?" he asked.

"I'm looking for Count Pergen's office," I said.

His brows shot up. "The minister of police? What would you want with him?" He studied me, suspicion written on his face. "Are you one of his spies?"

"No, no! There's been a crime, a murder. I believed—I remembered—no, I must be in the wrong hallway." As I turned away, I stumbled.

The bureaucrat caught my arm. "Wait, sir," he said. "You are in the correct hallway. But Pergen's ministry moved last year. This is the tax reform office now."

"Do you know where I can find Count Pergen?" I asked.

"Yes. His offices are in the imperial chancellery wing, right beneath the emperor's rooms. But take my advice, my friend. You should stay away."

"I must speak to his assistant. There's been a murder," I said.

"Well, if you insist on going there—when you leave this building, go through the arch on the right. That will take you into the main courtyard. Go in the first door on the left. Ask any of the guards to direct you to the ministry offices."

I thanked him and hurried out the door. I made my way into the courtyard of the Hofburg. The long expanse was dotted with groups of bureaucrats, soldiers, and citizens of the empire who had business with the various ministries. I made a sharp left and entered a small door flanked by over-sized statues of young men wrestling a bull and a lion into submission. Once inside, I asked directions from a guard, who pointed me up to Pergen's second-floor suite of offices.

I hesitated outside the door that led to Pergen and Troger. What was I doing? I had hoped never to encounter either man again. Perhaps I should take the bureaucrat's advice, and stay away. I closed my eyes. A vision of the surprised expression on my dead friend's face appeared. I opened my eyes and hurried through the door.

The anteroom was ornate and lavishly furnished with stuffed armchairs. A middle-aged secretary clad in a severe black suit sat at a large mahogany desk. He looked up as I approached.

"I am Lorenzo Da Ponte, the theater poet. I must see Captain Troger immediately. It's about the man who was killed at the Stephansdom this morning."

He motioned me toward one of the armchairs. "Let me see if Inspector Troger is free," he said.

I put down my satchel, sank into a chair, and looked around. I had been in just one room during my former en-counter with Pergen and Troger, and it had been sparsely furnished and dimly lit. This office was its extreme opposite. It looked more like one of the salons in which I occasionally met with the emperor than a police office.

After a few minutes, the secretary returned. "I'm sorry, Signor Da Ponte," he said. "Inspector Troger is in an important meeting and cannot be disturbed."

"I'll wait for him," I said.

"I wouldn't advise it, signore," the man said, frowning.

I leaned back into the comfortable chair. "I'll stay until he is free. I must speak with him. I don't care how long it takes."

The secretary sighed, went over to his desk, and picked up a small bell. Moments later, a barrel-chested guard appeared.

"Please escort Signor Da Ponte to the Court Theater," the secretary said. He looked at me, his face apologetic. "I'm sorry, signore. Inspector Troger does not wish to see you."

At the main gate of the Hofburg, I assured the guard I could make my own way to the theater. Nevertheless, he stood watching until I entered the front door.

Six large candelabras had joined the ladder and mandolin in the narrow hallway to my office. I maneuvered past them, opened my door, threw down my satchel, and collapsed onto my desk chair. I rested my head in my arms. The horrible vision of Alois's body sprawled at the base of the chancel, above him Saint Francis, his foot on the defeated Turk, came unbidden to my mind. Had my friend really just encountered a violent thief? Or had he been confronted by someone much more sinister, a minion of the devil with an evil purpose? I shuddered as I imagined Alois's last moments. I hoped that God had taken him quickly.

I cast my thoughts back to the times I had spent with my friend—our first meeting, in the aisles of an old bookshop in the Jewish quarter of the city; the many hours we had sat in his spartan office, discussing our favorite books; the many meals shared over a bottle of his favorite Tokay. A sob lodged in my throat as I recalled his continual yet gentle scolding of me—sometimes trying to draw me back to the church he loved so much, other times urging me to work more on writing poetry and less on writing for the theater.

I took a deep breath and tried to calm my swirling emotions. I reached into my satchel and pulled out the notes I had scratched out the other day, ideas for the burlesque scene Mozart had agreed to add to *Don Giovanni*. The words on the paper swam before my eyes.

After a few futile hours I gave up and threw down my pen. My grief for Alois had turned to anger at Troger. He and I had been uneasy allies two years ago, but I had solved the case that had been put to me. The least he could have done was to allow me to wait today, and not had me escorted from his office under guard. Why was the Ministry of Police interested in Alois's death? It usually concerned itself with more important matters affecting the security of the empire and, these days, censorship, leaving the city constabulary to handle crime. I determined to go back to the Hofburg tomorrow morning and refuse to leave until I spoke with Troger.

I put my work into my satchel, left the theater, and went

home. My landlady was setting a vase of flowers on a small table in the foyer of the house when I entered.

"Signor Da Ponte! You are home early today," she greeted me.

"Good afternoon, Madame Lamm," I mumbled.

"You are just in time for dinner. Professor Strasser is downstairs already with Sophie. Please come down. There is plenty for one more."

I opened my mouth to decline, to claim that I had no appetite, but she had already caught sight of the misery on my face.

"Signore! What is wrong? You look terrible. Are you ill?"

I shook my head. "No, madame. I've just heard about the death of a close friend." My voice broke.

She bustled over to me and took my satchel. "You poor man. No wonder you left work early. Was your friend ill?"

Her face was full of concern. I could not share the horror of the scene at the Stephansdom with her. She would hear about it from the neighborhood gossips soon enough. "No," I replied. "It was sudden. But he was an old man."

"Let me take this up to your room," she said. "You need a good dinner and an afternoon reading in the garden. It feels as though it might rain later, but you should have a few hours. I'll make sure that Sophie and her friends do not disturb you."

I started to protest, but shut my mouth. It was comforting to have someone directing me about. "Thank you, madame," I said.

I took the back stair down to the comfortable, cheery kitchen. My fellow lodger, Erich Strasser, a professor at the university's Oriental Academy, was already seated at the long table. Sophie Lamm was at the hearth, ladling stew onto large plates.

"Signor Da Ponte! Good afternoon. Are you joining us?" she asked.

I nodded. I slid into the chair across from Strasser and greeted him. The fifty-year-old professor had an exotic air about him, his closely cropped light gray hair contrasting with thick, almost ebon brows.

"Get the wine from the cupboard, Sophie," our landlady said as she entered the room. Sophie set a steaming plate in front of Strasser and went over to the cupboard.

"A special treat for my favorite lodgers," her mother said. She set a plate of stew in front of me. Sophie poured a glass for each of us from a large jug, and took a seat across from her mother.

I bit into a piece of soft meat. Madame Lamm was a good cook, but today the food tasted like sawdust. I sipped my wine slowly and picked at my plate as the others conversed.

"Have either of you gentlemen heard any news about the emperor's troops?" Madame Lamm asked.

Strasser shook his head. "As far as I know, madame, they are still outside Belgrade, waiting for the Russians to get to Galicia to distract the Turkish army," he said.

"Still? Well, at least they are keeping the Turks away from Vienna," the landlady said.

"I don't believe the Turks wish to invade Vienna, Madame Lamm," Strasser said. "We are the aggressors in this war."

The landlady frowned. "Oh! But I'm sure the Turks would love to take the city, if they were able. They've attacked us so many times. I remember my grandfather talking about the last one. He was just a boy of ten when it happened, but when he was an old man, he used to tell me stories about how we almost lost the city to the Turks, how his family had to scrabble to find food during the siege, how terrified everyone was that the city walls would fall and the Turks would massacre everyone. I still shudder when I see one of their cannonballs stuck in a building, like that one over in the Am Hof. We came so close to losing everything then!"

"Is it true, Professor Strasser, that you've lived among the Turks?" Sophie asked.

Strasser nodded. "Yes, Miss Sophie. I spent many years in Constantinople as part of my training. I've traveled to many parts of the Ottoman Empire."

Sophie gave a sly glance in the direction of her mother. "Is it true what they say?" she asked Strasser. "That their sultan keeps a stable full of women?"

"His religion allows the sultan to marry many wives," the professor explained. "The women all live together in a wing of the royal palace. It is called a harem."

Sophie's eyes glittered with excitement. "I've heard stories about it. They say the women, especially the young beautiful ones, are kept chained to the walls in the harem. They are only released when the sultan sends for them, to sate his needs—"

"Sophie Lamm! Watch your mouth!"

"Oh, Mother. You must have heard the stories yourself.

Are they true, Professor? I've heard that the Turkish pirates capture ships and kidnap Christian women. They sell them as concubines. If a woman resists, she is tortured to death."

"I have heard no such thing!" her mother said.

"Those are just tales, Miss Sophie," he said. "The truth is actually the opposite. Most Turkish women have more freedom than do women here in Vienna."

Madame Lamm frowned. "But Professor, how can that be? The Turks are not Christians. Everyone knows they have no morality. Why, even their religion is based on violence. They are bloodthirsty barbarians!"

Strasser sighed. "Ah, madame, I'm afraid you've fallen right into the emperor's trap."

"What do you mean?"

"It serves the emperor well if you have no real understanding of the Turk. By getting people riled up with all these stories, he keeps you in fear, and assures your support for his plan to grab some of the Ottoman Empire's lands for Austria."

The landlady opened her mouth to retort, but then shut it. She glanced over at me. "Would you like another glass of wine, signore?" she asked.

I shook my head. "No, thank you, madame. If you will excuse me, I'll just go up to my room and rest."

"Of course. Let me know if you need anything, signore."

I went up to my room, took off my coat and waistcoat, and rinsed my face at the basin. I sat at my desk and stared at some work for a while, but concentration eluded me. Sighing, I went over to the cupboard, rummaged through the small collection of beloved books I kept there, and pulled out my tattered copy of Dante's *The Divine Comedy*. I returned to my chair, opened the book, and read: "In the middle of the journey of our life, I found myself in a dark forest, for I had lost the straight path." Soon I walked in Dante's world, traveling with him and the poet Virgil through the circles of Hell.

I must have dozed a bit, for when a soft knock sounded at my door, I was surprised to see that darkness had fallen. I put down the book and opened the door. A folded paper sat on the floor. I drew in a sharp breath, leaned over and picked it up. My landlady was at the end of the hallway, about to descend the stairs.

"Madame Lamm," I called.

She came over to me. "Yes, signore?"

"This message, where did it come from?"

"A boy delivered it an hour ago. I am sorry, signore. I thought you were sleeping. If I had known you were awake, I would have brought it up earlier."

"What type of boy?" I asked. "What did he look like? How old was he?"

My intensity startled her. "Let me think, signore. Young, about eleven or twelve. Blond hair."

"One of the neighborhood boys? Was he wearing livery?"

She looked at me quizzically. "Is something wrong with the message, signore?"

I sighed and ran my hand through my hair. "I am sorry, madame. I did not mean to interrogate you. I am just tired."

She nodded. "I understand, signore. You need not apologize. You have had a terrible day." She thought for a moment.

"No, I've never seen the boy before. He wasn't wearing any uniform. I wish I could tell you more. Is it important?"

I shook my head. "Probably not. Thank you, madame."

"I will say good night, signore. I am sorry about your friend."

I went back into my room and threw the message on the desk. I was not in the mood for another mysterious communication tonight. I took the volume of Dante over to my bed, lit a candle on my small bedside table, and resumed my reading, but soon found that I could not regain my interest in the poetry. I glanced over at the desk and shook my head. I was being silly. It was a piece of paper, that was all, as were the other two messages I had received. It was simply my imagination that made me think they were a threat to me. Someone—perhaps one of my enemies at court or at the theater—was merely playing a vexatious prank on me.

I went to the desk and picked up the message. Now that I examined it closely, I could see that it was different from the previous two. This paper was crisply folded and neatly addressed to me here at the house. When I turned the packet around, I saw the imperial seal stamped into the wax. My fingers trembling, I ripped the message open and read it. My attendance was requested by Count Anton Pergen, tomorrow morning at ten, at the offices of the Ministry of Police.

I changed into my nightshirt, snuffed out my candle, and climbed into bed. Exhaustion seeped through me, but I did not fall asleep. Reminiscences of my good times with Alois jostled with darker memories of my encounter with Pergen and Troger two years ago. Outside my window, a crash of thunder ushered in the storm. Soon raindrops hit the glass and flashes of lightning lit up my small room. I tossed and turned, finding no comfortable position that could lull my weary body to rest. A loose shutter on the house across the street banged in the wind. I lay and listened to it for hours, waiting for the dawn.

Four

"So now you see, Da Ponte, why we suspect there is more to Father Bayer's murder than a mere robbery gone wrong." Count Pergen, the minister of police, looked tired, as if, like me, he had been up all night.

I had presented myself at the requested hour, and this time the secretary had taken my cloak and led me into the minister's office. The room was even more lavish than the anteroom, grand and airy, with damask wall coverings and large paintings hung around the walls, a setting fit more for the emperor than for one of his ministers. Thorwart's worries about the budget of the theater briefly crossed my mind, but I shook them away. The count must have paid for the expensive adornments himself. The emperor was too humble a man and frugal a ruler to allow treasury monies to be spent on decorating imperial offices.

Pergen had been seated behind a large, ornately carved desk. Troger sprawled in one of two chairs on the opposite side. He had gazed stonily down his hawklike nose at me as the count gestured me to take the remaining chair. In the corner of the room, staring out one of the tall windows that lined an entire wall, stood the blond-haired, stocky man I had seen the other day in the cathedral with Christiane Albrechts, the deceased general's daughter. Pergen had introduced her fiancé to me as Count Richard Benda. The count had greeted me in a softly accented voice, shaken my hand, and then returned to his station by the window.

Now I was reeling at the information Pergen had just related about the death of my friend. "I don't understand," I said. "Alois's face was disfigured?"

"Yes," Troger said. "His throat was cut first, with a short, thin dagger. The carvings in his forehead were made with its tip. The markings were strange—a straight line, from the bridge of his nose to his hairline. To the right of that, a half circle."

A shiver ran down my spine.

"We believe the carving was done after Father Bayer was dead," Pergen said gently. "He must have gone quickly, after the killer cut his throat."

I nodded dumbly to keep him from saying more. My poor, gentle friend. What had he possibly done to deserve such a gruesome death?

"There's more you should know, Da Ponte," Pergen continued.

I sagged in my chair. What more could the monster have done to a poor, defenseless old man?

"Father Bayer was not the first man to die in this manner," Pergen said. "General Albrechts's body was found last week in the Am Hof, sprawled at the base of the Marian Column. His throat had been cut in the same manner."

I frowned. "I heard that he died of a seizure," I said.

"That's the word we put out," Pergen said. "His body was found in the very early hours of the morning, before the market square became busy. We removed the body immediately and instructed the papers to print the story that the general had been taken by a seizure."

I sat speechless.

"The general's forehead was not carved, like your friend's was," Troger said. "But his body was also defiled. The killer burned his legs and the lower part of his torso, up to his waist."

I sat silent, my mind grasping to understand the horror Troger described.

"His throat had been cut in the same manner, with what looks like the same weapon as killed Bayer," Troger continued. "And his body was arranged around the base of the Marian Column, exactly the same way as Bayer's was around the Capistran Chancel."

"It must be the same person committing these crimes," Pergen said. "Someone with a vendetta against these men."

"I don't understand," I said. "I can imagine that the general might have had enemies. But Alois? He was a simple, peaceful priest. Why would anyone want to kill him?"

Count Benda turned from the window. "Was he involved in politics at all?" he asked me.

I shook my head. "No, I don't believe so. He was a scholar. He spent his days studying ecclesiastical philosophy. His books and work were his life. In all the years I've known him, I've never heard him speak about political issues."

"What was his view of the war?" Pergen asked.

I shrugged. "I have no idea. We never spoke of it."

Troger raised an eyebrow. "Never? Why, everyone in the city is talking about this war. It seems that is all people talk about. Surely you two must have discussed it once or twice."

"We talked about books and poetry," I said. "Are you saying that some madman killed Alois because of his political views? That is ridiculous."

Pergen glanced at Benda.

"It could be that the old priest represented something to the killer," Benda said. "The fact that he was murdered at the base of the Capistran Chancel—below that statue of the saint subduing the Turk—might be important. The killer may be attacking symbols of Austrian greatness."

I opened my mouth to interrupt, but Benda raised his hand to stop me.

"He has already murdered the general, the country's greatest war hero," he continued. "Perhaps he wished to attack the church next. He may have lurked outside the cathedral last night, waiting for a priest—any priest—to come by. Your friend might just have been in the wrong place at the wrong time."

Pergen nodded. "That's as good a theory as we have," he said. He turned to me. "Da Ponte, I have a proposal for you."

I slumped in my chair.

"I was very impressed that you found the killer in the Palais Gabler two years ago," he said smoothly. "We are shorthanded here at the ministry. Many of our staff investigators are with the emperor in Semlin. We have our hands full with other matters of great importance to the future of the empire."

My heart sank. I knew where this was leading.

"Count Benda is going to lead the investigation of these murders for us," Pergen continued. "When Troger mentioned that you had come here yesterday, I realized that you would be a good candidate to assist him. He knew the general well, and you were close to Father Bayer. You have some experience solving a murder, which he does not."

"But—"

"I'm confident the two of you can solve this case for me." He studied me. "What do you say? Will you help us find the killer of your friend?"

I shook my head. "I cannot—"

"If you are worried about the danger, you may rest assured that I will guarantee your safety," Pergen said.

I sighed. I wished I were anywhere in the world but here, slumped in this chair in this opulent office. It had taken me a long time to recover from my ordeal two years ago. I didn't believe I had the strength to go through such a challenge again. And could I trust Pergen and Troger to protect me from harm? But then I remembered the look on Alois's bloody face. The fear I felt right now was nothing compared to what he must have felt when he had encountered his killer, and realized that his life had come to an end. He had been a second father to me. How could I not attempt to find his murderer?

I sat up straight.

"I'll do it," I said.

. . .

Benda and I made our way to the pastry shop in the Michaelerplatz. At this time of the morning, the small, cheery café was bustling with patrons. The proprietor recognized Benda and led us to a small private room.

"Have you been here before?" Benda asked as we sat. "The cream slice is my favorite. But the doughnut puffs are also delicious. If you prefer something lighter, I'd suggest a fruit ice."

I shook my head. "I don't have much of a sweet tooth," I said.

"Oh, but you should try these. The owner, Dehne, came here from Württemberg two years ago." He gestured toward the busy main room. "As you can see, he has built a following. He caters all of the society parties now."

A waiter approached. Benda ordered a cream slice, and I asked for coffee.

"I had to use all my connections to get Pergen to agree to let me investigate the general's murder," Benda said after the waiter left. "I promised Christiane—my fiancée, the general's daughter—that I would find her father's killer. She is distraught with grief, as you may well imagine."

The waiter brought my coffee and Benda's pastry. The crust crunched as the count's fork cut into it. He took a bite and smiled. "Delicious, as always. Would you like a taste?"

I shook my head. I had no appetite.

"Pergen's busy tamping down the protests against the war and implementing the new censorship rules. He's also involved with suppressing the uprisings in the Netherlands. When the general's body was found, the ministry believed it was just a vicious robbery. They were content to let the constabulary investigate. Of course, that department is useless—they are hopelessly understaffed."

He paused to shovel another large bite of pastry into his mouth.

"Christiane was indignant. She believed that one of her father's enemies had murdered him. I was at my estate in Bohemia when it happened. I rushed here to be with her. When I learned about the burns on the body, I agreed with her."

I took a sip of coffee.

"Christiane had already asked the police to say that her father had died of natural causes. When I made inquiries, I found the constabulary had done little to investigate the crime. When your friend was found yesterday, Pergen was forced to pay attention to the similarities in the deaths."

He ate the last bite of pastry, then scraped the remaining cream off his plate with his fork and popped it into his mouth.

"Ah, I could eat two more of those," he said.

"Which day was the general's body found?" I asked.

"Last Wednesday morning. As I was saying, once Pergen's office became involved yesterday, I went directly to Prince Kaunitz." Kaunitz was the emperor's chancellor, who was running the government while the emperor was away at the front. "He agreed with me that these killings had a political motivation. He instructed Pergen to let me lead the investigation."

"I don't understand the politics," I said.

"There is a lot of opposition to this war," Benda said.

"No, not many are as vocal as these young men who stand shouting in the streets, but in the private rooms of the city, there is a great deal of discontent." He scraped his fork along the surface of the empty plate. "I believe the killer is murdering his victims as an expression of opposition to the war, to the government, to everything the country stands for."

I thought for a moment. "I accept that someone might have seen the general as a symbol of the country, but what about Alois?" I asked. "He was just a simple priest, a scholar."

"First the killer murdered the general, a great war hero. He struck at the heart of Austria's power, the army. For his next murder, he aimed at the church, another powerful institution."

"But Alois wasn't involved in running the church—"

Benda shrugged. "As I said back in Pergen's office, I think the killer wanted a priest, any priest. Father Bayer just had unlucky timing. The killer would have chosen any priest he encountered that night."

I gritted my teeth at his dismissal of Alois as merely a random priest, but I knew there was no purpose in arguing with the man. His mind was made up. "Where do we begin?" I asked.

"Yesterday Troger's men finally questioned people who live and work around the Am Hof, where the general was killed. They found a witness who says he saw the general early Wednesday morning. He's a baker who has a shop near the plaza. Do you have time to go see him now?"

I nodded. Benda called for the waiter and paid the bill. We left the shop and walked down the busy Kohlmarkt, then turned left and continued down the Naglergasse, the narrow street that had been home to the city's needlemakers in the Middle Ages. At the very end of the street, just before it joined the Heidenschuss, the baker's sign hung over the entrance to a small shop. As we approached the door, it opened, and a tall, red-faced man rushed out.

"You'll pay for this, Vetter!" he shouted back into the shop. He waved a loaf of bread in our faces. "Look at this! This is what he calls a loaf of bread! It's half the normal size!" He spat on the ground. Benda took a step back.

"He's a goddamn thief!" The man stormed off toward the Am Hof.

We entered the shop. There were not many loaves left on the shelves at this time of day. Baskets of stale crusts for soup and bags of crumbs sat on the long counter. To the side, charcoal left from the baker's ovens sat in tubs awaiting sale to those whose budget did not include fresh wood.

"I'll be with you in a moment." The baker was leaning over his baskets, his back to us. When he turned and saw Benda's fine clothes, he hastily stood to attention.

"Gentlemen, how can I help you?" He glanced at the door. "I apologize for my last customer."

"You must hear a lot of that these days," Benda said.

"Oh yes, sir," the baker said. He shrugged. "But what can I do? Everyone in the city knows that the wheat from Hungary is now sent to the troops. I spend half my day trying to locate new sources of flour. And no one wants the darker loaves; everyone wants the nice white bread. So I am forced to make my loaves smaller. What else can I do?"

We nodded our sympathy.

"How may I help you, sirs?"

Benda introduced himself and then me, and explained that we had some questions about the general's death.

"Ah, yes. The constable told me to expect someone," Vetter said. He sighed. "The poor general. My father served with him in the war. To think that I might have been one of the last to see him before he died." He frowned. "Funny, though. He didn't look ill when I saw him."

"What time was this?" Benda asked.

"It was one o'clock Wednesday morning, sir. I know because I was on my way here to the shop, to start work."

"You don't live upstairs?" I asked.

"No, sir. I know it's odd. And to be honest, it isn't easy for me. I live with my wife's family around the corner in the Tiefer Graben. Her mother refused to leave her own house to come live here with us when my father-in-law died. My Johanna wants to be close by, to keep an eye on the old lady. So I must come here every night."

"Tell us where you saw the general," Benda said.

"I was coming down the Tiefer Graben. I had almost reached the corner when I saw a man hurry by. It was the general."

"Are you sure of that?" Benda asked.

"Oh yes, sir. I'd seen him once or twice before, so I recognized him. And it was a clear night. The moon wasn't full, but there was still plenty of light to make out faces."

"Which direction did he come from?"

"From the Freyung. His palace is right down the street from here."

"Did he say anything to you?"

"No. He nodded at me, and then hurried toward the Am Hof."

"Was there anyone else in the street?" Benda asked. "Did you see or hear anything else?"

"No, sir. No one else was about. I was unlocking the shop when I heard voices coming from around the corner, in the Am Hof."

"How many voices?"

"Two. Two men shouting."

"Could you hear what they were saying?"

"No, sir. Their voices sounded angry, as though they were arguing. But I couldn't make out what they were saying. A moment later, I heard footsteps—a man running. I turned to look. A man ran out of the Am Hof, toward the corner right here."

"The general?"

"No, another man, younger. He stopped for a moment and saw me, then ran down the street toward the Freyung."

"Did you get a good look at him? Could you describe him?" Benda's voice was eager. "Was he tall? Heavy? What color hair did he have? What was he wearing?"

The baker held up his hand to stop Benda. "I can tell you more than all that, sir. You see, I recognized him. It was that protester—the young ragged one who is always standing on that crate yelling about the war."

"Did you hear any screams?" Benda asked.

Vetter shook his head. "No, sir, just the argument. As soon as the protester ran off, I came inside and went downstairs to check on my leaven. I was down there the rest of the night, doing my baking. I was shocked when I heard from my customers that afternoon that the general had died."

He peered at Benda. "Why are you asking me these questions, sir? I heard the general had a seizure, at home in bed. What is going on?"

"None of your concern," Benda said.

We thanked the man and left.

"Let's look at the spot where the general was found," Benda said. We walked around the corner to the Am Hof. The largest square in the city, the plaza was busy as fruit sellers and bake stands were discounting their wares at the end of the morning. We made our way to the center of the plaza, to the Marian Column, a monument dedicated to the Virgin Mary, who legend says aided the Viennese in re-sisting invasion by Sweden a hundred years ago. The lady stood atop a tall bronze pillar that rose from a large stone plinth. The entire structure was surrounded by a low balus-trade wall, below which sat three short, shallow stone steps. At all four corners of the plinth, pudgy bronze cherubs, clad in armor, trampled upon creatures that represented the four scourges of humanity—war, heresy, famine, and plague.

"The general was found lying here." Benda pointed to the right-hand corner of the monument. "His body was draped across the steps, his right arm propped against the wall here. His left arm was limp against his side."

I leaned in to examine the wall. Although the light-colored stone had been scrubbed, faint specks of blood remained. "Alois's body was in the same position," I mur-mured. I looked up at the cherub who guarded this corner of the statue. He held a sword in his right arm, and his body was twisted, ready to deal the death blow to the large serpent under his foot. He stared down at me with scornful eyes. I moved to the right a bit to avoid his gaze.

"We have to find that protester," Benda was saying. "If he's not our killer, he might have seen something the baker did not."

"He's often over in the Graben or the Stephansplatz," I said as I stepped away from the monument. The back of my neck tingled as the cherub's contemptuous eyes followed me.

"I'll send a message to Troger," Benda said. "He should be able to find the man's name and address." He drew his watch from his coat pocket. "I have an appointment at the chancery," he said. "Why don't we meet tomorrow morning, Da Ponte? Come by Christiane's house around ten. I stay there when I am in town. Her steward saw the general leave the house early Wednesday morning. I've questioned him, but maybe another telling of his story might elicit new details. Do you know the house?"

"The Palais Albrechts?" I asked.

"Yes. It's in the Freyung, the second to last palace on the left, right across from the Scottish Church. You cannot miss it."

We said our good-byes and Benda hurried through the arch on the northeast side of the square, toward the Bohemian Chancery. I started toward the other end of the plaza. After I had taken a few steps, I looked back at the site of the general's murder. The cherub gazed down at me with disdain. I shuddered. He seemed almost alive.

I turned and hastened out of the square toward the Kohlmarkt.

Five

I picked at my dinner in a catering shop in the Graben, and spent a few hours in my office preparing libretto booklets for upcoming performances at the theater. As theater poet, I was responsible for editing and printing all of the librettos. This part of my job was tedious, yet had its pecuniary rewards, for I collected a percentage of each booklet sold. And today, the detailed work brought with it an extra blessing— it distracted my thoughts from my meeting this morning with Pergen, Troger, and Benda.

I finished correcting errors in *La modesta raggiratrice,* a libretto by Lorenzi, which would premiere next week. I went out to the small cupboard in the hallway to check that there were still copies of my own work, *Axur,* and of Petrosellini's *Il barbiere di Siviglia* to last the rest of the month. I frowned. A large black scythe, which was carried by the figure of Death in my opera *Axur,* had joined the other props in the narrow hallway. I must speak to Thorwart. His workmen could not continue leaving the props here.

Back in the office, I drew the notes I had been making for the *Don Giovanni* burlesque scene from my satchel. As I stared at my scratchings, my respite from the horror of Alois's murder came to an end. I could not prevent the vision of the gash in his throat and the surprised expression on his face from filling my eyes. I wished that Pergen had not told me that my friend's body had been mutilated in such a grotesque manner.

A knock on the door stirred me from my dark thoughts.

"Come in," I called.

Felix Urbanek, the priest from the Stephansdom, entered. "Ah, Da Ponte, I've finally found you. This place has more hallways and crannies than the cathedral!"

I stood to greet him and motioned him to the chair I keep for visitors.

"I am here to offer my condolences on the death of Father Bayer," Urbanek said. "I know that you and he were close friends."

"He was like a father to me," I said.

"The body has been taken to the cemetery in St. Marx. The burial will be tomorrow. I told the mortuary director that I thought Father Bayer would want a simple, modern burial—in the common grave without any coffin or marker."

I nodded. "Yes, I agree with you. He was a humble man, but modern in his outlook. I'm sure that is what he would have chosen."

"I am organizing a memorial service for him," the priest

continued. "Father Krause has agreed to lead it. We have a slight problem, though."

"What sort of problem?"

"It seems we don't know all that much about Father Bayer, even though he spent most of his life at the cathedral. He came here before we instituted the new system of recordkeeping. Would you know if he has any family?"

"He has—had—a sister in Innsbruck. They hadn't seen each other for years, but she should be notified. I doubt she would be able to make the trip, but I'm certain Alois would want her to be told of his death." I paused, thinking. "Anna, her name is. Her married name is Wex. Yes, Anna Wex."

Urbanek took a small notebook from his pocket and wrote down the name. "I'll send a message to her right away." He sighed. "I don't enjoy being the bearer of such sad news. The way he died—" He shivered. "Perhaps I should just tell her he died suddenly. There's no need for her to know the horrific details."

"Yes, I think that would be wise," I said.

Urbanek stood. "Well then. That is all I needed. I'll let you know when the date of the service is set."

I gathered my papers and put them in my satchel. "I'm ready to head home. Are you going back to the cathedral? I'll walk with you."

We climbed the stairs to the lobby and went out into the Michaelerplatz. We strolled down the Kohlmarkt and into the Graben, sharing our memories of Alois. I told Urbanek how I had met Alois the first time, when both of us had reached for the same copy of Petrarch's epistles in a bookshop in the Jewish quarter. "He was a great companion," I told Urbanek. "We both loved the same things—books, poetry, fine wine."

"He was a good priest," Urbanek said. "I was sorry to see him retire to his little room, to bury himself in his studies." We passed by the Baroque plague column. The young protester was nowhere to be seen.

"You are a priest yourself, Da Ponte, are you not?" Urbanek asked.

I did not answer.

"I hope you don't think I am intruding. I am merely curious. Why do you no longer practice?"

I sighed. "It's a long story, Father. I took minor orders when I was young. My father was a leatherworker with three young sons. When he remarried, the local monsignor took our family under his protection, and sent me to the seminary to be educated. It was there that I discovered my love of poetry." I did not add that my family was Jewish, and that the monsignor had converted us to Christianity.

Urbanek nodded. We continued into the Stock-im-Eisen-Platz, the small square between the Graben and the Stephansplatz.

"Our patron died suddenly when I was sixteen, and the seminary informed my father that if I were to continue there, I must train for the priesthood. I knew that I was not suited for the profession, but my father insisted. He had remarried, and no longer had the means to support me."

"Yet I've heard you served the church when you lived in Venice," Urbanek said.

"Yes, I did. I must confess I found serving as a parish priest an easy way to earn some money. But I knew the church was not my calling."

"Are you sure you wouldn't change your mind?" Urbanek asked. "The church needs intelligent priests like you."

I laughed. "Now you sound just like Alois, Father!"

As we entered the Stephansplatz and approached the great front portal of the cathedral, an angry voice greeted us.

"No, you listen to me, you goddamn Turk-lover!" The crippled nobleman I had seen arguing with the war protester earlier in the week stood in front of the doors. "Don't tell me you love this country!"

My fellow lodger, Erich Strasser, put up his hands to shield himself from Hennen's anger. "I merely said—"

"If you were a true patriot, you wouldn't be sitting in your comfortable office over at the university, feeding propaganda and outright lies to those young boys you teach!"

"I am not lying to my students," Strasser replied. "I am teaching them to look at this war from both sides."

Hennen waved his stick in front of Strasser's face, and then lifted it over his head. "If you truly loved Austria, you'd be in Semlin with the emperor and his brave men. You are just a coward, posing as an intellectual!" As he brought the stick down, Strasser ducked to avoid the blow.

Urbanek rushed forward and took the nobleman's arm. "Baron Hennen," he said. "Please, no violence. This is holy ground." Strasser glanced at me, turned, and hurried away.

The baron shoved the priest's hand off his arm. "I am sorry, Father. I just hate cowards. He has a lot of nerve, always talking about how Austria is the aggressor in this war. I am tired of hearing it." He gestured toward Strasser's back. "See, there he goes, slinking off. He doesn't even have the courage to stay here and argue with me."

"Come inside, my son," Urbanek said. "Come in and sit with me a while. We will pray together. You will find some peace."

"No, thank you, Father. There is nothing in there for me," Hennen said. "Excuse me. I must get home." He turned and clumped toward the Stock-im-Eisen-Platz.

Urbanek shook his head as we watched him go. "That man is always angry," he said.

"He seems to pick a fight with anyone who doesn't agree with him about the war," I said.

Urbanek thought for a moment. "No. He's angry at God, I think—because he is a cripple."

I said good-bye and watched Urbanek enter the cathedral. When I rounded the corner of the building, I saw Strasser at the far end of the side plaza. I ran to catch up with him.

"Are you all right, Erich?" I asked.

"Oh, Lorenzo! Good evening. Yes, I am fine. Are you headed home?"

I nodded. We turned into the Wollzeile. "That's the second time this week I've seen Baron Hennen arguing with someone about the war," I said.

Strasser let out a deep breath. "Yes. My work makes me an easy target for these prowar zealots. And it doesn't help that I look like a Turk."

"Are you opposed to the war?" I asked.

"Yes, Lorenzo, I am. It is not a just war. The Ottomans

are not the aggressors here. They are merely defending their borders from the empress of Russia's plans to dominate the Black Sea." We walked past the medieval university building and the pleasant square that fronted the university church.

"I thought the emperor was imprudent to sign the treaty promising to support Catherine," Strasser continued. "His decision was shortsighted. He's alienating all of our allies in western Europe with this war. Many of them were already dismayed by his expansionist policies in Bavaria and the Netherlands."

We walked through the Stuben gate. Ahead of us, on the banks of the narrow river, a team of oxen was pulling a barge. The long, flat boat was loaded with two large howitzer guns.

"How many times have you traveled to the Ottoman Empire?" I asked. "It is clear that you love the place."

"I was born there," Strasser said. "My father was an engineer here in Vienna. He was sent to Constantinople by the old empress to map some of the territory around the Ottoman capital. My mother was a Turk, the daughter of a merchant. They had a brief, hard marriage. My mother was ostracized from her family for marrying a Christian. She died a year after I was born. My father sent me here to Vienna, to live with his aunt and uncle while he continued his work for the empress. I never saw him again. He died in Constantinople two years later."

We turned into our street.

"I suppose that's why I've committed my life to studying the Ottomans," Strasser said. "It's my way of staying close to the memory of my parents. When the empress established the Oriental Academy to foster the study of the empire, I was one of its first pupils. I've been there ever since."

I was silent. I had lost my own mother when I was five years old, and had few memories of her.

"I've dedicated my life to encouraging an understanding between our two peoples," Strasser continued. "But it is difficult. So many Viennese are eager to believe the tales—like our landlady and her daughter."

I laughed. "Yes, their ideas were a bit silly."

Strasser smiled. "Miss Sophie may seem silly to us, Lorenzo, but that boy Stefan had better take care. She could be the ruin of him someday."

"Yes. He is besotted with her," I agreed.

We entered the house. All was quiet. The stairs creaked as we climbed the stairs to our rooms and said good night. I entered my room, put down my satchel, and hung my coat in the cupboard. A message sat on my desk. I snatched it up and saw the familiar scrawl and mess of wax. I quickly broke the seal and read the contents, which by now I knew by heart.

33 27 54 71 52 33 61 33 28 55
Verrò
21 aprile

Six

I knew it was foolish of me to read the mysterious messages as portents of approaching troubles, but nevertheless, I spent a sleepless night racking my brain, trying to decipher their meaning. The row of numbers was obviously some sort of code, but I had no idea how to interpret it, and had no clue as to the identity of the person who persisted in announcing his arrival on April 21, just two days from now. The messages had been delivered both to my office and to my home. Someone obviously knew where to find me. Perhaps the sender had an innocent intent, but still, the fact that the messages were written in Italian nagged at me. Could they have been sent by someone in Venice? Was my past catching up with me?

I left my lodgings in the morning with that strange feeling one has when one hasn't slept well—a combination of physical exhaustion and a racing mind. I knew that by the end of this day, I would be dragging, longing for my bed.

The cinnamon roll and cup of coffee I had at my favorite coffeehouse in the Graben did nothing to revive me. I spent an hour in the office and then took my satchel and walked over to the Freyung, the large triangular market area near the old Scottish Church.

Eight years ago, before I arrived in Vienna, the Benedictine monks who occupied the medieval monastery—it was popularly referred to as a church but was actually one of the few monasteries left in the city—had pressured the city government to remove the busy fruit and vegetable market that had thrived in the plaza. The vendors had merely moved their stalls away from the steps of the church into the wider southeastern end of the plaza, and on this pleasant Saturday morning, they were conducting a brisk trade in cabbages, onions, and peas.

The Palais Albrechts stood on the left side of the plaza, and appeared to have been designed by the same architect who had planted tedious, bulky stone boxes all over the city. I walked through a short passageway into the courtyard. Four lackeys were carting panniers heaped with clothing, linens, and kitchen goods out of the palais and standing them in large wagons. A bald-headed, jug-eared man in the uniform of a steward directed the activity.

Benda came to the door. "Don't forget the boxes in the library," he called to the steward. He looked over and, seeing me, came out to greet me. "Good, Da Ponte, you found us. Thank you for coming." He gestured toward the carts. "We're preparing to move out to Christiane's summer palace."

I nodded. I had heard that General Albrechts owned a

large, luxurious estate called the Belvedere, directly outside the city walls in the southeastern suburb of Favoriten.

"I tried to convince Christiane that she wasn't up to all this trouble," Benda continued. "But she insisted the work of packing would help assuage her grief— No! You there! Those are not mine. Those go to the cart over here, the one for the church." He leaned toward me and lowered his voice. "The general's clothes," he murmured. "She didn't wish to part with them, but I convinced her that the church would benefit greatly by selling them."

He called over to the steward, and turned back to me. "After we marry, we'll sell this house and the Belvedere estate and move to Prague. I must take Christiane away from all of these painful memories."

The steward joined us. "Altmann, tell Signor Da Ponte what you told me, about the night the general died," Benda instructed.

The man nodded a greeting at me. "Well, sir, I saw the general leave that night. It was very late, a little before one in the morning. It was quite strange to see him."

"He did not often leave the house at night?" I asked.

"No, sir. The general kept to a strict schedule—a habit from his military days, I suppose. He went to bed at ten o'clock every night. He claimed a good night's sleep kept him fit for battle." The steward smiled sadly at the remembrance of his master. "He was an old man, but I think he secretly hoped the emperor would call on him once more."

"What time do you close up the house?" I asked.

"Before midnight, sir. As I said, the general always retired at ten. The young mistress often stayed up later, talking with the count in the salon. And she likes to read late into the night, those sentimental novels about love all the young ladies enjoy these days. Sometimes when I am making my rounds before I lock up, I'll see the light still on in her chamber. Her maid Charlotte scolds her, telling her she'll ruin her eyes. But other than that, it is a quiet household."

"Why were you up at one that night?" Benda prompted.

"The weather that day had been very windy, as though a storm were coming. I always sleep with one ear cocked, since the palais is my responsibility. I heard a door slam. My first thought was that I had forgotten to secure one of the doors, and the wind had blown it shut. But a few moments later I heard footsteps, someone running. I dressed and went down to check."

"Was that when you saw your master?" I asked.

"No, sir. No, I heard the noise a few minutes before I saw him. When I got down here to the courtyard, I saw no one. I went out into the street to see if anyone was about, but everything was dark and quiet. I tested the doors here. They all were locked." He pointed toward a small door set in the right-hand side of the courtyard. "I had just entered the servants' door to return to my room when I heard the front door open. I cracked the servants' door open a bit so I could see. I heard the door close, then I saw the general cross the court and go out through the passageway."

"Did you call to him?" I asked.

He shook his head. "No, sir. Oh, no. The general would not have appreciated me inquiring into his business. It wasn't my place to ask where he was going in the middle of the night."

"Did you notice anything strange about him? How was he dressed?"

"He was wearing a suit, sir, but no cloak. That night was the beginning of this warm spell. He looked as if he were going out on business for the day." He thought for a moment. "Now that I think about it, there was something odd. He was carrying an object in his hand."

"A satchel? A bag?" Benda pressed.

"No. Please, sir, let me think. No, not a bag. Ah, I remember. It was a piece of paper."

Benda glanced at me.

"How did he seem to you?" I asked the steward. "Could he have been sleepwalking?"

The man stared at me with surprise, and then laughed. "Ah, sir, I see you've never served in the army. Generals never walk in their sleep. My master slept deeply all night, and was a man of action during the day. No, I'd swear he was wide awake. He was walking briskly, with purpose—as if he were going to an appointment."

"No paper was found by the general's body," Benda said as we entered the palais.

"And none by Alois," I said. "Troger would have mentioned it."

"I've sent him a message, asking him to find that war protester. You know, Da Ponte, the more I think about it, the more I believe that these two killings are definitely connected. The murderer is making some sort of pronouncement against the war."

I wasn't so sure. I paused to gather my thoughts as we

entered a large foyer. A grand staircase, its balusters and newel posts made of red stone veined with white streaks, dominated the room. Benda gestured for me to leave my satchel on the floor, and then led me up the wide marble stairs.

"Well, I agree with you that it is the same man committing these murders," I said. "The victims were killed with the same type of weapon, and each body was mutilated in some way. Both victims were killed near some sort of monument, and the bodies were found in the same position. But—"

"Yes," Benda said excitedly. "It's as if the killer were arranging each victim in a sort of display. That's why I believe the murders are related to the war. Both murders were committed in busy areas of the city—he wants all of Vienna to see his handiwork."

We reached the first landing and stopped between two large doorways.

"But what about the differences in the treatment of the bodies?" I asked. "The burning of the general's legs and lower torso, and the strange marks on Alois's forehead? What could those mean?"

Benda waved off my objections. "We just don't understand it all yet. But after we question that protester, we'll know more. Remember, the baker heard him argue with the general, and saw him running from the scene of the murder."

My thoughts returned to the horrible morning outside the cathedral. The protester had arrived soon after Alois's body had been discovered. Had he simply been attracted by the size of the crowd, seeing a large audience for his speeches, or was he the killer, standing on his crate exulting in the scene beneath the Capistran chancel? I couldn't imagine that such evil could exist in another human being.

I wasn't ready to agree with Benda's theory, however. While I could understand that if a killer wished to murder for political reasons he might choose a great war hero like the general as a victim, I could not fathom the reason he had also killed my dear friend, who had never involved himself in politics, and who had wished for nothing but to pass his remaining days with his beloved books. Benda was grasping at conclusions too quickly. I sighed. It was clear to me that I would play the uncomfortable role of challenger to his speculations. But if I must, I would. Jumping to conclusions had gotten me nowhere in my investigation two years ago, and my myopia had resulted in the death of someone I had held dear.

I opened my mouth to voice my disagreement. "I think—"

Benda motioned me toward a smaller door on the right-hand side of the landing and shook his head. "Ah, there you are, my love!" Benda cried as he entered the room. I followed him into a large salon. The room was square, its walls covered with rich blue damask, its high ceiling painted with a complicated scene of buxom young women cavorting in a pine forest. Tall windows draped in the same damask as the walls lined the right-side wall. A long sideboard sat along the left wall. The seating had been pulled to the center of the room to make the space more intimate. Two sofas colored the deep blue of the walls faced one another, while a large armchair sat under the window. An elegant, tall clock cabinet faced with blond wood and ivory marquetry stood alone on the farthest wall.

The woman I had seen with Benda in the cathedral rose from the armchair. Her tall, slender frame still wore the black satin of mourning.

"Christiane, this is Lorenzo Da Ponte. Da Ponte, my fiancée, Christiane Albrechts," Benda said.

She came to me and offered her hand. I bowed, and then looked up into large violet eyes full of sorrow. Her raven hair was pulled back into a chignon. Gone was the extraordinary emotion I had witnessed in the cathedral days ago. It was as if she were a balloon fallen to the ground, all of its roiling, hot air cooled, leaving just a limp cloth shell. "I am pleased to meet you, Signor Da Ponte," she murmured. "Richard has explained that you will be assisting him with his investigation."

"It is an honor to meet you, mademoiselle," I said. "May I offer my heartfelt condolences on the loss of your father?"

"And mine to you, for the loss of your friend," she said.

Benda sat on the nearest sofa. "Come, sit down, Da Ponte," he said.

"I'll ring for some coffee," Christiane said. I remained standing until she had rung the service bell and sat back in the armchair.

"Please make yourself comfortable, signore," she said. I took a seat next to Benda.

"I'm sure Richard has already explained to you that Count Pergen wishes to keep the true circumstances of my father's death from the public," she said.

I nodded.

"That is also my wish. I do not want my father's name involved in sordid gossip." She leaned forward and studied me intently. "Can you think of any possible relationship your friend could have had with my father?"

"Come, love, we have discussed this," Benda said. "We believe Father Bayer was just in the wrong place at the wrong time. The killer wanted to strike at the church by murdering a priest—any priest."

Christiane gazed at him. "I know that is what you believe, Richard, but I—" She looked over to the door as a servant entered the room. "Yes, what is it?"

"Excuse me, mademoiselle. Baron von Gerl is downstairs. He wishes to present his condolences."

Her thin hand flew to her throat. "Von Gerl is here?" She looked over at Benda, who had stood. "I don't think I'm ready to receive anyone yet."

"It's just von Gerl, my love," Benda said. "He's probably come to offer his assistance."

"No, Richard, please. I don't think I am able to see anyone else, not today." She sat upright in the chair, her body stiff.

"We should receive him, Christiane. He is your neighbor. It would not be proper to send him away." Benda addressed the servant. "Send the baron up." The man glanced at his mistress, who sat wringing her hands together, then nodded at Benda and left the room, closing the door behind him.

"But Richard," Christiane protested. "My hair, my dress, I am not prepared to receive guests—"

"Nonsense," Benda answered. "You look beautiful. No one expects you to be dressed à la mode when you are in mourning." He went to her, squeezed her hand, and moved to gaze out the window.

A moment later the door opened once more. A tall, lissome man with short, curly black hair and a cropped dark beard bounded into the room.

"Baron von Gerl, mademoiselle," the servant announced.

Von Gerl rushed to Christiane's chair and bowed to her. "Mademoiselle Albrechts," he said. "I have just this minute returned from taking the waters in Baden. My valet told me about your father's unfortunate demise. No, no, please. Do not get up."

I watched as he leaned over, took her hand, and kissed it, his lips lingering a bit too long than was neighborly. Her violet eyes widened.

"Is there anything I can do for you?" he asked. Christiane shook her head.

"Had he been ill? What happened?"

Benda glanced over at me and shook his head slightly, warning me not to discuss the murders in front of this man. He moved to stand by his fiancée's chair. "It was a seizure," he said. "It was very sudden."

Von Gerl released Christiane's hand and grabbed one of Benda's. "Benda! I'm glad you are here with her." Christiane's hand trembled as she idly fingered the lace at the collar of her dress. The newcomer turned to me.

"Von Gerl, this is Lorenzo Da Ponte, a friend of mine," Benda said. "Da Ponte, Valentin von Gerl."

The baron's eyes widened. "Da Ponte? The theater poet?" he asked.

I nodded.

"It's a pleasure to meet you!" von Gerl said, shaking my hand.

"The pleasure is mine, sir," I replied.

"I loved your latest with Salieri. I'm afraid I missed your big hit, the one with the Spaniard, Martín. I was living abroad when that was performed. And the one you wrote before that, the one based on the Beaumarchais play—" He scratched his head. "What was the name of that composer?"

"Mozart," I said.

"Of course! Mozart. I've never heard his work. Maybe someday, now that I am in Vienna to stay. I'm a great fan of the opera."

The door opened and a servant entered with a large tray containing a pot of coffee and four cups. He placed it on the sideboard, poured four cups, and brought one to Christiane. Her hands trembled as she accepted the drink.

Von Gerl settled on the sofa across from me, at the end nearest his hostess. "How long have you been in Vienna?" he asked me.

"Almost seven years," I said. "Why do you ask?"

"I can still hear the Veneto in your speech," he answered.

I raised an eyebrow. "I am impressed, sir."

"Venice, I would guess," von Gerl continued. "Am I right?"

"Yes, I lived several years in Venice, before I came here." The baron beamed. "Hah! I could tell."

"Very good, von Gerl," Benda said. "Very impressive." He returned to his place on the sofa and turned to his fiancée, who was gazing at her neighbor. "Don't you think so, Christiane?" Benda asked.

She leaned toward him and murmured an unintelligible reply.

"I was in Venice about six months ago," von Gerl said.

"On business?" I asked.

"No, just traveling. It was my last stop on my grand tour, before I had to come back here."

"The baron's father died recently," Benda explained to me.

"Yes," von Gerl said. "I am the second son—the troublesome one." He grinned. "My brother was the heir. I was intended for the priesthood, if my sainted mother had had her way. She made my father swear on her deathbed that he would send me to a seminary. Luckily for me, my father knew I was not fit for the church. Once my mother was gone, he sent me on a tour of Europe, with the idea that when I returned, he would use his connections to find me a position in the government."

Christiane slowly ran a fingertip up and down the bodice of her dress.

"Once I was away from my father's beneficial influence, I determined not to return to Vienna until I had seen some of the world," von Gerl continued. "My father and brother were busy managing our estates and paid little attention to my whereabouts. I stayed away for ten years. I traveled everywhere, all over Europe, and to the east also. I returned a few months ago, when I received news that both my father and brother had been taken by the pox." He shrugged. "That is my story. I am now Baron von Gerl, stuck here in Vienna with a big, empty palace."

"Christiane was wondering a few weeks ago how you were settling in," Benda said. "Weren't you, my love?"

She started. "Yes, yes I was," she said.

"You must come over and see!" von Gerl said. "Of course, not before your mourning period is over. But after that, I could use some feminine advice."

The servant returned with a fresh pot of coffee. Benda rose and took it from him. As her fiancé leaned over to refill her coffee cup, Christiane looked over his shoulder at von Gerl with desperation on her face. He grinned at her. *Did I imagine a slight, teasing lift of his dark brow?*

Benda came over and refilled my cup. Christiane put hers on a small table beside her chair and rose. "Richard, I am suddenly very tired," she said.

Benda rushed to her side. "I'll ring for Charlotte," he said.

"No, I am fine."

"I'll take you up, then," Benda said.

Von Gerl and I rose.

"Signor Da Ponte, it was a pleasure to meet you. We will meet again soon, I hope," Christiane said. I bowed.

Von Gerl reached for her hand. "My most beautiful friend, please—if I may be of service to you, I await you in my house," he said.

She pulled her hand away and took Benda's arm. Von Gerl's eyes followed them out the door. He opened his mouth to say something to me, but changed his mind. He sprawled in Christiane's big armchair.

"I've just finished having my father's old things carted away," he told me. "I've picked up a large number of items in my travels and I'm eager to display them all." He thought for a moment. "You must be a poetry lover."

I nodded. "Of course. The great Italian poets were among the first books I read as a child. And I write poetry myself."

"You should come over to the house and take a look at my collection. I've purchased some books, but the library in the house is huge, so I'm going to need many more. Perhaps you could help me fill it, by guiding my purchases."

"I'd be honored to consult with you, sir," I said. There was little I liked more than spending time in a library.

"The Italian poets?" von Gerl asked. "Petrarch and the like?"

"Yes. Petrarch is my favorite. I esteem him as the greatest of all poets."

"Greater than Dante? He's my favorite."

"To me, yes, Petrarch is a better poet than Dante." I smiled. "But of course, they were both geniuses. I suppose it depends on the reader's mood."

Von Gerl laughed. "You should come over today." He pulled his watch from his pocket. "It's almost dinnertime. Why don't you come dine with me?"

"Thank you, sir," I demurred. "But I have work—"

"No, I insist. I'd love your company. Besides, I have something you should see. You must know about the prints Botticelli made to illustrate *The Divine Comedy*. I own two of them."

My eyes widened. "You own some of the Botticelli cycle?" I asked. At the end of the fifteenth century, the great artist had prepared over one hundred drawings illustrating his fellow Florentine's work. I had heard about them, but had never seen one.

"They are right next door," von Gerl said. "Please, come

have dinner with me. I assure you it won't be any trouble. I'm always on the lookout for someone to show off my collections to."

I paused. Perhaps I should go. A fine dinner and the diversion of the baron's collections might be just what I needed after the gruesome last few days. Work could wait. "I'd be delighted to come," I said.

Benda returned. "I apologize for Christiane," he said. "She is taking her father's death very hard."

"You must let her grieve," von Gerl said. "No worry, Da Ponte and I have become fast friends. He is coming with me to see the collections and have dinner."

Benda accompanied us downstairs to the foyer, where a servant waited with my satchel, von Gerl's pale gray velvet cloak, and a hat with a large gray plume the likes of which I had not seen anywhere in Vienna.

"Tell Christiane I will come by again when she is feeling better," von Gerl said.

Benda nodded. "She will enjoy that. Thank you." He turned to me. "I'll communicate with our friend about that issue we discussed and let you know what he says."

I stood, puzzled, for a moment, until I realized that he was telling me he would find out more about the war protester from Troger. I nodded, and von Gerl and I walked out the door.

In the courtyard the bustle of packing had died down. The last cart was pulling through the archway, on its way to the Belvedere. For a moment I was grateful for my lack of worldly possessions. I could not imagine the trouble of packing and moving between two houses twice a year.

Von Gerl and I walked into the street. "My house is up there," he said, pointing to the left, where the Herrengasse merged with the Freyung to form the highest point of the triangular plaza. I scurried to keep up with the baron's long strides as we approached his palace. It was a twin of the Palais Albrechts except for the choice of ornaments on its façade. We paused outside the entry arch, where von Gerl took a deep breath. "Ah! Can you smell that, Da Ponte?"

"Smell what?" I asked.

"That scent—floral, but not heavy. It is familiar. Yes, I remember. I once knew a woman—"

"There you are, you monster!" a voice screamed. A small shape rushed past me and pounced on von Gerl. I moved to come to his aid and a moment later found myself sprawled on the ground.

"You fiend! You traitor!" A young woman pounded the baron's chest with her fists as he held her by the shoulders. I stood up. A small valise sat at my feet. I must have tripped over it when she had seen von Gerl and flung it to the ground.

"I'm going to kill you!" she cried. "I'll tear your heart out!"

"Marta, calm yourself," von Gerl said. The woman twisted in his grasp, unable to free herself. Her pleasingly plump figure was fitted into a modest woolen traveling cloak, which rode up as she attempted to escape von Gerl's hold. Her small cap had gone askew on her head, revealing tendrils of silken red flecked with gold.

I glanced across the plaza to the front of the Scottish Church. A small group of bystanders stood gawking at us. A sturdy, dark-haired young man wearing a forest-green cloak lounged on the steps of the monastery, watching the scene. As our eyes met, he gave me a slight, sardonic smile.

"Perhaps we should go inside," I said to the baron.

He looked down at his attacker. "Marta," he said, as if addressing a recalcitrant child. "If I let go of you, will you promise not to kill me until we are inside?"

She pounded on his chest once more. He leaned over and whispered in her ear. She took a deep breath and ceased her assault.

"That's better," von Gerl said. "Now, since you say you are here to kill me, I must ask you—do you have a knife or pistol with you?"

She shook her head.

"Good," he said as he released her from his grasp.

She put her hands on her shapely hips. "I've come all this way to see you." She gestured toward the church. "I've been waiting over there for an hour already. Where have you been?"

"Paying a condolence call," von Gerl answered. He beckoned to me. "And making a new friend. Lorenzo, this is Marta Cavalli. Marta, my friend Lorenzo Da Ponte."

I bowed to her. Her features were unremarkable—the face a bit too wide, the nose too short and full. But her green eyes were luminous and full of emotion, and her mouth was ripe, the color she had applied earlier in the day now smudged, as if she had just been kissed. My heart turned in my chest.

She glanced at me and turned back to von Gerl. "I must speak with you," she said.

"Of course you must," he replied. "But you are dusty from your travels and you must be hungry. Come inside and have dinner." He took her arm and led her through the archway into the courtyard.

I picked up her valise and followed.

Seven

The foyer of von Gerl's palace had the same design as that of the Palais Albrechts—a monumental staircase rising from a vast floor of smooth marble. A single bench sat on the right side of the large room. Von Gerl removed his cloak and hat and placed them on the bench, then helped Marta Cavalli out of her traveling cloak. He pulled a rope on the wall.

"Why don't you freshen up while I show my new friend my collections?" he suggested. "Then the three of us will dine."

A door in the back of the foyer opened and a servant appeared. His build and height resembled his master's, but he had none of the baron's handsome looks.

"Ah, Teuber. Look who's come to visit." Von Gerl passed Marta's cloak to the servant.

Teuber's eyes widened. "Miss Cavalli," he said, bowing slightly toward her.

Color rose in her cheeks. "Don't call me—"

"Come, my dear," von Gerl said. "Let Teuber draw you some water. You can wash and change your clothes." He smiled at her.

"All right, Valentin," she said. "I won't be long." I handed Teuber her valise and the servant led her up the stairs.

Von Gerl looked after them. "Complications, I'm afraid," he said. He rubbed his hands together. "But nothing that cannot be handled. Come, Da Ponte. The collection rooms are upstairs. Leave your satchel on the bench there. Teuber will take care of it later."

I followed him up the marble staircase. At the first landing, we turned right and passed through two large salons, both empty of furniture and decoration.

"I emptied the place out when I arrived," von Gerl explained. "My father's furniture was so heavy and dark. But I haven't had time to buy anything new yet. I've been too busy setting up my collections."

The third room was a library lined with tall wooden shelves, just one of which was full of books. I crossed to it and examined the volumes. Von Gerl's collection was eclectic— Dante's *The Divine Comedy* shelved beside the old chestnuts *Robinson Crusoe, Moll Flanders,* and *Gulliver's Travels*; Palladio's *The Four Books on Architecture* next to the sentimental novels *Pamela, Tristram Shandy,* and *The Sorrows of Young Werther*; a few volumes of the *Encyclopédie*; and works by Voltaire, Diderot, and Rousseau. I smiled when I saw a copy of Beaumarchais's play *The Marriage of Figaro.* I had spent a long time with my own copy, adapting it into my first opera with Mozart. On the middle shelf stood a row of large volumes, all bound in the same dark leather.

"As I told you, I have a small book collection," von Gerl said. He waved his hand around the room. "We have plenty of work ahead of us, Da Ponte." He noticed me eyeing the large leather volumes. "Those are my catalogs," he said, pulling one off the shelf and opening it. He turned the page toward me. "My travel expenses, for each day since I left home ten years ago." He replaced the volume on the shelf and took another. "This is a list of all the animals I've shot on hunting expeditions. I started this when I was a boy."

He returned the book to its place on the shelf and ran his fingers over the spines of its neighbors. "This one contains a list of every book I've ever read. Now this one, this should interest you." He pulled out a volume and handed it to me. "A list of all the operas and recitals I've attended."

I opened the heavy book's cover.

"And this last one, this is a list of every acquaintance I've made in my travels. I've just started a new page since I came home to Vienna. I will add your name." He took the book over to a desk and wrote in it.

"Come, Da Ponte. Leave that one on the desk here. You must see my scientific collection. This way."

I left the book on the desk and followed him into the next room. Rows of empty glass display cases filled the large space. Piles of cartons sat along the walls. "I'm just getting started in here," von Gerl said. "Let me show you some of the things I have." He led me over to the cartons along one wall. "This box is filled with herbal specimens I collected during my travels in the east," he explained. I looked down into the carton, which contained a number of small wooden boxes. "And over here are my stones, my playing card collection, oh, and here are my astronomical instruments. I spent a small fortune on them when I was in Italy."

He pulled a bronze astrolabe from one of the cartons and shook his head. "I really must get these unpacked," he said. He set the instrument aside and opened another carton. I peered into it. It was full of mismatched shoes. "I collect women's shoes wherever I go," he explained. He grinned. "You think it odd? Some of them are works of art!"

We retraced our steps to the central staircase and entered the large salon on its other side. "My paintings are in here," von Gerl said.

I drew a sharp breath as I entered the room. Each wall was covered with framed paintings from floor to ceiling. My eyes took in a dark-haired, voluptuous woman reclining on a sofa, her breasts partially exposed, her lips parted to receive the kiss of her lover; the nude goddess Diana, attended by a nymph, drying her feet after bathing, her auburn hair clasped in a tiara, a delicate string of pearls in her hand; and a cozy scene of a young noblewoman, clad in a peignoir, serving coffee to the family priest in her boudoir.

"I just purchased this one last week," von Gerl said, directing my attention to a large canvas. "I've been pursuing it since it was painted three years ago." I studied the picture. A fountain of light poured through the vaulted ceiling of a ruined basilica as two cowherds led their charges through the rubble of the ravaged building.

"Amazing," I murmured. I turned to the opposite wall. The paintings here were uninteresting, pedestrian depictions of the muses, the seasons, and the senses most likely done by students—the type of art purchased by the cartload

by the newly wealthy merchants of Vienna who were decorating their homes.

Von Gerl noticed my disdain. "I know, I know," he said.
"There is nothing special about these. But when I saw
them, I couldn't help myself. I had to have them." He gestured to the next room. "Come, there are two in here you
must see."

The long gallery contained but two paintings, which hung
side by side on the right wall. The first was of a raven-haired
male nude, his body stretched out on a saffron cloth, his head
at the left bottom corner of the large canvas, his crossed feet
at the right top. One hand rested behind his head, the other
was splayed out to his side. I leaned in to study the lifelike
muscles on his chest.

"Hector, the great Trojan warrior," von Gerl murmured.
"And over here, Patroclus."

I gazed at the second painting. Achilles' bosom friend
sat on a red cloth, his torso twisted away from the viewer.
"The brushstrokes depicting the muscles are amazing," I
said.

"The artist is the rage in Paris right now," von Gerl said.
"His name is David. I bought these at an auction, and I
must tell you, I paid dearly for them."

We contemplated the paintings.

"Come, the Botticellis are upstairs," von Gerl said.

"I've never seen anything like this," I said as we climbed
the wide steps to the next floor. I couldn't imagine the expense of shipping the collections to Vienna.

Von Gerl beamed at me. "Thank you. I'm proud of it. I
must confess that sometimes I worry I have gone too far,

but I enjoy owning all of these things. To view a fine painting whenever I wish, to study an anatomical object, to read a great book—I love being able to do that. I am never bored!"

He led me down a long hallway on the right. "We'll go through my chamber," he said. We entered a large, airy room, its ceiling decorated with elegant gold and white medallions. An enormous bed, its posters swagged with red velvet, stood in the center. A large fur throw lay across the well-stuffed mattress. We passed through von Gerl's closet, a room twice the size of my room at Madame Lamm's. Open cupboards filled with suits of the finest fabrics lined the walls. The plumed hat sat on a bench in the middle of the room. I lingered to admire a dark blue velvet coat with golden braided trim.

"In here, Da Ponte," von Gerl called. I continued into a much smaller room lined with waist-high display cases. I approached the one nearest to me. A collection of butterflies of varying sizes, all in shades of gray, lay pinned to the felt under the heavy glass.

"Those are just the carpet moths," von Gerl said. "They are all local. The more interesting ones are over here." I crossed over to him. The case held more butterflies, these in shades of blue, some with violet dusted on the edges of their wings.

"I caught these when I was in Spain."

I tried to avoid a grimace as I studied the poor creatures, their brief lives ended so that this man could enjoy their beauty. I looked up and gestured around the room. "You've caught all of these?" I asked.

"Many, but not all of them," von Gerl answered. "I've bought a few from other lepidopterists." He reached for a dark leatherbound volume on a shelf underneath the nearest case. "I have them all cataloged here," he said, showing me the pages.

"How many are in the collection?" I asked.

He flipped to the middle of the book and ran his finger down the page. "As of today, 527." He replaced the volume. "Come, let us see those Botticellis. They are this way, in my art cabinet."

When I entered the next room, I gasped in delight. The cabinet was long and narrow, with a low coffered ceiling trimmed with gilt. Fine light wood paneling lined the walls, which were hung with small paintings. I wandered around, looking into the glass cases that displayed small, delicate objects—boxes inlaid with amber; elaborate miniature clocks; a chess set formed from ivory; perfume bottles made of the glass blown by the skilled artisans of Murano, in my own beloved Venice; and small animals sculpted from jade and marble. In the center of the room stood a long table, its surface inlaid with an elaborate, multicolored mosaic of marble.

"I reserve this part of the collection for myself alone," von Gerl explained. "I love to spend the evenings in here, with a glass of brandy, looking at these things."

"It's beautiful," I breathed.

Von Gerl opened a large, elegant wooden cabinet and pulled out a portfolio. "Here are the Botticellis," he said, carrying it over to the table. He drew two pieces of parchment from the folder and spread them on the mosaic. I leaned over and examined the first. The illustration had been drawn in pen and ink, the lines still legible on the yellowed parchment. It showed the punishment of the heretics, from Dante's *Inferno*. Small groups of men walked among a field of burning coffins. In the center of the illustration, a heretic stood in the flaming lid of his bier.

"'For among the graves flames erupted, firing them all with glowing heat—no smith could ask for hotter iron,'" I murmured. I turned to the second parchment. The lines on this one were even more delicate and painstaking than on the first, as the great artist depicted the terrace of the lustful from Dante's *Purgatory*.

"'There the bank hurls its furious flames, and a spiraling wind from the ledge reflects them and constrains their way,'" I said.

"You certainly know Dante," von Gerl exclaimed. "I am impressed."

"Where did you get these?" I asked.

"In Berlin. They were a gift from a grateful widow. Her husband had collected them. She had sold most of them, but had kept these two." A wistful smile came over his face as he carefully placed the parchments into the portfolio. "Now, there is one more thing you must see. I bought these prints while I was living in Paris."

He placed the Botticelli portfolio in the cabinet and brought out a smaller folder. Back at the table, he unfastened the ribbon on the folder. "These are the finest specimens of their type," he said. "I share these with special friends." He spread a number of colored drawings across the table.

I leaned over to examine them. The first showed a naked woman astride a man, her ample derriere lifted in the air as he moved to enter her. I laid it aside and reached for the second. A man, clad only in an unbuttoned shirt, sat on a bed, his hand pulling up the skirts of the woman on his lap to reveal the muff of fur between her legs. My loins stirred as I took the third drawing. A nude woman, her torso tangled in a pure white bedsheet, writhed with pleasure on a soft bed—

"There you are!"

Von Gerl and I started as Marta entered the room, wearing a simple dress. I flushed.

"What are you two gawking at?" she asked.

"Come see," von Gerl said, flashing me a wicked grin.

She approached the table and stood next to me. My pulse raced as her hand brushed mine. She reached for the first print and looked at it. "What is—oh! Oh, my!" She turned to von Gerl. "You monster! I should have known!"

My cheeks burned, but von Gerl merely laughed. "Come, let's go down to dinner." He took Marta's arm and led us back to the first floor, where a large dining salon was tucked behind the art galleries. The walls were covered with faded, flocked gold paper, and velvet draperies of the same color festooned the windows. A small platform for musicians was tucked into the farthermost wall. Otherwise, the room was empty except for a large table, three chairs, and a tall ebony clock with golden trim and a large gilt and steel face.

"That's an astronomical clock," von Gerl told me. "It used to belong to one of the monasteries here in Vienna."

Von Gerl held a chair for Marta and motioned me to take the one opposite her. He took a seat at the head of the table and rang a bell. The manservant Teuber entered from a door behind his master and placed plates of fish in a white cream sauce in front of each of us. I found I was famished, and I ate the delicious dish with due speed. Marta picked at the food, occasionally glancing at von Gerl.

"Tell me about your grand tour," I said to my host. Teuber brought a bottle of wine, opened it, poured us each a glass, and stationed himself behind Marta.

"I started and ended in Italy, where I spent a total of three years," von Gerl said.

"There were hundreds like you there, miss," Teuber said in a low voice as he leaned over Marta's shoulder and poured another bit of wine into her glass.

"Where in Italy?" I asked.

"Everywhere. I saw the whole country."

"Especially the country girls," Teuber said sotto voce. Two red spots appeared on Marta's cheeks. She raised her glass and sipped the wine.

"Then I went to Germany for a year, after that France. I spent most of my time in France in the capital."

"Waiting maids, beauties of the city, countesses, he had them all," Teuber told Marta in a loud whisper. She hissed and turned her head away from him.

"May I have some wine?" I asked him. He nodded and hurried over to me, pouring me a glass. He topped off his master's drink, cleared the plates, and then left the room, returning a moment later with a large platter of carved pheasant. He leered at Marta as she took a portion.

"After France I traveled for a year in the Ottoman Empire," von Gerl continued. Teuber came around the table and offered me the platter. I took a small piece of the roasted bird.

"Then on to Spain for two years," von Gerl said.

Teuber served von Gerl, and then hurried back to Marta. I strained to hear his voice as he again leaned over her and refilled her glass. "Over a thousand ladies there—baronesses, princesses, anyone who would have him." She waved at him to shoo him, but he merely took a step back and stood at attention behind her chair.

"I ended the tour in your home city, Da Ponte," von Gerl said. "La Serenissima. That's where Marta and I met."

"Yes, last winter. He likes plump ones like you in wintertime, but in the summer, he likes them slender," Teuber said in a low voice from behind Marta. Her hands trembled.

"But generally, anyone who wears a skirt," Teuber said. Marta's fork clattered on her plate. She clamped her hands over her ears.

Von Gerl looked over at his servant. "Stop that, Teuber," he ordered. "Bring in the dessert."

Teuber smirked at Marta, piled the soiled dishes on a large tray, and left the room. We sat quietly, sipping our wine. A few minutes later, the manservant returned with a small tray on which sat two glass goblets filled with lemon ice. He placed one in front of Marta and one in front of me, and then whispered in his master's ear. Von Gerl nodded, stood, and placed his napkin on the table.

"I'm afraid I've forgotten that I have an important appointment this afternoon," he said. "I am so sorry. Please stay and enjoy your dessert."

"But you promised that we would speak," Marta sputtered.

"I apologize, my dear. But I cannot stay. Please sit as long as you like. You two should discuss Venice. We will speak soon, I promise." He turned to me and bowed. "Signore, it was an honor to meet you."

"Thank you for having me," I said. "I enjoyed seeing the collections."

He smiled. "I'll contact you about the library project soon." He nodded and the two men left us.

Marta took a bite of her ice and put down her spoon. She stared down at her hands.

"Have you lived in Venice your whole life?" I asked her.

She looked up. "I beg your pardon?" she asked.

"I was just asking if you have lived in Venice for a long time," I said.

"Yes, I was born there," she said. She picked up her spoon and took another bite of the dessert.

"I lived there for many years myself," I said. "But I was born in Ceneda, in the Veneto. Have you heard of it?"

"No, I haven't."

I squirmed in my seat, stifled a sigh, and transferred my

attention to my own dessert. I was relieved when Teuber entered a few minutes later. He swept our half-eaten ices away.

"I haven't finished that," Marta protested.

"I am sorry, miss, signore," he said. "You must go now." He pulled Marta's chair from the table so swiftly that she almost fell to the floor.

"But I must unpack—let go of me, you oaf!" Marta attempted to shrug off Teuber's grasp as he hustled her out of the dining room and down the stairs. I jumped up from my chair and followed them. In the foyer, he handed Marta her cloak, then gave her valise and my satchel to me. "I've taken the liberty of packing your other dress, Miss Cavalli," he said. He opened the door and pushed us out into the courtyard.

"Wait!" Marta cried.

The door slammed behind us. She pounded on it. "What is he doing? That rogue! Valentin will hear about this!" She banged on the door again, but there was no answer. She gave a cry of frustration.

I knocked loudly on the door and called the manservant's name. "He must have gone to the cellar, or is in the back and cannot hear us," I said.

Marta looked around the courtyard. "Valentin will be back in a few hours, I am certain. But where can I wait? There is no place to sit out here. I'll have to go back to the church."

We walked out into the street. "You can't stand around the Freyung the rest of the day," I said. "Come, where are you staying? I'll take you there." A hansom cab was letting passengers off a few doors up the street. I signaled to the driver.

"I just arrived today," Marta said.

"Shall I have the driver recommend a hotel?" I asked. She flushed. I guessed she did not have the money to afford a hotel. Besides, a hotel was no place for a young gentlewoman to stay alone.

"I don't know. I should wait here," she said.

"Why don't you come with me?" I asked. "My landlady has extra rooms. She is an upstanding widow with a daughter. You'll be perfectly safe there. You could stay there, at least for tonight."

She thought for a moment. She glanced back into the courtyard of von Gerl's house. "All right. Thank you. I am sorry, I've forgotten your name."

"Lorenzo. Lorenzo Da Ponte," I said.

"Thank you, Lorenzo. I'll send a message to Valentin tomorrow."

I handed her into the cab. Across the plaza, outside the church, the young man I had seen earlier leaned against a pillar, wrapped in his green cloak, looking at us. I gave the driver Marta's valise and the address of my lodgings and climbed into the cab. It rumbled down the Freyung and turned left onto the Tiefer Graben. Marta gazed out the window.

"Have you been in Vienna before?" I asked.

"No," she said. "It's lovely. I think I will enjoy living here very much." Her mouth curved into a smile. "The palace is beautiful, don't you think?"

For a moment I was confused, as the cab was taking the

back streets around the various markets of the city on its way to the Stuben gate, and there were no noble houses to be seen. Then I realized she was talking about von Gerl's house.

"It needs a woman's touch, don't you agree?" She smoothed her cloak on her lap. "As soon as I settle in, I'll replace that nasty manservant and hire a real staff. I'll have to find someone to advise me on how to decorate. Valentin will know who is the best in the city."

The cab jolted a bit as it drove over a pit in the road. I sat there, befuddled, as she chatted on about furniture, fabrics, and window decorations. Her face had grown animated and had taken on a subtle beauty. I forced myself to look out the window.

As the cab crossed through the Stuben gate into the suburb, I turned back to Marta. I could not think of a delicate way to phrase my question to her, but I proceeded anyway. "The baron did not seem to be expecting you," I said.

"I know. That was my fault. I shouldn't have surprised him." She sighed. "I should have written, but I wasn't sure what his address was, or even whether he had made it back here from his travels yet. When we parted, he had told me he was going home to Vienna. I sold everything I owned to raise money to come."

"But what if he hadn't been here at all?" I asked.

Her eyes widened. "Oh, I never considered that. I suppose I could have stayed in a convent here in the city, waiting until he arrived." She unpinned her cap and placed it on her lap. Her silky red-gold hair fell loose around her shoulders. I sat on my hands to resist the urge to reach over and touch it.

"He's just surprised to see me, I think. I'll give him a few days, and then I'll move into the palace."

"You seem certain that he'll welcome you in," I said.

She smiled. "Oh, he will. Of course he will." She ran her fingers through her hair. "You see, I'm his wife."

Eight

I slept late the next morning, and woke to find the sun streaming in my window. I stretched my toes to the end of my bed. For the first time in days, I had had a good night's sleep. Today was Sunday, and I planned to go to my office to do a bit of work, and then join the Mozart family for a pleasant afternoon.

I washed and donned my second best suit. I liked to dress up a bit when I visited the Mozarts. Although Wolfgang always teased me about my formal attire at his casual dinners and musical get-togethers, I knew that Constanze was pleased when I arrived in a nice suit. I also had to admit that I was hoping to run into Marta downstairs at breakfast.

As I left my room, my foot kicked a small object on the floor of the hallway. I looked down to see another message, with my name hastily scrawled in the familiar handwriting. I brought it into my room, tore it open, and read the numbers and words I had now learned by heart. Once again my enigmatic correspondent announced his arrival on April 21—tomorrow.

I put the message in my cupboard and went downstairs to the kitchen, where my landlady was setting out breakfast.

"Good morning, signore," she said, smiling at me. "Did you sleep well?"

"Yes, madame," I said. She gestured me to sit at the table. "Madame Lamm—the message that was outside my door this morning. Did you put it there?"

"I took it in, Signor Da Ponte," Sophie said as she entered the room with a loaf of bread in her hand. "I left it outside your door about an hour ago."

"Who delivered it?" I asked.

"A young boy," Sophie said.

I did not bother to ask what the boy had looked like, or if he had been wearing livery that could identify him. The sender of the messages was taking great care to ensure that I could not trace him.

Sophie sliced the bread and placed it on the table, then brought a bowl of stewed fruits and ladled some onto my plate. She joined her mother and me at the table.

"Has Miss Cavalli been down yet?" I asked. Madame Lamm had welcomed Marta when we arrived last evening, immediately noticed her fatigue, and bustled her upstairs to a room. I had spent the evening working, occasionally slipping down here to see if she had reappeared. But she must have washed, unpacked, and gone straight to her bed, for she never came, and my questions about her marriage to von Gerl were answered by nothing but my imagination.

"She was so tired last night, signore," my landlady said,

as if reading my thoughts. "I drew a bath for her and made up a bed. She fell asleep right away." She looked at me with a twinkle in her eye. "Such a lovely young lady, signore. Her bearing is so dignified. Is she a noblewoman? And she is very pleasant. She thanked me over and over for letting her stay." She paused, and her brow wrinkled. "But she was so pale, and I sensed a sadness in her, signore. Something about her filled me with pity. Do you know what was bothering her?"

"No," I said, shaking my head. "I just met her yesterday. I was visiting a friend when she arrived. She had nowhere to go. I appreciate your taking her in, madame. I will pay for her room until she decides what to do."

"Another lodger is always welcome, signore," Madame Lamm said. She hesitated. "Food prices are going up so fast, I'm afraid I may have to raise the rents. I hate to have to do that. So your friend is welcome for as long as she wishes to stay." She passed the bowl of fruit to me. "Why would a young gentlelady be here in Vienna all alone?" she asked. "She told me she had come to find her husband."

I shrugged and said nothing. The last thing I wanted to do was gossip about Marta and von Gerl.

"Come, Sophie. Finish your breakfast. It's time for church," my landlady said. The two women took their plates over to the large sink. I sat and chewed on a slice of soft bread, thinking of Marta's soft hair and full lips. But after a few moments my mind turned to the messages, and then to Alois's murder. By the time I finished my meal, my optimism and pleasure in the morning had disappeared. I sat glumly listening to the women's chatter.

"I think I'll wear my pink dress," Sophie said as she wiped the plates clean. "Perhaps I'll sew some bows on it. That would be fancy enough."

"No, not that one," her mother replied. "The neckline is too low. Wear the blue one."

"Oh, Mother." Sophie sighed with the universal weariness of the young, who were often called upon to explain to their elders how the world really worked. "The blue one is hopelessly out of fashion. This is my first fancy ball. All of the other girls will be wearing new dresses. The neckline of the pink one is perfect. What do you think, Signor Da Ponte?"

I stirred from my dark thoughts. "About what, Sophie?"

"The ball tomorrow night at the Redoutensaal. Will you be going?"

The Hofburg Palace's Redoutensaal were large party rooms that the emperor had opened for public dances and concerts. When he had left to join the troops outside Belgrade, he had ordered that the balls continue, to keep up public morale during the war.

"I don't believe so, Sophie," I answered. "I'm not much of a dancer."

"Who are you going with?" my landlady asked her daughter. "Is Stefan taking you?"

"Yes, if he can get away from work early enough. If he cannot, I'll go with Teresa and Liesl," Sophie answered.

"You will not," her mother replied. "Stefan will take you, or you will stay home."

"But Mother—"

"I don't want you going there without him. Look what

happened to Barbara. You will not go to any parties or balls without Stefan. Now go fetch your shawl." Sophie bade me good morning and ran up the stairs.

Her mother looked after her and sighed. "May I bring you anything else, signore?" she asked. I shook my head. She took my plate. "I don't know what to do about that girl. She's too high-spirited." She sat down next to me and lowered her voice. "I hope Stefan is planning to propose to her soon. I need to see her settled." She shook her head. "That friend of hers, that Barbara, I never liked her. A lazy girl, always putting on airs in front of Sophie. Her mother could not control her. Barbara went to all the balls. She met a man there, a nobleman. Now she is expecting his child, but of course, he won't have anything to do with her." I recalled the forlorn pregnant girl at Sophie's party.

"The way people behave these days," my landlady clucked. "I just don't understand it. Everyone does what he or she wants, without a care for anyone else. People of all ranks together at parties and dances—it's not right. No one knows his place in the world anymore. It's no wonder children like Sophie get fanciful ideas."

"I'm sure Stefan will look after her," I said.

"I wish her father were still here," Madame Lamm said. "She needs a strong hand. I cannot very well ask Stefan what his intentions are, can I?"

"He seems very much in love with her," I said. "Perhaps he is waiting until he has saved enough money to marry."

"Do you think you could talk to him for me, signore? Find out for me what his plans are?"

"I don't see very much of him," I said. "I'm very busy at the theater."

"Oh, I would not ask you to take time from your work, signore, of course not. But if you should happen to run into Stefan sometime, here at the house—well, you are a clever man. You could easily find a way to turn the conversation to Sophie and his plans." She looked at me with pleading in her guileless face. "If you could just bring me some assurance, to ease a mother's worries—"

"I'll see what I can do, madame," I said.

I tarried in the garden for another half hour in case Marta should awaken, and then made my way through the Sunday-morning traffic to the theater. Once in my office, I put the finishing touches on the idea I had for the *Don Giovanni* burlesque scene. When the bell in St. Michael's Church sounded the noon hour, I took my satchel and went into the Michaelerplatz. Well-dressed aristocrats streamed from the old wooden doors of the church. The pastry shop across the way had flung its own door wide, tempting the church-goers with the scent of baked butter and vanilla. I walked up the Kohlmarkt and then up the Tuchlauben. A block before the street entered the Hoher Market, Vienna's oldest market square, I turned into the entryway of a nondescript building. On the ground floor, rows of jars filled with powders and potions sat locked behind the grate of a dark apothecary shop. I climbed worn, steep steps to the fourth floor and knocked on the door farthest from the landing.

Mozart opened the door. "Lorenzo!" he cried, ushering

me into the apartment. "I'm glad you came." A young maid appeared behind the composer and took my satchel. The mewls of a baby came from the room on the left. Constanze Mozart's rich voice gently soothed her child.

"Come into the study," Mozart said. I followed him into the room, which was filled with furniture. The large table Mozart used as a desk was pushed along the left wall, and was surrounded by armchairs. The composer's fortepiano sat in a dark corner next to an empty birdcage. Two sofas sat underneath the small windows. A young boy had found a space on the crowded floor, and was playing with a small terrier.

"Hello, Carl," I said.

The boy looked up and grinned at me. "Unc' Renzo!" he cried.

"Hello, Lorenzo," Constanze said as she entered the room, carrying the baby. She leaned up to kiss my cheek. "I'm so glad you could come. I haven't seen you for a while."

I looked down at the bundle in her arms. The babe's skin was pale and waxen. She gazed at me with dark eyes, and stuffed her tiny fingers into her mouth.

"How are you, *piccola principessa*?" I asked her. She answered me with a whimper.

"She's still sick," Constanze said. "This catarrh has lasted all winter."

"She'll be four months old in a few weeks," Mozart said, coming over and stroking the baby's wispy hair, which was the same color as his own. "The winter was so cold. But she'll be better soon."

"Come, Carl," Constanze said. "Bring Gauckerl. It's time for a nap."

The little boy opened his mouth to protest, but seeing the stern look on his mother's face, instead stood and grabbed the dog's collar.

"Dinner in a half hour," Constanze said to us. Boy and dog followed her out of the room.

Mozart sprawled on the nearest sofa and motioned for me to sit. "I solved the mystery of Morella," he said.

I raised a brow. "Not the dry air in the theater after all?" I asked.

The composer smiled. "No. I had him here the day after the rehearsal. After some coaxing, he admitted that he was nervous about singing the coloratura part of the aria. I should have guessed that was the problem. We wrote that part for Baglioni in Prague. Not every tenor can sing the way he can. I told Morella we would cut the aria and write something better suited to his voice."

"What did you have in mind?" I asked.

"I don't know—something contemplative, peaceful. We can put it in anywhere, so don't worry too much about context."

I nodded. "I have an idea for the burlesque scene," I said. "Tell me what you think. After the sextet, when Don Giovanni's servant escapes from the rest of the cast, everyone will exit. In a few moments, a door will open and the peasant girl will enter wielding a large razor, dragging the servant by the hair."

"I like it already," Mozart said.

"She threatens to do all sorts of violence to him and his

manhood," I continued. "She ties his hands with her handkerchief, and fastens him to a chair with a cord. She twists
the other end of the cord around the latch of the window
and leaves, telling him that when she returns, she will shave
him without any soap."

Mozart winced.

"While she is gone, he struggles frantically to free himself. There'll be no aria here, maybe just some frenzied
sounds from the orchestra. Just as the audience hears her return, the servant jerks hard on the cord. The window crashes
down off the wall and he hops off, dragging the chair and
the window with him."

Mozart laughed. "I love it! Finish it up and I'll set it right
away."

A bell rang from the other side of the apartment. "Dinnertime," Mozart said. "Constanze's gotten a bell to summon me. She says she is tired of calling me three or four
times when dinner is ready. If I don't come within two minutes, she starts without me."

We crossed the foyer into a small games room, where
a dining table sat alongside Mozart's prized billiards table.
As I sat with my two friends and ate a rich stew with dump-
lings and drank a delicious Rhine wine, the trials of the past
few days receded from my mind. Constanze was a charm-
ing hostess and a very good cook.

"Do you expect a large crowd at the premiere, Lorenzo?"
she asked as the maid served a light dessert of almond milk
and biscuits.

"I think so," I replied. "Even with the war going on, the

theaters are still full most nights. I only wish the emperor could be there to see it."

"He'll see one of the later performances," Mozart said. "This war is going to be a short one. He had better come home soon," he added. "I'm writing a lot for his private chamber orchestra, and it will take him several weeks of listening for six hours a day to catch up with me!" A few months ago, the emperor had appointed Mozart as court composer, a position that included a nice stipend, although according to gossip I had heard around the theater, not as much as Salieri had been paid when he held the post.

"I wrote some dances for the ball tomorrow night," Mozart said. "Are you coming?"

I shook my head. "Probably not. I'm not feeling very frivolous these days."

Constanze studied me, a puzzled look on her face, and then realized the cause of my distress. "Oh, Lorenzo—that priest they found dead in the Stephansplatz. You knew him, didn't you?"

"He was a close friend," I said.

"Do the police know yet what happened to him?" Mozart asked. "I heard he interrupted two Turkish spies plotting to kill the archbishop and they slit his throat."

"Hush!" Constanze told him. "I'm sorry for your loss, Lorenzo. Please, if we can do anything for you, let us know."

I nodded my thanks.

"Now, on a happier subject," she said. "Is there anyone special in your life since I last saw you?"

The gleam in her eyes made me laugh. "I'm afraid not," I said.

"Then you should come to the ball," she said. "There will be many beautiful ladies there."

"I'll give it some thought," I said, smiling at her.

"Good, I'll save a few dances for you," she said, patting my hand. She rose and went into the next room to check on her sleeping children. Mozart and I took the remainder of the bottle of wine and our glasses and drifted back into the study.

"Have I played you my war song?" he asked me. I shook my head. "I used an old poem by Gleim." He sat down at the pianoforte.

"'I'd love to be the emperor!'" he sang, banging on the pianoforte. "'I'd love to be the emperor! I would shake the Orient, I would make the Muslims tremble, Constantinople would be mine!'"

I laughed.

"You have to imagine it with the wind band, the cymbals, and the drums," he said. "'I'd love to be the emperor!'" He resumed singing. "'I'd love to be the emperor! Athens and Sparta shall become, like Rome, queens of the world! Ancient times shall be reborn!'"

I applauded.

"Wait, there's more," he said. He leaned over the keyboard. "'I'd love to be the emperor! I'd love to be the emperor! I'd engage the best poets to—'" He looked up. Constanze stood at the door. From the depths of the apartment, the baby howled.

"Now look what you've done!" she said. She hurried off to comfort the child.

Mozart gave me a sheepish grin.

"I should go," I said. "I must get to work on the new aria for Morella." The composer accompanied me to the door. As the maid handed me my satchel, Constanze reappeared, cradling the fretful baby. "Thank you for the delicious meal," I said, kissing her cheek. "Take good care of the *principessa*."

I returned to the theater, worked for a few hours, then walked home as dusk was turning to night. A group of students stood at the Stuben gate, bidding each other good night. Out of the corner of my eye, I noticed the dark-haired young man in the forest-green cloak whom I had seen outside the Scottish Church yesterday loitering in the doorway of a darkened tailor shop. Frowning, I quickened my pace and walked through the gate. As I crossed over the wooden bridge that spanned the *glacis*, I paused at the railing, pretending to admire the scenery. I glanced back at the gate, but saw no one following me. I sighed and continued on to my lodgings, scolding myself for letting my overactive imagination get the better of me. Just because I happened to see the same man twice in two days, I was sure he was after me. I shook my head. Benda was probably right—the killer sought victims who represented Austria's greatness. He would not come after a lowly theater poet.

As I entered the courtyard of my lodging house, Marta rose from the bench in the garden and came to greet me.

She was wearing the same plain dress as yesterday. Her silken hair was bound in a velvet ribbon.

"I've been wondering when I would see you again," she said.

"Have you had a pleasant day?" I asked, following her back into the garden. We sat on the small bench. The full moon bathed the small corner of the yard with silver light.

"I've been out here resting and reading all afternoon," she said. She looked around the neat space, where Madame Lamm had enclosed her young vegetable seedlings with clipped short shrubs set in a diamond-shaped pattern. "It is so beautiful, and the day has been so mild."

I leaned toward her slightly and breathed in her floral scent. I longed to take her hand.

"You should see some of the city while you are here," I said. "The Prater is very beautiful this time of year, and very good for watching people, if you enjoy that."

She smiled. "I expect I'll be here a long time," she said. "I've sent a message to Valentin telling him where I am. He'll be coming for me anytime now, I expect."

A pang of jealousy stabbed me. I opened my mouth, and to my surprise, found myself inviting her to attend the ball in the Redoutensaal. "A friend of mine has composed some dances," I said. "You'd enjoy meeting him and his wife."

She hesitated.

"It's a chance to see the glittering side of Vienna," I said.

"Oh, Lorenzo, it sounds wonderful. But I shouldn't. What if Valentin comes for me while I am out?"

"He'll leave a message with Madame Lamm, and I'll deliver you to him myself," I said. "Please. I would love for you to come. You would be doing me a favor."

"What do you mean?"

"I recently lost a dear friend. I could use a nice evening to take my mind from my sorrow."

She sat silently for a moment. "Well, I suppose I could go with you. You've been so kind to me," she said. "But no, wait, I have nothing to wear. I brought just one gown with me. It's very simple, not suitable for a fancy ball. And I have no jewelry. I sold it all to pay for my carriage fare from Venice."

"You'll look beautiful in anything," I blurted.

She blushed and looked down at her hands. My hand reached for hers, but I drew it back before I made a fool of myself. I took a deep breath. What was I doing?

Nine

Although I tried to convince myself over breakfast in a coffeehouse that my worries about the anonymous messages were groundless, my stomach churned as I sipped coffee and chewed on a roll. It was April 21, the day my enigmatic correspondent had promised to arrive.

I turned my thoughts to the murder investigation. Benda must have heard from Troger about the background of the war protester by now. I sighed. The count seemed determined to blame the murders on the protester, but the evidence was thin. True, the baker had overheard an argument, and seen the man hurrying from the Am Hof the night the general was killed. Perhaps Benda was right, and the protester had murdered the general. But what about Alois? Benda's theory that my friend was killed because he was a symbol of the church seemed fantastical to me. I had been involved in the investigation of only two murders, but my experience had taught me that people kill for reasons deep in the human heart, not to make political pronouncements. Or so I chose to believe.

I dug a few coins out of my pocket, left them on the table, and went out into the Graben. It was clear that Benda wasn't going to give much consideration to the circumstances surrounding Alois's death. That was left to me. I was tired of waiting to get information secondhand. I walked over to the Stephansplatz, entered Alois's office building, and made the long climb to his little room. To my surprise, when I turned the door handle, it was locked. For as long as I had known him, Alois had never locked his door. He had once told me that if a thief was determined to steal a book, the man was welcome to the knowledge within it.

I went downstairs to the cellar and found the porter supervising a pair of boys who were stacking fresh firewood. I introduced myself. "I'm a friend of Father Bayer's," I said. "I was just up at his office. The door was locked."

He looked me up and down, his eyes suspicious. "Father Bayer is dead, sir. He was robbed just outside here, over by the cathedral. The ruffians cut his throat."

"I know. I lent him a book before he died. It's a valuable volume. I wanted to get it back," I lied.

"Well, sir, you'll have to go across to the cathedral and find that priest. He locked the door to Father Bayer's office and took the key."

"Father Urbanek?" I asked the porter.

He shook his head. "No, the new one. What's his name? Dauer. Father Dauer."

I thanked him and walked over to the front of the cathedral. I was spending more time here than I desired these days. I entered, hailed a passing deacon, and asked for Father Dauer.

"I haven't seen him today, sir," he said. "There is usually a meeting over at the archbishop's residence every Monday morning. Chances are he's over there. Is there something I might help you with?"

"I was a friend of Father Bayer's," I said. "I wanted to get a book from his office, but the porter says Father Dauer locked it and has the key."

The young man sighed. "Poor Father Bayer," he said. "He was a gentle old man." He looked around and lowered his voice. "Is it true what I've heard, sir? That he interrupted a gang of thieves who were breaking into the treasury room, and they butchered him?"

"I don't know anything about that," I said. "Would you know where Father Dauer has left the key?"

"No, sir. He probably has it in his office. You'll have to come back and speak with him. The meetings last until mid-afternoon. Come back then."

As I walked over to the theater, I tried to think of anything I knew about Alois that might link him to General Albrechts, but nothing came to mind. I entered the theater and took the stairs down to my office. I groaned as I turned into the hallway. Thorwart had gone too far. All of the soldiers' helmets, swords, and elaborate Asian headdresses worn by the choristers of my opera *Axur* were piled against the wall with the ladder, mandolin, candelabras, and scythe. A path about a foot wide led to my office door. I picked my way down it and opened the door.

I drew in a sharp breath. A tall, muscular man stood

with his back to me, studying the collection of librettos on my shelves, his shoulders slumped like those of a child who has just lost a game of hoops to his closest friend.

"You! What are you doing here?" I said.

The man turned and straightened. I may have imagined a flash of sadness in his heavy-lidded eyes and a sagging in his aged-lined, olive cheeks, but a moment later they were supplanted by a broad smile. He enveloped me in a smothering embrace.

"Lorenzo! There you are! I was afraid you weren't coming into work today."

"Giacomo? What are you doing here?"

He frowned. "Didn't you get my notes? I sent several, telling you I was arriving in Vienna today."

My knees felt weak. I grabbed the edge of my desk to steady myself, nodded toward my guest chair, and fell into my own seat. "You sent me those notes?"

"What do you mean, Lorenzo? Who did you think sent them? I put my name right at the top. "Casanova is coming to see you.""

I stared at him, my mouth wide open.

"Don't tell me you couldn't decipher the code." He laughed. "It's basic kabbalah. I hoped you'd have some fun with it."

I let out an exasperated sigh. "Fun? I didn't know what to think! All I could understand was that someone was coming today, April 21. Your name was nowhere in the messages!"

"It was in the string of numbers, my friend. The fourth one, the 71. That's my name. It's a simple code. Assign the number 1 to the letter *a*, 2 to *b*, et cetera, all the way through the alphabet. But *i* and *j* share the number 9, *u* and *v* are 20, and *x* and *y* are 21. Add up the number for each letter to get the number for the word."

I put my head in my hands.

"It is simple—'My dear friend, Casanova comes to Vienna to see you.'"

I looked up and swore softly.

He peered at me, his eyes full of concern. "I'm sorry, Lorenzo. An old man likes to think he can still play at games. It never occurred to me that you would be unable to decipher the code. Did I frighten you?"

"No," I said. "I've just been very busy. And a good friend of mine died recently."

He gazed at me with sheepish eyes, and after a moment the famous charm worked its magic on me. "It is good to see you again, my friend," I said. "What are you doing here?"

"The count was coming, so I rode along with him. I'll take any chance I get to escape from that awful palace." Casanova, now in his sixties, had recently retired to Dux, in Bohemia, where he worked in the employ of a count who paid all of his living expenses in exchange for my friend's administration of the palace library. "Are you free for dinner this afternoon?" he asked.

I shook my head. "No, I have a lot of work to do."

"What about tonight? Do you have plans? We have a lot of catching up to do since we met in Prague last fall."

"I'm going to a ball at the Redoutensaal. Mozart has written some dances that will be played."

"How is the little fellow?" Casanova asked.

"He is fine, but he wouldn't enjoy hearing you call him that." I smiled.

"I'll address him as the little genius. He'll like that."

I laughed. "Why don't you come tonight? I am taking a friend, but you are welcome to join us."

He raised a brow. "Interfere with a liaison? Never!"

"It's not like that. She is just someone I met the other day. She is from Venice. I'm sure she'd enjoy meeting you."

"Are you in love, Lorenzo?"

I waved him off. "No. Her interests lie elsewhere."

"Poor you! I can give you some tips about how to change her mind, if you'd like."

"Thank you, but no."

Casanova stood. "I have some visits to make this afternoon. I'll get a cab and pick the two of you up tonight. Are you still living in the Graben?"

"No, out in the Landstrasse." I frowned. "You should know. You sent a boy to my house a few times."

He looked at me blankly, and then his eyes widened. "Oh, with the notes? I have a good friend here in the city. I'm staying with her while I am here. Her husband is in the diplomatic service. He is stationed near Dux. Luckily for her, he seldom comes home to Vienna. I sent the notes to her through the diplomatic pouch—it goes on the mail coach every day. She must have instructed a servant to find out where you lived and deliver them."

I chided myself for my foolishness, my suspicions that someone was threatening me. The simplest explanation is usually the correct explanation, it is said. I must keep reminding myself of that.

Casanova and I exchanged addresses and agreed that he would pick Marta and me up at eight this evening. After he left, I settled in for a long, quiet afternoon of work.

At quarter to eight that evening I was downstairs in the courtyard of my lodgings, clad in my finest dress suit, waiting for Marta to appear. Outside in the street, Stefan was wiping stone dust off the driver's bench of his humble cart. I walked over to greet him. Before I could engage him in a discussion, Sophie, resplendent in a low-cut pink dress, emerged from the courtyard, a cloak on her arm.

"There you are!" she said to Stefan. "Why didn't you come to the door? I've been waiting inside." Her pretty face fell when she saw the cart. "I thought we were taking a cab," she said.

Stefan looked at his feet and mumbled something I could not hear. I silently prayed that Casanova would not appear at that moment in the hansom cab. Sophie sighed and put her hand on her admirer's arm. "It is fine, Stefan." She looked at the passenger side of the bench. "At least it is clean. We'll leave it in the Neuer Market and walk back to the Redoutensaal. What are you waiting for, silly? Help me up!" She gave me a jaunty wave as she rode down the street.

"The poor boy," Marta said behind me. I turned. She was clad in a simple sapphire-blue gown, her hair piled on her head and bound with a matching velvet ribbon. She carried her traveling cloak in her hand.

"You look lovely," I said as I helped her into the cloak.

Her cheeks colored. "Thank you, Lorenzo. I wish this dress were not so plain."

"It is not plain, it is elegant," I said.

She smiled. "Who is this friend of yours who is coming for us?" she asked.

"His name is Giacomo—Giacomo Casanova. He's also from Venice, but he's led an adventurous life. He's traveled all over Europe, and has written a few books. We met about ten years ago, when I was secretary to Count Zaguri."

"Casanova? I've heard of him. Isn't he the one who escaped from the doge's palace? My father used to tell me the story."

"Yes, but that was years ago. He's an old man now. He's retired from traveling. He spends his days tending to a count's library in Bohemia."

A hansom cab turned into the street and pulled up at the house. The door opened, and a moment later, Casanova climbed down. He smiled at me and bowed deeply to Marta.

"Marta Cavalli, may I present my good friend Giacomo Casanova."

I was pleased to see Marta's eyes twinkle. "I am honored to meet such a famous personage, sir," she said.

Casanova took her hand and kissed it. "The honor is all mine, my dear. I have been locked away in a dusty dark library for many months. Your smile is a sunbeam lighting the corners of my pitiful life."

Marta blushed.

"Marta," Casanova murmured. "A lovely name. I knew a Marta once, years ago, when I was a young, innocent priest. She led me astray—" He waved his hand. "But enough of her. She's retired to a convent now."

"Shall we go?" I asked.

Casanova took Marta's hand again. "I am delighted that you have agreed to allow me to accompany you and Lorenzo this evening, my dear. To be seen in the company of such a beautiful young woman will enhance my reputation."

"That's enough," I said, laughing. I helped Marta into the cab. Casanova climbed in after her. As I prepared to join them, there was a tug on my sleeve. I looked down to see a young boy.

"Are you Da Ponte?" he asked. "I have a message for you."

I peered into the cab, where Casanova was settling in too close to Marta for my taste. "Another mystery message, Giacomo?" I asked. "Don't you ever stop?"

He shrugged. "I know nothing about this, Lorenzo, I swear."

I exchanged a few coins for the message, and the boy ran down the street. I unfolded the single sheet of paper, read it, gave instructions to the driver, and climbed into the cab.

"Would you mind if we make a brief stop before we go to the Redoutensaal?" I asked Marta. "I must see someone."

"Of course not," she replied.

The carriage rolled down the street, over the bridge, and through the Stuben gate into the city. I listened idly as Casanova entertained Marta with tales of his travels. The driver took the back streets, and it was not long before we arrived in the Freyung. As it turned to enter the courtyard of the Palais Albrechts, Marta craned her head out the window. I sighed inwardly. What a dolt I was. I had forgotten that von Gerl lived right next door.

As the cab pulled up at the front door of the palais,

Benda emerged. I climbed out of the cab and turned back to my companions. "I'll just be a moment," I said.

"Good evening, Da Ponte," Benda said, shaking my hand. "Thank you for coming promptly." He looked past me into the cab. "I see I've interrupted your plans." He leaned forward and introduced himself to Marta and Casanova. "Please, there is no need to sit outside. Come in." He reached in to help Marta down. Casanova followed. I asked the driver to wait, and followed the three of them into the palais.

A servant appeared and took Marta's cloak. Benda murmured an order to him, and then led us up to the first floor and into the salon, where Christiane sat in her armchair. She rose as we entered.

"Look who I've found, my love," Benda said. "Signor Da Ponte and some friends." I bowed and introduced Marta and Casanova to her.

Christiane smiled and beckoned to Marta. "Please, Miss Cavalli. Come sit by me," she said. "I seldom see any gentlewomen my own age these days. Are you all going to the Redoutensaal?" Marta nodded and took a seat on the sofa near Christiane. The servant entered carrying a tray of glasses filled with champagne. Casanova took one and sat nearby.

Benda handed me a glass and pulled me aside. "Troger has found the name of the protester," he said. "Michael Richter. He lives over in the Judenplatz."

"When do you want to question him?" I asked. "Tomorrow morning? I am free—"

"I've already spoken to him," Benda said. I struggled to keep annoyance from my face. I glanced over at Marta, who was chatting happily with Christiane. "He claims he was nowhere near the Am Hof that night."

"But the baker seemed so sure the man he saw running was him," I said. Christiane rose, took Marta's hand, and led her out of the room.

"Richter is lying," Benda said. "That's a sure sign of guilt. We'll have to find a way to corroborate the baker's story."

"How?" I asked.

"I've asked Troger to find out more about Richter's past. Meanwhile, I'm told he lives with his mother. She might know something. We should talk to her."

I nodded. I sipped my champagne. After a few minutes, the two women returned.

Marta came to me, her face glowing with delight. "Look, Lorenzo," she said. "Mademoiselle Albrechts has loaned me a pair of her earrings." I glanced quickly at a pair of crystals hanging from her delicate ears. She returned to the sofa and sat by Casanova.

"They look wonderful with your dress," Christiane said. She looked down at her mourning dress. "I won't have a chance to wear them anytime soon. Please keep them as long as you'd like."

Casanova leaned over and fingered one of the stones. "They are beautiful, but mere stars to the moonlight of your eyes, my dear," he said. Marta giggled.

I turned back to Benda. "Let me know when you are ready to proceed," I said quietly.

He nodded. "I'll check my diary and send you a message." I noticed Casanova regarding us, speculation in his eyes.

We stayed for a few more minutes, chatting and finishing the champagne, then gave our thanks to our hosts and walked downstairs. The servant brought Marta's cloak. I helped her into it, and the three of us walked into the warm moonlit night.

Ten

The cab dropped us near the front entrance to the Redouten-saal. The windows of the long, elegant wing of the imperial palace blazed with light. The plaza in front was jammed with gilded private carriages egesting members of high society dressed in the latest fashions. Behind them, more modestly dressed members of the public climbed from hansom cabs and carts and joined the throng heading toward the door. As the three of us climbed from our cab, Casanova discovered he had left his purse behind in his room. I dug into my pocket to pay the fare.

We followed the crowd into the lobby and up the wide staircase to the ballrooms. The building contained several large connecting rooms, and thus could be used either for small, intimate concerts or for large dances like the one to-night.

At the landing, Marta excused herself to refresh her powder. "I'll check your cloak and get us a drink," I said.

"More champagne?" She nodded and disappeared into a large group of chattering ladies moving down the hallway.

"She is a lovely young lady," Casanova murmured in my ear. "I believe there is a chance for you there, my friend." I shook my head. We checked Marta's cloak and entered the first ballroom. The light, airy space was filled with dancers, their jewels glittering as they reflected the candlelight from the chandeliers that hung from every part of the expansive ceiling. At the far end of the room, a band of musicians struck up a minuet. The dancers formed two long lines, the ladies facing their partners, and began the graceful movements forward and backward, never touching one another.

"Da Ponte!" Valentin von Gerl, dressed in an elegant satin suit the color of plums, approached and pumped my hand. "We meet again so soon! I'm sorry I had to run off the other day."

"No apologies are necessary," I said. "It is good to see you again, sir."

Von Gerl turned to Casanova. "Excuse me, have we met before? You look very familiar to me," he said.

"Von Gerl, this is my good friend Giacomo Casanova," I said. "Giacomo, Baron von Gerl." The two men bowed to one another.

"Casanova!" von Gerl exclaimed. "It's an honor to meet you, sir. I've read your translation of the *Iliad*."

Casanova beamed at him.

"And of course I've heard the story of your escape from Venice. You must tell me all about it—"

I glanced around the room as they chatted, hoping that Marta would not appear too soon.

"Oh, I beg your pardon," von Gerl said. "I see someone I must speak to—a book dealer, for my collections." He bowed to Casanova. "It was a pleasure meeting you, sir. You must come have dinner while you are here and tour my collections." We watched as he hurried into the next room.

"A very interesting man," Casanova said. "Excuse me, Lorenzo. I too see someone I must greet. I will see you later."

I wandered through the crowd, searching for the bar. A voice called my name. I turned to see Salieri. I bowed to his wife and shook his hand.

"You are not dancing?" I asked.

"No, we are on our way out," he replied. "Theresa has a headache." He looked around. "It is so crowded—one would never imagine the country is at war."

"Have you seen the bar?" I asked him.

He gestured toward the door leading to the next ballroom. "The champagne is in there," he said. "I haven't seen the punch tables." He nodded to me and led his wife away.

I looked around the room for Marta, but did not see her, so I wandered into the next room to get the champagne. The band in here was playing a contredanse. The dancers lined up in the middle of the room, each dancing around his or her partner, the petty merchants and workers energetically to the beat of the music, the nobles more sedately, to their own rhythm.

I saw a punch table at the side of the room, but no champagne, so I went into the last room, where I found the bar. As I stood in line, watching couples move in a large circle to the lively music, Mozart and Constanze twirled by, his hand around her waist. They stopped to greet me.

"This is one of my dances," Mozart said. "What do you think?"

"It's very sprightly," I said.

"Sprightly, sprightly. I like that," Mozart said. He clasped Constanze's arm. "Come, my love, let us dance to the sprightly music your husband has composed." Constanze laughed as he pulled her away. "If he didn't write music, he would be a dancer," she said. "We'll talk later, Lorenzo." I waved as they rejoined the large circle.

The line for the champagne was not moving. I looked around and saw another one across the room. Sophie Lamm stood alone at the end of the table. I worked my way through the crowd to greet her. When I was a few feet away from her, I passed a pair of well-dressed women. One of them glanced over at Sophie.

"I don't know what the emperor was thinking, opening this place to the public," she sniffed to her friend, her loud voice aimed toward my landlady's daughter. "Look, the peasants are taking over." Sophie's cheeks flushed. I hurried toward her, but before I could reach her, von Gerl swooped in and took her hand. He leaned his head close to hers and murmured in her ear. She smiled.

I moved to the other side of the bar, where the line seemed shorter. Ahead of me, two noblemen were prognosticating the effects of the war. "Taxes will go up, mark my word," one said. Behind me, a young man with a high-pitched voice complained to his companion. "I never thought I would miss Hungarian wine," he said. "The bilgewater they sell here now isn't fit to feed the hogs on my father's estate."

I glanced over to the end of the long table, where Stefan

had joined Sophie and von Gerl. He said a few words to Sophie. She shook her head. He glanced at von Gerl, who still held Sophie's hand, then reached for her other arm, as if to lead her away. She shook her head again. Von Gerl put out his hand to stop Stefan from grabbing the girl. The young stonemason flushed with anger, said a few words to Sophie, and then stomped away. The baron laughed and took Sophie's other hand.

Across the room I saw Marta dancing with Casanova. I looked at the line of people ahead of me. I could be here all evening and my old friend would have persuaded Marta to elope to Paris with him. I quit the line and walked toward them. The music had stopped and people were milling about, chatting.

"This war is going to last years . . ."

"Have you seen the prices at the market?"

"Our cook just heard that her son died in the field hospital in Semlin."

"It's time for us to approach the emperor and urge him to end this war. I don't know about you, but I have a warehouse full of fine porcelain that no one is interested in buying."

"Kaunitz must be replaced. This war is his idea."

"Shhh . . . careful . . . the walls have ears."

I passed my fellow lodger, Strasser, who was deep in conversation with two other professors from the university. He nodded a greeting at me.

"There you are, Lorenzo," Marta said. She looked at my empty hands.

"The lines for the champagne are too long," I said, coloring with embarrassment.

"It's all right," she said. "I doubt it was French champagne, anyway. Will you dance with me?" I led her onto the floor and put my arm around her waist. We joined the circle of dancers, stepping back and forth briskly. My heart pounded—more from my enjoyment of holding her than from the strenuousness of the dance steps—as we whirled around the room to Mozart's music.

As we passed along the longer side of the room, Marta stiffened. I followed her gaze to the end of the champagne bar, where von Gerl stood laughing with Sophie. I turned her away from the sight and hurried her around the room, but it was too late. She had grown quiet, and her feet no longer matched my steps.

We danced by Strasser and his colleagues. Baron Hennen had joined them, and was arguing loudly with two of the professors. A third man took his arm and led him away. "You are drunk, sir," I heard him say to Hennen.

"Can we stop, please, Lorenzo?" Marta asked. "I'm very tired." She looked over to the spot where von Gerl had stood with Sophie. They had disappeared.

I led her to a chair across the room. "Sit and rest for a while," I said. "Would you like a cold punch?"

She nodded.

I gestured back to the middle room. "I have to go in there to get it. Stay right here. I'll be back soon."

As I entered the adjoining ballroom, a wave of heat passed over me, and a hammer began to pound in my head. I walked out of the room into the wide hallway that ran the combined length of the ballrooms. I felt a breeze coming from the left, so I walked down the hall toward an open window to get a breath of fresh air. As I approached, I heard a familiar voice.

"Brrr . . ." my landlady's daughter said. "There's a draft. Can't we move away from these windows?"

"Put your arms around me. I'll warm you," a man's voice said. I heard a giggle, then a loud sigh. A moment later, the man groaned.

I peeked around the corner. Sophie stood in a small vestibule, her slim arms clasped above her head, pinned against the wall by a male hand. The bodice of her dress had been untied and her chemise pulled down. Valentin von Gerl's face was buried in her downy breast. His left hand moved expertly to lift her pink skirt.

I stepped back into the hallway, coughed loudly, waited a moment, and then entered the vestibule. "Oh, there you are, Sophie," I said, trying to keep my eyes away from her breasts. She started, and then, seeing me, reddened and clutched at her chemise. Von Gerl released her, pulled down her skirt, and smiled at me.

"Marta is feeling ill. Come, I promised your mother I would see you safely home."

She glanced at von Gerl as she fumbled with the ties of her bodice.

"I'll take you home in my carriage later," he said.

She looked from him to me. I raised a brow. She chewed on her bottom lip. "Oh, I had better go with Signor Da Ponte," she told von Gerl.

He bowed and kissed her hand. "If that is your wish," he murmured. "I will say good night for now, my beautiful Sophie." He nodded to me and left.

Sophie gazed after him and sighed.

"Take a moment to compose yourself," I said. "Where is Stefan?"

"Oh, we had an argument," she said. "He was angry because I wanted to talk with Valentin. He can be such a jealous booby sometimes."

"Come along," I said, taking her hand. I dragged her down the hallway into the third ballroom. The band had granted my throbbing head some mercy and stopped its playing. Mozart and Constanze had left. I saw no sign of Casanova, but was not concerned. He could see himself home. Marta sat forlornly on the chair where I had left her.

"I'm afraid we must leave," I told her. Sophie directed a small wave across the room, where von Gerl stood chatting with a pair of merchants.

Marta's eyes followed the girl's. "Yes, I see," Marta said. She took Sophie's arm. I marched them through the two front ballrooms, collected their cloaks, and led them downstairs and outside.

A line of hansom cabs waited at the edge of the plaza. "Wait here," I told the ladies. I walked over to hail one. As I returned, Baron Hennen came out the door. The cab I had signaled for halted suddenly as a fancy carriage, drawn by four horses wearing golden plumes, cut in front of it and pulled up at the door. Four very drunk, fashionably clad young ladies stumbled out of the Redoutensaal. The driver descended and helped them into the carriage, taking time to admire the heels of the first and the cleavage of another.

"You whores!" Baron Hennen lifted his cane and shouted at the young women. "Wasting four good horses for your silly entertainment! The troops in Semlin could use those horses!" The girls gawked at him from the windows of the carriage, and then collapsed into fits of giggles. The baron swore loudly at them and hobbled out of the plaza, heading down one of the narrow streets leading to the Neuer Market.

Our cab pulled up and I helped Sophie and Marta in. Sophie stuck her head out the window and looked wistfully at the departing carriage. "Did you see the blond one's necklace?" she asked Marta. "And the dark-haired one's purse. It must have been silk." She sighed. "My friend Barbara met a nobleman at one of these balls. He fell madly in love with her. He gave her jewels like that, and drove her around in a fancy carriage just like that one."

Marta pulled Sophie back into the carriage. I gave the driver the address and we drove away. Marta sat quietly, staring out the window into the dark streets, as Sophie babbled on about the ball. Exhaustion seeped through me. My head throbbed.

After a while, Marta spoke. "You must be careful of these noblemen," she told Sophie. "A girl in your situation can easily get into trouble. Trust me. I know what I am talking about." Sophie looked at her blankly. Marta's warning did not spend much time in that pretty young head.

"'There with tokens of love and embroidered words he deceived Hypsipyle,'" Marta murmured.

"Who?" Sophie asked.

"Hypsipyle, the queen of Lemnos. She was seduced by Jason, the leader of the Argonauts—oh, never mind," Marta said. She shook her head and returned to staring out the window.

Back at the house, I helped the ladies down from the cab and paid the driver. We walked into the courtyard, where a sole lantern burned at the door.

"Please, Signor Da Ponte," Sophie said. "Don't tell my mother that you had to bring me home. If she finds out Stefan left me there she'll never let him come here again."

I sighed. How had I become involved with all this female drama? "All right, Sophie," I said. She bade us good night and tiptoed into the house.

I turned to Marta. "Would you like to sit in the garden for a moment?" I asked. "We've had no time to talk all evening."

She followed me to the garden bench and sat beside me. Her floral scent wafted to my nose.

"It's so dark out here," Marta said. "I'm not used to it. It is like being out in the countryside."

"It is not Venice, that is certain," I said. "Tell me, where did you read Dante?"

She looked at me, puzzled for a moment, then laughed. "Oh, what I told Sophie, about Hypsipyle? My father provided me with a fine education. He was a younger brother of the family. If you lived in Venice, I'm sure you've heard of us."

I nodded. The Cavalli family's palace was near the church where I had led mass when I lived in Venice.

"My mother died giving birth to me. I was my father's

only child. He encouraged me to read everything—Dante, Petrarch, even Shakespeare."

"Does your father know you've come to Vienna?" I asked.

"No. He died when I was fifteen. Since then I've lived with my uncle's family. I am the poor relation, I'm afraid. That's how I met Valentin. My uncle collects butterflies. Valentin came to the palace to purchase a part of his collection."

"Are you really married to him?" I blurted. She looked at me sharply. I flushed. "I am sorry. That is none of my affair."

"No, you have been so kind to me, I owe you an explanation," she said. "When Valentin came to my uncle's house, I found myself attracted to him immediately. I had never felt that way about any man. I tried to control my feelings, but I could not." Her eyes took on a faraway look. "He promised to marry me. I pledged myself to him, and let him seduce me. I was deliriously happy. I bribed one of the servants to leave the palace door unlocked, and he would come to me late at night. We planned to announce our marriage when my uncle returned from a long trip to Asia. Then Valentin received a message from Vienna. He told me his father and brother had died, and that he had to return to assume the title. He promised he would send for me when his affairs were settled."

She sighed. "As you know, six months passed, and I did not hear from him. That is why I came here. To answer your question, yes, we are married. No, not with the full pomp of ceremony, but the old way. He promised to make me his wife, and I gave myself to him. The church would agree that we are married, I believe."

I sat there, a hollow pit in my stomach.

She shivered and drew her cloak around her. "But he's not ever going to send for me, is he?" she asked in a small voice.

As her tears began to fall, I took her in my arms. She sobbed into my shoulder. I brushed my hand over her soft hair.

Finally, when her tears were spent, she raised her head and looked into my face. "I'm all alone here, in this dark place," she whispered. "What shall I do?"

"I don't know," I said. "But I am here to help you." I ran my finger over her cheek to wipe away her tears. She gently pulled away from me and stood. "I had better go in. Thank you, Lorenzo, for the evening. Good night."

"Good night, Marta," I said. I sat on the bench staring at the shadows the moonlight cast against the walls of the small garden. The door to the house opened and closed. I stood and looked up at the house. A moment later, a light appeared in her window. I turned back to the garden and stood there for a long time, staring into the night.

Eleven

A soft knock on my door roused me from sleep. The gray light of dawn filled my room as I wrapped myself in my dressing gown and opened the door to find my landlady, her hair still bound in her nightcap, her brow furrowed with concern.

"Signore, there is a carriage waiting for you downstairs," she said, pulling her shawl around her worn wrapper.

"Thank you, madame. I'll be right down."

I glanced out my window and saw a black carriage standing in the mist. The driver lounged in the street. I washed hastily, dressed, took my cloak and satchel, and hurried down the stairs.

The driver tipped his cap and held the door for me. "I'm from the Ministry of Police, sir. I'm to take you into town. Inspector Troger and Count Benda are already there."

"What is it?" I asked him, although I had already guessed the terrible answer to my question.

"There's been another one, sir. Another murder."

. . .

The carriage clattered loudly through the Stuben gate and onto the deserted, silent streets of the city. I turned my head away from the north side of the Stephansdom as the driver pushed the horses around the cathedral, into the empty Stock-im-Eisen-Platz, and past the curved apartment building that marked the entrance to the Graben. The stalls of the cloth market, which would soon be busy with vendors selling fabric, buttons, ribbons, and thread, sat closed, dark and still.

The carriage halted. The driver climbed down to open the door for me. "I'm afraid I'll have to leave you here, sir. They are closing off the Graben at both ends."

Ahead of me, constables were setting barricades along the width of the large plaza.

The driver shouted to one of the constables. "Just go in there, sir, before he places the barrier. You'll find the inspector and the count straight ahead."

I thanked him and trudged into the Graben. A light rain had begun to fall, and despite the warmth of the early morning air, I was grateful for my cloak. A small group of men huddled around the plague column. Benda saw me and came over to greet me.

"Good, you came quickly. We want to get him out of here before the city wakes up and we have a furor on our hands."

"Who is it?" I asked. "It is the same?"

Benda gestured toward the base of the large monument. Walther Hennen lay on the steps at the base, his gnarled right leg splayed off to the side at a sharp angle. His right arm rested against the bloodstained, squat balustrade wall that separated the plinth of the huge pillar from the stones of the plaza; his left arm lay at his side. He stared unseeing at the sky, his mouth shaped in the same surprised rictus as Alois's had been, his throat slashed from ear to ear. Blood seeped over the coat of the dress suit I had seen him in just hours before at the Redoutensaal. His ornate stick lay several feet from his body.

Troger nodded at me. "It's our killer," he said. "The placement of the body, the slashes on the throat are the same. And his forehead—the cuts are the same as those on the old priest."

My empty stomach heaved, but I forced myself to look carefully at Hennen's body. His forehead was covered with blood. "Could someone clean off his forehead?" I asked.

Troger opened his mouth to object, but then nodded at a constable, who leaned over the body and gingerly wiped the crimson mess off the dead baron's head.

My legs shook as I knelt and examined the forehead.

"It's the same man, for certain," Benda said. "The pattern fits. First he attacks a great war hero, next a priest, and now an aristocrat."

The markings were the same as Troger had described to me when he and Pergen had told me that Alois's body had been mutilated. A shallow, straight line stretched from the spot in the center of Hennen's eyes to about a half-inch below his hairline. To the right of the straight line, the killer had cut a broad arc beginning at the top of the straight line and ending halfway down it, in the middle of the baron's forehead. I squinted, trying to avoid Hennen's vacant stare as I studied the cuts. A memory niggled in the back of my brain. Something about the shapes was familiar—

"You must arrest that protester, Richter, right away," Benda told Troger.

"On what evidence, sir? I need more than your theory and intuition before I can convince Count Pergen to issue an arrest warrant," Troger replied.

I stared at Hennen's forehead, racking my brain to remember where I had encountered this figure before. I looked up at the statues on the plinth of the monument, and then down at Hennen's forehead again. Then it came to me. A ball of ice settled at the pit of my stomach. I knew that Benda's theory was wrong. We were not confronting a man who, motivated by his hatred of the war, was killing symbols of the country's might and power. No, the devil committing these crimes was driven by urges that were much more malevolent.

PART II

Women and Good Wine

Twelve

Benda and I walked down the Kärntnerstrasse to the Himmelpfortgasse, where Hennen had lived. We said little, each of us lost in our thoughts.

"I saw Hennen just last night, at the Redoutensaal," I finally said as we turned into the street. "He was wearing the same clothes."

"He must have met his killer on his way home," Benda said, as we walked by a large, opulently ornamented palace that was now used for ministry offices.

"No, I don't think so," I said. "He left early, as did I. I heard him berate some girls in a fancy carriage as I was hailing a cab. He was angry that they hadn't donated their horses to the war effort. He stalked away, in this direction, not toward the Graben. And besides, the Graben would have still been busy that time of night. This man waits until everyone in the city has gone to bed before he comes out to commit murder."

Hennen's palace stood at the end of the next block. It was a bit smaller than its neighbors, and not as well maintained. There was no courtyard entrance, just a large, plain wooden door. The paint on the façade had peeled off in large patches in some places, and the stone caryatids that flanked the large doorway were each missing several toes.

Benda knocked on the door. We waited in the light rain for a few moments. There was no answer.

"It's early, but there must be servants about," Benda said, pounding on the door.

A window directly above us on the top floor opened, and a round face swathed in a frilly white nightcap looked out.

"Who is there?" the woman called.

"Are you the housekeeper?" Benda shouted.

"Yes, sir. What is this about? Please keep your voice down. You'll wake the baron," she said.

"We must speak with you. Please let us in."

"Let me dress, sir. I'll be down in a moment." The window slammed shut.

Benda stomped his foot in irritation. "Surely she could send a lackey down to open the door, so we could get out of the rain," he said.

We stood for five long minutes, and then the door opened to a large woman in a threadbare uniform. I could tell from the look on her chubby face that her irritation with us had turned to fear on her way down the stairs. She stepped back and ushered us into a large, cold foyer.

"What is it, sirs? If you are here to see the baron, he is not at home."

"Where are the other servants?" Benda demanded, looking around the room, which was barren of any decoration. A simple wooden bench sat against the right wall.

"I am alone here, sir," she said.

"In this big house?" I asked. "You do everything? That must be a lot of work."

She cast me a friendly look, and nodded. "The baron doesn't need much, sir. He is a bachelor. Most of the rooms are closed up, so I dust them just once a week. It's so expensive to keep the fires going in them, you see—" She saw the look on our faces and put her hand over her mouth.

"Something has happened to the baron," she whispered.

"Yes," Benda said. "He was found in the Graben this morning."

"Is he dead?" Her voice trembled.

Benda nodded.

Large tears rolled down her ruddy cheeks. "What happened, sir? Did he fall and hit his head?" she asked. "He rushed everywhere, leaning on that stick. I was always afraid he would fall."

We did not answer. I pulled out my handkerchief and handed it to her. She nodded gratefully.

"How long have you worked for him?" I asked.

She wiped her eyes. "Twenty-five years, sir, since he was a boy. I was hired to watch him after his mother died. The former baron, Walther's father, had no interest in the boy after his wife died. He drank and gambled." She sniffled. "But I shouldn't speak ill of the dead, sir. All of that happened a long time ago."

"Was Walther married? Is there any other family?" Benda asked.

"No, sir. He was an only child. It was just the two of them, Walther and his father, until the old baron died a few years ago. Walther never married. There was an engagement, five years ago, but after the accident—"

"When he was lamed?" I asked.

She twisted my handkerchief in her chapped, plump hands. "Yes, sir. Walther was a joyful, handsome boy, but very lonely. When his father sent him off to school, he suffered from melancholia. He was never able to overcome it. That's why I was so happy when he became engaged to Mademoiselle Albrechts."

Benda gasped.

She glanced at him and frowned, and then returned her attention to me. "She was from an excellent family. Her father was a war hero. He passed away recently. Walther adored her." Her voice broke. "Then the carriage knocked him down over in the Michaelerplatz. Both of his legs were broken. The doctors could not set one of them right. The young lady changed her mind after that."

She sighed. "Poor Walther never recovered from the blow. When his father died a year later, Walther discovered that the old baron had lost most of their lands at the gambling tables. Walther was left with almost nothing, just this house and its contents. He let the rest of the staff go, but kept me on to look after him. He's had to sell the furniture and all of the art to support us."

She began to weep.

"When did you last see him?" Benda asked.

"Last night, sir. He had gone to that ball at the Redoutensaal. I was happy that he had decided to go. He usually avoids parties. 'No one wants to dance with a cripple, Marthe,' he would say. But he didn't stay very long. I've heard those parties let out well after midnight. He came home at about eleven. He'd been drinking. I could smell the whisky on his breath."

"What did he do when he came in?" I asked.

She blew her nose into my handkerchief. "A message had been delivered earlier in the evening, sir, after Walther had left for the ball. I gave it to him when he arrived home. He read it, and then told me to leave the front door unlocked. He said that he would be going out again later."

"Who delivered the message?" I asked. "Was there an insignia on the seal?"

"Oh, sir, I didn't look at it. The baron's correspondence is none of my business." She thought for a moment. "A young boy delivered it."

I stifled a curse. These damned anonymous boys! How many were there in this city? "What happened after he read the note? Did he tell you anything about its contents?" I pressed.

"No, sir. He took it up to his room. I went to bed a few minutes later."

"Did you hear him go out again? Did you hear him come back?" Benda asked.

"No, sir. You see, I sleep on the top floor. I can't hear anything that goes on way down here. But when I was coming to let you in just now, I looked in his room. His bed hasn't been slept in."

"We'll need to search the house," I told her.

"But I don't understand, sir. What is it you are not telling me? You said he tripped and hit his head."

"He was murdered," Benda said. "We found his body at the base of the plague column this morning. His throat had been cut."

Her face crumpled. "Like the old priest by the cathedral?" She staggered. I grabbed her arm before she fell. As I guided her toward the bench, I glared at Benda, who was already halfway up the stairway.

"What is going on, sir?" she asked me. "Is there a maniac on the loose? Why would anyone kill Walther?" She rocked back and forth, sobbing. "My poor little boy, my poor boy," she moaned. I sat next to her and put my arm around her shoulder. Benda continued up the stairs.

She wiped her eyes and turned to me. "Who could have done such an evil thing, sir?"

"That's what we are going to find out," I said. "Can you tell me which rooms he used?"

"The salons on the first floor are all closed up. He used the rooms on the second floor. His chamber is there, and the library is next door. He spent most of his time in the library. Lately, he even took his meals in there. Do you want me to show you?" she asked.

"No," I said. "You stay here. We'll go up ourselves."

I joined Benda at the first landing. "We should look in all the rooms in case she's hiding something," he said.

We walked through the grand public salons on the first floor. Every room was empty of furniture. Tattered velvet drapes hung at the tall windows. Large dark rectangles on the faded damask wallpaper were the only evidence that the Hennen family had once owned a large art collection.

On the second floor, we walked through more empty rooms until we finally reached the baron's library. The walls here also showed the telltale marks of treasured paintings sold, and most of the books had been removed from the shelves.

Benda hurried over to the writing desk at the center of the room. He shuffled through a pile of papers on its top. "Look here, Da Ponte," he called to me. "Here's a letter Hennen was writing, to send to one of the newspapers, I imagine." He scanned its contents. "It's the usual arguments in favor of the war."

He picked up another paper and read it. "He's been writing a pamphlet in support of widening the draft," he said. He slapped the table. "Yes! Hennen was a logical victim for our killer—a nobleman, highly vocal in his support of the war. Yet another symbol of the greatness of our country."

"But the victims are not very strong symbols," I objected.

He arched a brow. "What do you mean?"

"General Albrechts was an old man, his days of glory already faded. Alois was also old. He hadn't been involved in church affairs in over ten years. Hennen was a minor nobleman who had to sell off his family's possessions simply to survive." I waved my hand around the bare room. "Where is the greatness your killer is supposedly attacking?"

Benda thought for a moment. "All you say is true," he said. "But consider this. The people the killer actually wants are out of his reach. The high-ranking officers in the military and most of the nobility are in Semlin with the emperor. The senior members of the cathedral staff are usually sequestered in the archbishop's residence. The killer chooses victims whom he can confront and murder easily."

I shook my head, but said no more. Benda's theory was far-fetched, but I did not want to argue with him until I could mull over the ideas that had begun to form as I had examined Hennen's body.

We quickly finished our search of the library, but found no paper that could have been the message Hennen had received last night. We moved next door to the baron's chamber. Most of the furniture that once had filled the large room was gone, and like the other rooms in the house, no art graced the dark bedroom's walls. A small bed sat in one corner, a stuffed reading chair in another. Next to the chair was tucked a small table, upon which sat a lamp and a pile of papers. I riffled through them as Benda searched Hennen's meager wardrobe.

The first item in the pile was a political pamphlet, the type one saw in every coffeehouse in the city. I scanned the front page and snorted.

"What is it?" Benda asked.

"It's a broadside entitled 'Chambermaids: A Cautionary Tale for Young Gentlemen,'" I said. "The author is warning wealthy young men against their servant girls, who are looking to seduce their masters and improve their social standing."

"You shouldn't laugh," Benda said. "That's happening everywhere these days." He smirked. "But I don't think Hennen had anything to fear from that one downstairs."

I thumbed through the rest of the pile, which included a bill from Hennen's tailor for the repair of a dress suit, a receipt from a pawnshop in the Jewish quarter for a gold watch, a notice of a meeting in one of the Masonic houses in the city, and a letter from a nearby bookshop informing the baron that the proprietor could not take the baron's remaining books on consignment because the market for histories of the wars at the turn of the century had dried up.

At the bottom of the pile I found two sheets of paper of a lighter color than the ones in the rest of the pile. Both sheets were of fine rag with an elaborate watermark. Each contained a few lines written in black ink in a neat hand. I studied the contents of the top sheet. "But you have fixed your mind solely on earthly matters; you harvest only darkness from the true light," it said.

I put the sheet aside and took up its companion. "That infinite, indescribably good that dwells above, speeds itself to love, like rays of light to a shining body." My pulse began to race. "Come take a look at these," I said to Benda. He came and read the lines over my shoulder.

"Quotations of some sort," he said. "I don't recognize them. Do you?"

I took a deep breath. "Yes. The lines are from Dante, from his *Purgatory,* part of *The Divine Comedy.* Have you read it?"

Benda shook his head. "Is this Hennen's handwriting?" he asked.

"I don't know. Everything else here is correspondence from others." I took the two sheets and replaced the rest of the pile on the table. "I'll go into the library and compare these with the draft of the letter he was writing."

"I'll meet you downstairs," Benda said.

I carried the pages into the library, went over to the writing desk, and pulled out the draft of Hennen's letter. A glance told me that the documents were not written by the same hand. I went over to the bookshelves and studied the few volumes that remained, but could not find anything by Dante.

I went down to the foyer, where the housekeeper was standing with Benda. "Is either of these the message the baron received last night?" I asked, handing her the papers. She held the first one close to her face and studied it. I realized that she could not read. She peered at the second sheet of paper, and then handed them back to me. "No, sir. The paper on the message last night was different. These papers are a lighter color. The message that came last night was on a darker, thicker paper."

Benda took the papers from me, folded them, and tucked them in his coat pocket. We thanked the housekeeper and left. My mind brimmed with questions as we walked back down the Himmelpfortgasse and into the Neuer Market, the center of Vienna's flour and grain trade. We passed the Mehlgrube, a casino and concert hall on the site of the medieval grain storehouse, and the Donner fountain, a wide basin dominated by a simple sculpture of the imperial eagle—a replacement for its original elaborate statues of goddesses and nymphs whose lack of clothing had offended the old empress.

"Those Dante excerpts might be anything," Benda finally

said. "Perhaps Hennen belonged to a group that was studying the poetry."

I remained silent as we passed the Capuchin Church, where the monks tended the tombs of the Habsburg family, and turned into a smaller square. Outside one of the grand palaces, servants were tying canvases over the tops of large carts full of household goods.

"More people leaving the city for their estates." Benda sighed. "I wish I could join them. I've received some disturbing news about unrest among the peasants on my lands in Bohemia."

We continued past the Spanish Riding School stables toward the Michaelerplatz.

"Damn, Da Ponte," Benda said. "We are getting nowhere with this investigation! We have to work faster. Christiane refuses to leave Vienna until her father's murderer is found. She's determined to move out to the Belvedere at the end of the month. I don't understand what she is thinking!"

"It is difficult for a young woman to lose her father," I murmured.

"I know that," he snapped. His voice softened. "Of course I do. Her peace of mind is the most important thing in the world to me."

We approached the entrance to the Hofburg.

"I understand her grief. I feel it too. Watching her suffer wounds me to the center of my being. There will be no joy in my life until she gets over this sorrow, and is able to share a happy life with me."

I nodded. At the arch that led into the main courtyard to the Hofburg, Benda told me that he would come by tomorrow and we would visit the protester Richter's mother. We parted, he going to direct Troger to question Hennen's neighbors about the delivery of a message last night, and I heading to my office and work.

Thirteen

Caterina Cavalieri bore down on me as I entered the theater lobby.

"Ah, Lorenzo, there you are," she said.

I bowed.

"Antonio and I were discussing the opera last night," she said. "We believe my character is a bit underdeveloped."

I sighed inwardly. The bane of any theater poet is a soprano who is the inamorata of the company's music director.

"She just has that first aria, at the very beginning of the opera. The rest of the time I sing in ensembles."

I opened my mouth to speak but she put up her hand to stop me.

"Yes, of course, the music in the ensembles is beautiful. But Antonio and I agree that Donna Elvira needs something more. She's a much more interesting woman than Donna Anna, don't you think? And Donna Anna has two long arias! Not to say that Lange is not divine in that role." She sniffed.

"But she is still young. She doesn't have the experience to play a complex character like Elvira. The depths of her passion for Giovanni, the range of emotions she feels—I love playing her. And of course, your writing for her—your words are so expressive."

She batted her eyelashes at me.

"Antonio and I would love to see what you and Wolfgang can do to expand the role a bit," she continued.

"Madame—"

"I've been thinking. That spot in the last act, where Morella is supposed to sing his aria—the poor man, coloratura doesn't come naturally to everyone. I am so appreciative to God for my own gift. Why not put something for me there?"

She stopped to breathe and I was able to get a word in.

"I'll talk with Wolfgang, madame. I'm sure we could fit a short aria for you in the second act."

"Short? Oh, no. Antonio and I were thinking of a long scene. Elvira, alone on the stage. First a lengthy recitative, perhaps accompanied by one or two instruments. She will bare her soul to the audience, confessing that she still loves Giovanni. Then an aria. I'll need at least four stanzas to portray her raging emotions."

She put a bejeweled hand on my arm. "Wolfgang once told someone I had a flexible throat. Had you heard that? A flexible throat! You men make our art sound so mechanical."

"I will—"

"Well, you are the librettist. You know best. See what Wolfgang thinks. Tell him I'd like something similar to the arias he wrote for me when I was imprisoned by that awful pasha in the harem. He knows what I can do." She smiled at me and bustled off toward the main room of the theater.

"Dear God," I prayed as I headed downstairs. "Protect a poor poet from rivalrous sopranos!"

I picked my way down the cluttered hallway to my office. Once safely inside, I hung up my cloak and emptied my satchel onto the desk. I pulled out the new aria for Morella I had been working on. A wave of fatigue washed over me as I stared down at my jottings. I closed my eyes. The memory of Hennen's body sprawled at the base of the plague column, his blood mixing with the rain on the stones of the Graben, came unbidden to my mind.

I opened my eyes and pushed the paper away. Benda was right, we had to work faster on our investigation. But I was dismayed by the count's willingness to fit every fact to his theory. After the niggle of recognition I had felt while kneeling over Hennen's body, coupled with the Dante excerpts we had found in the baron's chamber, my own more terrifying theory was starting to form. I was certain that Benda would dismiss my inchoate musings. I wished I had someone to confide in, someone with experience in the world, who would listen to my speculations. I returned to the aria. Some moments later, an idea came to mind. I scribbled a note, folded it, and climbed upstairs to the lobby, where I gave a boy a coin to deliver it for me.

Back at my desk, I stared at the Morella aria for a few moments, then crumpled the page and threw it aside. I reached for a fresh sheet of paper and began to write.

On her peace of mind depends mine,
That which pleases her brings me life,
That which sorrows her gives me death.

Soon I was lost in my work, trying out phrases, crossing out words, slowly writing the plea of a man who loves a woman so desperately that he would do anything for her, but finds in the end that he cannot.

And I have no happiness if she has none.

When I finally lifted my head from the aria, satisfied with it, I was surprised to see that two hours had passed. I tucked the new work in my satchel, took my cloak from the cupboard, and left the theater.

"Three victims already!" Casanova's voice boomed across the table. I hushed him and looked around the busy beer hall. Our fellow patrons were laughing and chatting. No one seemed to have heard his outburst.

I had arrived at the establishment before Casanova, hoping that he would respond to the note I had sent earlier asking him to meet me here. As he had entered the room and threaded his way among the tables toward me, I noted that he looked tired and unhappy. After he had settled into a seat and ordered a beer, I asked him how his retirement in Dux was really proceeding.

He looked at me, his eyes lacking their usual enthusiasm. "I'll be honest with you, Lorenzo. It is not what I hoped for when I accepted the position. The count is often away, and I am left alone with the idiots the man has hired to serve him. The cook resents my presence and gives me tough meat. The steward does nothing I ask of him. The count keeps many dogs. They bark all night long."

"But surely, when the count is in residence, there are salons, parties," I said.

Casanova sighed. "Yes. He often invites guests to dine or for dancing parties, but they are provincial folk. They laugh at me, Lorenzo. They laugh at my poetry, at my writings. They laugh at my dancing. They even laugh about my clothes."

"The work in the library must be interesting, though," I said.

"The task the count has assigned me has proven impossible. The man is of no help to me as I try to organize his collection. He loans books to friends and never tells me. How can I properly catalog the volumes?"

When there was a break in the litany of complaints, I told him about the murders.

"What kind of monster kills a man and mutilates his body?" Casanova asked, shaking his head. "You mentioned you recognized the symbol that the killer had carved on Alois's and Hennen's foreheads. What was it?"

"The cuts were very crude, most likely made with the tip of the dagger the police believe the man is using," I said. "But when I saw the baron's forehead, I began to think that the killer is cutting the letter *P*. And after Benda and I found those excerpts from Dante in Hennen's chamber, I was certain."

Casanova took a sip of beer. "You think the killings are somehow related to Dante?" he asked. "I don't understand.

I've read *Inferno*. I don't remember anything about a letter *P*."

"It's in the second book, *Purgatory*. You should read all three volumes. Everyone is interested in Dante's depiction of Hell, but the work should be read as a whole. It is about a man's journey toward redemption and salvation—"

"I'll try the other two volumes sometime," Casanova said, waving away my lecture. "Tell me about the *P*."

"In the second volume, Dante and his guide, the poet Virgil, have climbed out of Hell and stand before the gate of Purgatory. They must travel up a steep, terraced mountain in order to meet Dante's love, Beatrice, in Paradise."

Casanova nodded.

"They must stop at seven terraces, where sinners committed to Purgatory are atoning for each of the seven deadly sins. Before they leave for the first terrace, an angel marks seven letter *P*s on Dante's forehead. As Dante passes through each terrace, one mark is erased from his brow. By the time he reaches Paradise, his brow is clean."

"Why the letter *P*?" Casanova asked.

"For the Latin *peccatum*—sin," I said.

"You think someone is committing these murders for some twisted reason linked to Dante's *Purgatory*?" my friend asked.

"Yes, although I don't understand it all quite yet. Only two of the victims had marked foreheads. I don't see how the general's murder fits into my theory. If I—"

"Lorenzo!" I looked up to see Mozart crossing the hall toward us. I shook my head slightly at Casanova, to signal that he was not to mention the murders to the composer.

"Well, who have we here?" Mozart said with a grin. He shook Casanova's hand. "Giacomo, it's good to see you again."

I patted the space on the bench next to me and beckoned the waiter.

After Mozart had ordered, he turned to Casanova. "I didn't see you after the premiere in Prague," he said. "What did you think of *Don Giovanni*?"

Last fall, I had traveled to Prague to work on *Don Giovanni* with Mozart. Casanova had been visiting the city, and had attended several rehearsals. I had missed the premiere myself, however, because Salieri had demanded that I return to Vienna to work on the libretto I was writing for him.

"I enjoyed it immensely," Casanova replied. "Although I was a bit disappointed that you didn't use my scene."

"What scene?" I asked.

Mozart and Casanova exchanged a glance.

"After you left Prague, I realized that something more was needed in the scene after the sextet," Mozart explained. "Giacomo was kind enough to sketch out an additional aria for the manservant character and a short piece for the ensemble."

"Why didn't you write to me—"

Mozart held up his hand to silence my protests. "In the end, though, I changed my mind and didn't use them. The cast performed the libretto the way you left it."

"I couldn't match your great literary talents," Casanova said to me. He winked at Mozart.

I took a sip of my beer. I had to confess that I was a bit annoyed that Mozart hadn't told me about this before.

"Look, Wolfgang," Casanova teased. "The great theater poet is sulking."

"Now you know how a composer feels when a singer insists on performing an aria written by someone else in the middle of his opera," Mozart said. The three of us laughed. Mozart had written plenty of such arias for insertion into the work of other composers.

"Oh, by the way, about changes," I said. "Madame Cavalieri cornered me this morning at the theater. She and her darling Antonio would like a solo scene for Elvira—a long recitative and a long aria, featuring as many vocal acrobatics as she can muster. So you had better go home and start writing, maestro!"

Mozart thought for a moment. "That's actually not such a bad idea. The character of Elvira is so ambiguous. Who is she? A crazy, spurned woman? One of the Furies, or a victim who truly loves her seducer? She's obsessed with Giovanni. She has an image of him in her mind—she makes him into what she wants him to be."

"I know that type of woman," Casanova murmured.

"Yes," Mozart said. "I like the idea. See what you can come up with, Lorenzo."

I nodded and reached for my satchel. "Since we are discussing the opera, I've written the new aria for Morella," I said, passing the page to Mozart.

He studied it and hummed a few bars of music. "This is good," he said. He tucked the paper in his coat pocket and turned back to Casanova.

"So how are things in Dux?" he asked.

"Great," Casanova said. "Just wonderful. The count

treats me as an honored guest, and is very involved in my work in his library. I'm enjoying it very much. It's a perfect place for my retirement. Of course, Dux is not Vienna, or Paris—"

"I hate Paris," Mozart muttered. "Italy, now that's a different matter. If I ever retire, I'd like to live there. I haven't been since I was fifteen. I'd love to go back someday."

"Oh, you must go back," Casanova said. "Tell me, were you in Venice as a boy?"

"Just for a few days," Mozart said. "I don't remember much about it, just that it rained the whole time we were there."

"You must go," Casanova said. A gleam came to his eye. "The ladies in Venice are in a class by themselves. Ah, I remember one from years ago, a dark-haired beauty who lived on the Campo San Barnaba. I spent many evenings in a gondola on the canal outside her window, attempting to woo her."

I winced. I had spent a lot of time in the campo myself as a young man in Venice. It was the heart of an area of the city the doge had set aside for young nobles who had lost their wealth through gambling. I had made love to such a man's sister. She had almost been the ruin of me.

"Alas, the young lady was one of my few failures," Casanova said. "She fell in love with a visiting merchant. I never saw her again."

"I already have a dark-haired beauty here in Vienna," Mozart said, winking at me.

"Where else in Italy did you visit on your tour?" Casanova asked.

"Let me think," Mozart said. "Verona, Bologna, Turin, Florence, Mantua—"

"Mantua! Such a beautiful city, surrounded by the three lakes. Did you happen to eat at that *osteria* near the gate of the old medieval wall? It was owned by a former singer, another great beauty. The Little Butterfly, we all called her."

"I played a recital at the brand-new theater around the corner from the gate," Mozart said. "I think we ate at that restaurant afterward. I remember a woman there. But she was old."

"Well, I was there several years before you." Casanova laughed. "How about Naples? Did you see it?"

"Yes, and Rome also. While I was in Rome, the pope made me a knight," Mozart said.

Casanova raised a brow. "You are a holder of the insignia of the Order of the Golden Spur?" he asked.

"Yes," Mozart replied.

"So am I! A few months after he was elected to the papacy, Carlo Rezzonico knighted me for donating the *Pandectorum liber unicus* to the Vatican Library. He was from Venice, you know."

"The what?" Mozart laughed.

"*Pandectorum*," Casanova said. "It was a collection of essays by Roman jurists. The emperor Justinian ordered its compilation."

I yawned.

"I haven't put on my sash and spurs for years," Mozart said.

"I didn't know we had so much in common, Wolfgang," Casanova said. He dug in his coat pocket and pulled out a piece of paper. "Tell me," he said slyly, looking over at me as he unfolded it. "Can you decipher the code in this message?"

Mozart studied the page. "33, 27, 54," he said. "Each number stands for a word?"

Casanova nodded.

"Let me think," Mozart said. "33. Give me a hint. How many letters in the first word?"

"Two," Casanova said.

"If each letter in the alphabet is assigned to a number, then the highest number cannot be more than 26. 26 and 7—that would be *z* and *g*. That's not a word. Let's try 25 and 8."

I sipped the rest of my beer as Mozart and Casanova worked through the puzzle. My bones felt weary, my mind exhausted. After about ten minutes of watching them, I placed some coins on the table, excused myself, and left the two knights to their fun.

It was raining lightly as I walked through the winding streets behind the university toward the Stuben gate. Dusk had fallen, and the torches in the street lamps sputtered in the moist air. Although it was still unseasonably warm, I pulled the collar of my cloak up around my neck as I made my way past the former church dedicated to Saint Barbara, which the emperor had recently given to the Greek community of Vienna. I was so tired that I could not think clearly about everything I had seen on this horrid day. I trudged down the street and turned into the short side street which would take me to the city wall. From there it would be a few steps to the Stuben gate.

The narrow street was unlit, its stones wet and slippery. I had only walked past the first of the darkened houses when the back of my neck tingled. Footsteps sounded behind me. I hurried past the next two houses, trying not to fall on the damp stones. The footsteps behind me quickened. Ahead of me the light on top of the city wall cast a welcoming pool of light on the street. I hastened toward it, my heart pounding. The footsteps kept pace with my own.

A moment later, I walked into the light and turned the corner. The Stuben gate loomed before me. A few more steps brought me to the gate. My shoulders sagged with relief as I joined a group of workers leaving the city. Before I crossed under the arch, I turned and looked back the way I had come. A man leaned against the wall of the corner house, resting in the pool of light. I could not make out his features in the distance, but a shiver ran down my back at what I could see of him—his sturdy build, his dark hair, and his forest-green cloak.

Fourteen

I was in my office the next day when Benda came in at noon.

"Any news?" I asked.

He shook his head. "Troger's men spent yesterday afternoon interviewing Hennen's neighbors, but no one saw a messenger come to the house, and no one saw the baron leave that night."

I sighed.

"I just passed Richter in the Graben," he continued. "He was headed toward the Stephansplatz with that crate of his. Now's a good time to visit his mother."

Although the rain had stopped late last night, the sky was still full of clouds. But the warmth continued, and I had left my cloak at my lodging house this morning. "I think we should consider a different theory about these murders," I said as we walked down the Kohlmarkt toward the Judenplatz.

Benda frowned. "What do you mean? The only evidence

that we have is the baker's claim that Richter and the general argued in the Am Hof before the general was murdered. What else is there?"

"Those papers we found in Hennen's chamber. I think the killer sent them to the baron."

"The Dante quotations? That's a leap!" Benda exclaimed. "As I said yesterday, they could be from anyone. They could mean anything."

"But there is more," I said. I explained about the symbolism of the markings on the victims' foreheads, and the link to Dante's *Purgatory*.

Benda was silent as we passed by the back of the Am Hof church. "There were no cuttings on the general's forehead," he reminded me. "His murder doesn't fit your theory."

"I know." I sighed. "I haven't thought the whole thing through yet. But I feel in my heart that there is a connection to Dante."

"Perhaps so. But how do we investigate that? Should we search the entire city for people who own *The Divine Comedy*? There must be hundreds. Even Christiane has a copy in her library, for God's sake."

My cheeks reddened. I made no reply as we walked down the Parisergasse and entered the Judenplatz. The small square had been the home to Vienna's synagogue in the Middle Ages, and was now lined with modest old apartment buildings. Benda led me to a cream-colored, narrow building on the right side of the square. A tailor shop occupied the ground floor. We entered the side door.

"It's at the top," Benda said. We climbed five flights of steep stairs to the attic. At the top landing, I struggled to catch my breath as Benda knocked on the door to our left. There was no answer.

Benda knocked again. "Frau Richter?" he called.

A loud clunking noise came from behind the door.

"She is blind," Benda told me.

"Who is there?" a frail voice called.

"Frau Richter, please open the door. We'd like to talk to you. It is about your son."

A minute later, the door opened. Richter's mother was small-boned, with a sharp nose, thin lips, and a fleshy wattle at her throat. Her brown eyes stared blankly at us.

"Good day, Frau Richter," Benda said. He pushed his way past her into the apartment. I followed.

The living quarters were tiny, just two small rooms. A small bed, a cupboard, and a small table with two chairs stood in the front room. I righted the chair that she had overturned in her haste to answer the door and placed it under the table. I looked through the doorway to the cramped second room. A small bed had been tucked under the sloping ceiling. Next to it stood a simple wooden table upon which sat a large clock.

"You gentlemen are friends of my Michael?" Frau Richter asked. She felt her way to the table and pulled out one of the chairs. "Please, sirs, sit down. May I offer you something to drink?"

Benda and I remained standing. "No, thank you, madame," I said. "We do not wish to bother you. We need just a moment of your time. Please sit."

She sat in the chair. Her hands quivered in her lap.

"We have a few questions about your son," Benda said.

Her hand flew to her throat. "Is he all right? Has there been an accident?"

"No," Benda said. "He is fine. We just saw him. We would like you to think very hard, back to two weeks ago, April 8. It was a Tuesday. Do you remember what your son did that night?"

Her head bobbed up and down as she pondered the question. "All of the nights are the same to me, sir. Which day was it?"

"Tuesday, April 8," Benda said impatiently.

"It was the first day of this warm weather," I offered, hoping to stir her memory.

"Oh, yes. Now I remember. It was so hot up here that day. Yes. Michael went to a meeting with some friends of his. He is involved in a group that opposes this terrible war. It lasted very late. Do you gentlemen know Michael from the group?"

Benda gestured for me to continue questioning her. He quietly moved into the next room and riffled through some papers on the table by the bed.

"Do you remember what time he came home that night?" I asked.

Her head bobbed up and down. "It was very late. He was upset when he got here. A man who had been with the troops at Semlin had spoken at the meeting. He told Michael and his friends how awful the conditions in the camp were. There has been a lot of flooding because of the spring rains, and it was beginning to get very hot. Many of the soldiers had watery bowels. Some had already died. Michael told me all about it. He was very angry."

"What time did he get home?" I asked gently. Benda had returned to the front room, and was gingerly opening the top door of the cupboard.

"Let me think. I remember it was late, much later than he usually arrives home. Yes, that's right. I hadn't had my supper. Michael is so busy attending meetings and giving speeches. But he always comes home before eight o'clock, to give me my supper and help me to bed."

Benda gently closed the cupboard door and opened the lower one. The hinges on the old wood creaked.

Frau Richter's head jerked toward the cupboard. "What's that noise? What are you doing?"

"It was nothing," I said. "My friend just brushed against the cupboard door. Michael didn't come home by eight that night?"

"No, he didn't." Her voice grew querulous. "I remember it clearly now. I waited and waited. I was worried that he might have been arrested or been injured in a fight. So many people don't want to hear the truths he preaches. But then he arrived. He was very upset, both about what he had heard at the meeting, and because he had kept me waiting."

I shook my head at Benda as he started to close the cupboard door. He left it ajar and remained standing there quietly.

"Do you remember what time it was?" I asked.

"About eleven, I think. Yes, I remember. I was sitting here at the table. Michael was preparing my supper. The clock in my bedroom chimed ten times."

"It was ten o'clock, then?"

"Oh, no, sir. The clock needs fixing, you see. It runs an hour slow."

"What happened after you ate?"

"Michael wiped the dishes, and we sat here at the table for a while. He told me all about the meeting. At midnight, he helped me into bed."

"Did he also go to bed?"

"No. He was restless. I heard him moving around in here for a bit. Then I drifted off to sleep."

Benda frowned, disappointed that the mother did not indict her son, as he had hoped.

"But now that I think about it, I remember waking up." She chewed her lip. "I thought I heard a noise—the latch to the door shutting. I called for Michael but he did not answer. He must have been fast asleep and didn't hear it."

"Did you get up?" I asked.

"No, sir. I lay awake for a few minutes, and when I did not hear the noise again, I fell asleep."

"Did you notice the time?" Benda asked sharply.

She turned her head to where he stood by the cupboard. "Yes, sir, I did. A moment after I called for Michael, the clock chimed twelve times."

Fifteen

"Was all that necessary?" I snapped as we hurried down the stairs and back into the Judenplatz.

Benda looked at me quizzically. "What?"

"Tricking that poor woman—allowing her to believe that we were friends of her son. Searching the apartment without her knowing. Taking advantage of her unfortunate condition!"

Benda stiffened at my criticism. "Pergen told me you had been involved in a murder case before," he said. "How can you be so naïve? We're dealing with a determined killer, one who is striking at the very heart of all that Austria stands for. You of all people should know that in situations like this, the ends justify the means. That woman is no poor innocent. She might be the mother of a vicious killer." His tone softened. "Consider what we were able to learn. Richter wasn't asleep when she was wakened by the noise. He had just closed the door and left the apartment. It was one o'clock in the morning. He was going to meet the general in the Am Hof, to kill him."

"We can't be certain of that," I protested.

"Where else would he be going, so late at night? None of the lodges meet that late. The taverns are all closed at that hour. No, I am certain that Richter is our man. Now we just have to link him to Alois Bayer and Hennen." He dug in his pocket and pulled out his watch.

"I have a meeting at the chancery," he said. "Afterward I'll tell Pergen what we've learned. Perhaps Troger has found more information about Richter. I'll contact you when I have news." He nodded at me and walked toward the street at the side of Richter's apartment house.

I gritted my teeth and went in the other direction, down the narrow, curving Currentengasse. I was tired of Benda's easy dismissal of all of my suggestions and concerns. Ahead of me, a small catering shop had set trestles out on the street. Uniformed lackeys and laborers sat on long benches eating dinner and drinking beer. The aroma of stewed meat rose from the tables, but I had no appetite. When I reached the end of the street, I heard a familiar voice around the corner.

"What do you mean, you are leaving me?" It was Valentin von Gerl.

"I'm quitting, sir," a second voice replied. "I've had enough of you."

"Don't be an idiot, Teuber," said von Gerl. "Is this about money? I don't pay enough? Here, take these."

I heard coins clink on the ground.

"Hello," I called, turning the corner.

"Da Ponte! We meet again!" Von Gerl, clad in the blue velvet suit I had admired at his palace last week, turned away from his servant and smiled. The plume on his hat bobbed up and down as he shook my hand. He showed no embarrassment at the memory of the last time we had seen each other, when his face had been buried in the young bosom of my landlady's daughter.

"I'm sorry I had to run off after dinner the other day," he said. "I hope you enjoyed viewing my collection as much as I enjoyed showing it to you."

"I did, sir." I glanced over his shoulder to see Teuber scowling at his master's back.

"You must come back, soon. And we must discuss plans for my library."

The bells of the Am Hof church sounded the hour.

"Is it two already? I must be off again, I'm afraid," von Gerl said. "Good to see you, Da Ponte. I'll send you another invitation to dinner soon!" He hurried away.

Teuber stood looking after him, his face sullen. I nodded at him and started down the street that led to the Bognergasse.

"Signore," he called.

I turned back.

"What happened to the young lady last week? Miss Cavalli?"

I stared at him. "I helped her find a place to stay. But why do you care? You threw us out of the house."

He reddened. "That was by order of my master, signore."

"His order? What do you mean?"

The manservant backed away from me. "I've said enough,

signore. But don't worry. He'll get what is coming to him someday."

"What did you say? What do you mean?"

"Nothing, signore. I said nothing. I meant nothing." He turned and scurried toward the Am Hof.

I ate dinner and worked the rest of the day in my office. As I was turning into my street a little before six, I met Erich Strasser. My fellow lodger was pale. Small beads of sweat lined his upper lip.

"Erich, are you ill?" I asked.

"Oh, good evening, Lorenzo." He took a handkerchief from his cloak pocket and ran it over his face. "No, I am merely tired—too much work," he said.

"We should have a glass of wine together some evening," I said. "I'd like to hear more about your experiences with the Turks."

"Let's do that, Lorenzo," he answered. "But now, if you'll excuse me, I am late for a lodge meeting." He walked in the direction of the city.

Stefan stood in front of the house, feeding a carrot to his horse.

"Good evening, Signor Da Ponte," he called to me.

"Good evening, Stefan."

"I wanted to thank you, signore, for seeing Sophie safely home the other night," he said. "I came back for her around midnight but could not find her. Her friend Liesl told me she had left with you and Miss Cavalli."

"Why did you leave her alone at the ball?" I asked.

He reddened and stared down at his shoes. "She was

flirting with that baron, von Gerl. I was so angry I had to leave." He looked up at me. "I swear, signore, I never would have left her there alone, without a ride home. But I couldn't control my temper. I wanted to punch the baron in the mouth."

The horse nudged his hand, and he gave it another carrot. "Sophie is young, signore. She can be very silly. She thinks she can manage every situation, but I knew what he wanted from her. But if I had hit him—well, I'm not stupid. Even a simple stonemason knows not to argue with a noble-man. I'd have been drafted and sent to Semlin the next day." He clenched his fist. "If it weren't for that, I'd take care of Baron von Gerl."

"Have you heard anything about the draft?" I asked. I knew that most young men Stefan's age had already been taken for the army. I was curious how he had managed to evade their fate.

"My master is protecting me," he explained. "When the bureaucrats came to register me, he reported that I was a necessary worker. But that won't last much longer. Our work is disappearing. No one is building anything new, with the war on, and the nobles are all leaving for their es-tates. They aren't ordering repairs or additions to their city palaces."

"Oh, Stefan, there you are," Sophie said, coming into the street from the courtyard. She gave me a flirtatious curtsy. "Good evening, signore." She put her arms around Stefan's waist and turned her cheek to receive his kiss. He stood stiffly, his arms at his sides.

"Are you angry with me?" she asked. "Whatever for?"

"Don't touch me," he said, pushing her away.

"What is it? Are you still upset because I was flirting with that baron? I already told you, he means nothing to me."

I took a few steps into the courtyard.

"You silly boy!" Sophie said. "Come on, why don't you beat me? I'll just stand here and take it. You must want to pull my hair out." Her voice was teasing. "Go ahead."

Stefan groaned. "You'll be the ruin of me," he said.

"But what is this?" Sophie's laugh was light and lilting. "You don't want to beat me after all? You no longer have the heart for it? In that case, you'd better forgive me, hadn't you?"

The courtyard and garden were empty. As I reached for the door, I heard the two young lovers kissing and cooing. I shook my head. I did not envy Stefan his long future with Sophie.

Inside, the house was silent. My legs grew heavy as I climbed the stairs to my room. The last week had been too horrible, too long. I entered my room and put my satchel on the desk. I hung up my coat and waistcoat, and lay down on my bed. As I closed my eyes, visions of Hennen's mutilated body came to me.

I got up and lit a candle, then took my Dante out of the cupboard. I sat on my hard desk chair and continued my reading of *Inferno*. Occasionally I closed my eyes to rest, but the vivid scenes of the murders soon returned to wake me.

I had read for about two hours when a knock sounded at the door. I opened it to find Marta standing there. Her red-gold hair flowed over the shoulders of her white nightgown. Her eyes were swollen, as if she had been crying.

"Marta? What is it?" I asked.

"Oh, Lorenzo," she whispered. "I'm all alone, all alone in this dark place. It is so cold. May I come in?"

For a moment, my heart stopped beating in my chest. Then I took her soft, small hand and drew her into the room.

Sixteen

The memorial service for Alois was held the next morning in the Chapel of the Cross in the Stephansdom. A few rows of chairs had been set up to accommodate the small group that had gathered: the priests Krause and Urbanek, a few of the workers from the cathedral staff, the porter from Alois's building across the plaza, and Franz Krenner, the proprietor of the bookshop where my old friend and I had first met.

I sat in the front row next to Krause, who would lead the service.

"Poor Father Bayer." He sighed. "I did not realize how much I would miss him. We had such heated debates about theology. He was a worthy sparring partner."

Felix Urbanek came over. "We might as well start," he said to Krause. "I think everyone is here. I'm not expecting Father Dauer to attend." His jaw tightened. "He said he would try to make it, but that he had meetings all day. One of the noble families is considering donating a large collection of sacred art to the cathedral treasury."

"'How brief the comedy of vanity that is committed to fortune,'" Krause murmured.

"It is a shame," Urbanek continued. "But after all, Father Bayer was just a simple priest. I suppose it is too much to expect that someone as busy as Father Dauer could fit this into his schedule."

Krause rose and went to the altar. As the familiar words of the service flowed up to the old vaulted stone ceiling of the chapel, I fell into deep thought. I wished to concentrate on my treasured memories of Alois, but my mind rebelled and wandered to the circumstances of his death and my failure to make any progress in finding his killer. I sighed inwardly. Perhaps Benda had been right to dismiss my idea that the murders were somehow related to Dante. I was grasping as desperately for answers as he was with his theory that the killings were motivated by the war. After all, Dante was everywhere, if one looked. Why, Krause had just quoted *Inferno* a moment ago. It was probably just my vivid imagination that saw some crude markings carved by a madman into dead men's foreheads as Dante's *peccatum*.

Krause intoned the final prayer for the dead and the small group of mourners stood. As I turned to leave the chapel, I saw Benda standing near the door.

"Thank you for coming," I said. We walked out into the Stephansplatz. Off to the right, near the archbishop's palace, Michael Richter, surrounded by a few spectators, stood on his crate.

"I've heard the terrible stories about the conditions in the camp," he shouted. "Men are dying there every day." He caught sight of us, climbed down from the crate, and charged over to us, his face purple with rage.

"You!" He grabbed Benda's arm. "What were you doing at my home yesterday?"

Benda shrugged off the protester's hand. "I don't know what you are talking about," he said. He turned to me. "Come, Da Ponte, let's continue our conversation in a quieter location."

"My mother told me two men came to talk to her—friends of mine, she said." Richter's lip curled. "I know it was you," he said to Benda. I shrank back involuntarily as he turned his anger on me. "Who are you? Were you there also?"

"I—"

"Is that what you two gentlemen consider amusing?" Richter sneered. "Harassing a poor blind woman?"

"Yes, we were there," Benda said coolly. "We are investigating a series of murders. We needed information from your mother."

"Murders! Murders of whom?"

"Of General Peter Albrechts, for one," Benda said. "You were the last person to see him alive, in the Am Hof."

"I told you the other day, I wasn't there," Richter said.

"You are lying," Benda said. I had to admit, despite his deficiencies as an investigator, the count remained calm and steady under pressure. His color was normal, his voice steady and confident. My own knees trembled underneath me.

"We have a witness," Benda continued. "Someone heard

you arguing with the general, and saw you running out of the square. The general's body was found hours later."

Richter gaped at him. "You think I . . . but you cannot . . . who is this witness?" He shook his head. "I don't believe you."

"An upstanding citizen saw a man running from the Am Hof a little after one o'clock the morning of April 9. He recognized you."

Richter opened his mouth to retort, then thought better of it and clamped it shut. A wary look came to his eyes.

"Your mother confirmed that you went out at about one in the morning," Benda said. "You lied to me the other day, and you are lying to me now."

The protester shook his head. "No! No, you have it all wrong! You are accusing me because I am not afraid to express my opinions about your war. I know all about you noblemen." He poked Benda in the chest. "You're probably making a fortune in the black market these days, aren't you?"

A constable hurried over. "Is this man bothering you, sir?" he asked. He pulled Richter away from Benda and shoved him. "Move on, you, before I arrest you." Richter glared at us and slowly walked away.

"Thank you, Constable," Benda said, brushing the front of his coat with his hand. He motioned to me to follow him, and turned toward the Stock-im-Eisen-Platz. I glanced back at Richter. The protester had retrieved his crate and stood at the opposite edge of the plaza, watching us. He saw me look at him.

"You will regret this!" he shouted after us. "You have it all wrong!"

Back in my lodgings that evening, I tried to expunge the emotions of the morning from my mind as I dressed in my best suit. I was going to a repeat performance of *Axur*, my latest opera with Salieri, accompanied by a beautiful young lady.

I took my cloak and went down the hall to Marta's room. Her door stood ajar, and I paused to admire her before I knocked. She sat on her bed reading a message. The light of the candle on the small side table danced off the glass at her ears and illuminated the golden flecks in her hair, which was bound with a sapphire-blue velvet ribbon. Two spots of pink colored her cheeks. She wore the same blue dress she had worn to the ball, and she toyed idly with its collar as she studied the missive.

I knocked.

She looked up and, seeing me, hurriedly folded the message. "Hello, Lorenzo. You look very handsome this evening." She stood, crossed the room, and put the message in the cupboard.

I took her in my arms. "Let's stay in tonight," I murmured.

She gave my chest a playful push. "Don't be silly. How often does a woman get the opportunity to attend the opera and sit next to the librettist?"

She took her cloak. I doused the candle and followed her out the door, beaming with pleasure at her excitement. We left the house and walked to the end of the street, where I hailed a cab. I paid no attention to the route the driver took, for I was preoccupied with my lady's kisses all the way into town.

When we arrived at the theater, I lifted Marta down from the cab and whisked her in the front door. Mozart was standing in the lobby chatting with another composer, my Spanish friend Martín. I introduced them both to Marta. Martín winked at me and excused himself. I took our cloaks to the checkroom. When I returned, the bell summoning the audience into the main hall sounded. Marta and Mozart were chatting companionably.

"You must come meet Constanze," he said to her. "You two would get on well." He bowed over her hand, raised an approving brow at me, and turned toward the main hall.

As I steered Marta to the stairway that led to the boxes, Casanova approached.

"Ah, I was hoping I would see you both tonight," he said, kissing Marta's hand. "My dear, you look absolutely ravishing this evening. If I were twenty years younger—no, maybe just ten—I would lure you away from this pedestrian poet and make you the Countess of Seingalt." He fingered the glass hanging from Marta's right ear. "But alas—"

I snorted. My friend styled himself as the Chevalier de Seingalt, but I knew he had been born to theater people in the warren of narrow streets between the Campo San Stefano and the Grand Canal.

Marta giggled. Her face was flushed with pleasure and excitement. For the first time since I met her, she looked happy. Perhaps I was succeeding in my goal to make her forget about von Gerl. I fervently hoped he would not make an appearance tonight. I took her arm.

Casanova leaned over to me. "We must continue our discussion of the other day," he said softly. I nodded.

Marta and I climbed the stairs to the boxes. Most of them were rented by the oldest aristocratic families in Vienna, but the emperor had directed that one always be held for the librettist and composer of the opera being performed. I opened the door to the box and ushered Marta inside. Salieri and his wife were already there. I introduced Marta to them and settled her into one of the comfortable armchairs.

The orchestra played the opening notes of the opera, and I settled back to enjoy my work and Marta's company. The opera was an adaptation of a libretto written by Beaumarchais, the French playwright, which Salieri had set to music last year in Paris. I had tightened Beaumarchais's flowery language and tendency to use too many words when I had translated the libretto into Italian for this performance. The opera had everything the Viennese audiences adored— an Oriental despot, a loyal soldier in love with a beauty from the despot's harem, the despot's schemes to kill his rival, and his final capitulation to the purity of young love. It had been very popular since it had premiered in January.

I stole a glance at Salieri, who leaned forward in his chair, his arms propped on the railing of the box, his eyes intently following the action on the stage. Next to him, his wife yawned. A wicked thought came unbidden to my mind. What was Caterina Cavalieri doing this evening, while her lover and his wife were at the theater? Did the music director leave his wife at home on those nights that his paramour was singing? I hoped so, for his sake. I wouldn't have wanted to be him should Cavalieri have glanced toward the box and seen him sitting there with Madame Salieri. I smiled to my-self. I was sure he would have heard plenty from that flexible throat when he went to the dressing room after the perfor-mance to congratulate his lover.

At intermission, I hurried downstairs to order cham-pagne for the four of us. When I returned, followed by a waiter with a tray of glasses, Marta was conversing with Ma-dame Salieri.

"Miss Cavalli was just telling us that she recently ar-rived from Venice," Theresa Salieri said to me. "Weren't you frightened, my dear, with the war going on?"

"I saw no indication there was a war," Marta said.

"You cannot miss it here," Salieri said. "The soldiers on the street, the protesters, the shortages—why, I went into Adam's the other day to order a suit and he told me he was having difficulty procuring satin."

"At least it will end soon," I said.

Salieri raised an eyebrow. "I would not be so sure. The troops have been sitting outside Belgrade for weeks now, with no progress to report." He sighed. "No, I believe this will be a long, expensive war, Da Ponte. You and I may not have many more chances to sit up here and enjoy our operas."

The crowd on the parterre below us buzzed as Count Rosenberg, the director of the theater and one of the em-peror's closest confidants, took the stage.

"Ladies and gentlemen," he said. "Forgive me for delay-ing the start of the next act, but I have just received excellent news. A few days ago, the emperor took the fortress of Sabac from the Turks. It will not be long now before Belgrade is ours!"

The applause was deafening. Some of the men in the audience, including Mozart, stood and cheered. I looked over at Salieri.

He sniffed. "Sabac is a small fortress, valuable for cutting the Turkish supply lines to Belgrade. But when will the emperor move on Belgrade itself?"

The music began and we settled back into our seats. Salieri's pessimism had left me unsettled. What if he were correct, and the war dragged on? Would the theater close? What would I do then? I had no large pool of savings to support me should I lose my position. I would have to leave Vienna and seek my fortunes elsewhere.

I willed myself to dismiss these black thoughts from my mind, and leaned back to enjoy the rest of the opera. I stole a glance at Marta. She sat entranced, her green eyes fixed on the stage. A tendril of silky hair had loosened from the sapphire velvet ribbon. As she reached to tuck it back up, her attention still on the performance below us, my pulse quickened. She must have felt me watching her, for she turned and smiled at me. My spirit lightened, I smiled back, and then spent the rest of the evening watching her, smelling her delicate floral scent, listening to her voice, and falling in love.

Seventeen

Marta and I breakfasted together the next morning in the Lamm kitchen. Although we tried to behave as though we were merely fellow lodgers sharing a meal, I believe Madame Lamm sensed there was something between us, for as we conversed idly about the opera, she glanced at us with approval in her twinkling eyes.

Finally I pulled myself away and rose from the table. "I'm afraid I must go to work, ladies," I said.

"On such a beautiful day? What a shame!" Madame Lamm said. "I was out at the market before you came down. It is almost like summer." She looked at me slyly. "Perfect for a long stroll in the Prater."

I sighed. "I agree, Madame Lamm. But unfortunately, I must attend a rehearsal of my next opera. We premiere in less than two weeks, and there is much work still to be done." I turned to Marta. "Do you have plans for today?" I asked her.

"Yes. Mademoiselle Albrechts has invited me to dinner this afternoon," she said.

"Christiane Albrechts?" Madame Lamm said. "You are acquainted with Christiane Albrechts?"

Marta nodded.

"Oh, my! She is such an elegant young lady. The poor girl—her father died suddenly, just a few weeks ago. He was a famous general, highly decorated by the late empress. Where did you meet her?"

"Signor Da Ponte introduced us," Marta said.

My landlady looked at me with new respect. "Have you been in her palace?" she asked Marta. "You must tell me all about it. Was it very lavish?"

"Oh, yes," Marta replied. "The rooms I saw were immense. The decorations are beautiful—and the furniture and fabrics, I've never seen any so fine."

"It sounds lovely," my landlady said. She joined Marta at the table. "But you know, that is just the family's city palace. Her father owned a large property right outside the city, outside the Karntner gate. It is called the Belvedere. It used to belong to Prince Eugene of Savoy, years ago. He built two palaces on the land, one at the top of the hill, another at the bottom. He lived in the lower one and used the one at the top of the hill just for parties! Can you imagine that? Of course, I've never seen it myself. I have no reason to travel out there, and even if I did, there are high walls all around it. But I've heard that the gardens are beautiful." She took a breath and sighed. "I suppose Miss Albrechts inherits it all now that her father is gone."

"I believe the household is readying for a move out there

any day now," I offered. I bade them both good morning and went up to my room for my satchel.

My landlady had been right—the day was summerlike, the skies clear. I hummed a tune from my last opera with Mozart as I crossed the bridge and went through the Stuben gate.

I had walked but three blocks down the Wollzeile when my happy mood vanished. I had reached the square that marked the entrance to the university. The onion domes of the Baroque church that had been taken from the Jesuits when that order had been abolished by the state fifteen years ago towered over the small plaza. Ahead of me, a stocky dark-haired young man in a forest-green cloak loitered near one of the two small fountains that flanked the entrance to the university administration building. My jaw clenched.

"You there," I called. "What are you doing there?" I marched over to him.

"I beg your pardon, sir. Are you speaking to me?" he asked. He stood at attention and stared back at me arrogantly.

"What are you doing here? Were you waiting for me?"

His brow furrowed. "Waiting? I don't understand, sir. I was just—"

"You were just standing by until I came, weren't you?" I snapped. "So that you could follow me again!"

"Do I know you, sir?"

"Don't behave like an innocent with me. You've been trailing me for days now."

He shook his head. "I don't know what you are talking

about, sir. I am just waiting for a friend." He bowed, turned his back on me, and sauntered toward the church.

I stared after him for a moment, and then continued down the Wollzeile, my face flushed. I had thought he was the young man who had been trailing me. But was I sure? There were many such young men in the city, and many forest-green cloaks. Might it have been mere coincidence that I had seen him so often the past few days? I shook my head. I didn't know what to think. I was losing my good judgment and reason.

When I reached the theater Mozart was standing outside chatting with the tenor Morella. After I greeted them, Morella excused himself to go in and warm up his voice.

Mozart stretched his arms over his head. "It is too beautiful a day to spend indoors rehearsing," he said.

"Does Morella approve of the new aria?" I asked.

"I just gave it to him. He seems to like it very much," Mozart said. "Oh, look!" He started toward the center of the Michaelerplatz.

"Where are you going?" I called. A man riding a small gray horse passed in front of the composer, and I suddenly understood. Mozart had owned a horse that color two years ago, but since the family had moved twice since then, first out to the suburbs and then back into town, they had sold the animal along the way.

Mozart returned to me, his face forlorn. "I hoped it might be Horse," he said. He sighed. "The army has taken so many horses for the war—he must be a soldier now."

We entered the theater and greeted the singers, who

were gathered on the stage in the main hall. As I removed my libretto from my satchel, Caterina Cavalieri beckoned to me. "Have you and Wolfgang given any thought to the matter we discussed the other day?" she asked, glancing toward Aloysia Lange, who was chatting with Benucci.

"Yes, madame," I said. "We are working on a long piece for you. It should be ready for you soon." She beamed.

"Come everyone," Mozart called as he sat at the fortepiano. "I want to start with the quartet in the first act. This is our last rehearsal without the orchestra, and I want to be sure everything is right."

The singers took their marks and the rehearsal began. After a few moments, I was caught up in the music, both the delight and annoyance of the morning temporarily forgotten.

We worked until dinnertime. After Mozart and the singers left, I walked down the Herrengasse to a large, bright café and had a light dinner.

As I left the café to return to the theater, I saw Casanova walking ahead of me. I ran to catch him.

"Do you have time to come with me for an hour or so?" I asked him.

"Is this about the murders?" he asked, his eyes agleam.

I nodded. "I want to search Alois's office." As we walked over to the cathedral, I reminded my friend about the contents of the messages Benda and I had found in Hennen's chamber. "They were lines from Dante's *Purgatory*, about the deadly sin of envy," I said.

"You believe Alois may have received similar messages?" Casanova asked.

"Yes." We reached the Stephansplatz. "I tried to get into his office a few days ago, but it was locked. We'll have to find Father Dauer in the cathedral. He has the key. I hope he hasn't had the office emptied yet."

"There is no need for a key," Casanova said. "I can break the lock for you."

"I think we'll try to gain access using legitimate means first," I said.

Casanova shrugged. "However you wish," he said.

Inside the cathedral, a deacon told us Father Dauer was in the treasury room, and directed us to the large room in the cellar of the cathedral. The low-ceilinged room was furnished with display cases and shelves filled with objects. The walls were hung with paintings of the Madonna and Child from all periods, the medieval ones embellished with gold. An ancient painting of the founder of the cathedral, Duke Rudolph IV, overlooked the treasure. Dauer stood alone in one corner, fingering an exquisite small marble sculpture of the Pietà.

"Signor Da Ponte, how good to see you again. May I offer you condolences on the loss of Father Bayer."

I thanked him and introduced Casanova.

Dauer gestured around the treasure room. "The archbishop has asked me to determine which items can be sold," he said. "I've just managed to acquire a large collection of valuable crucifixes from one of the noble families here in Vienna, so we must make room for them."

Beside me, Casanova shifted uncomfortably.

"Is there something I can do for you, gentlemen?" Dauer asked.

"I was told you had the key to Alois's office," I said. "I loaned him a book before he died. I'd like to retrieve it." To my surprise, I felt no remorse lying to the priest.

"Of course," Dauer said. "I haven't had the time to get over there and look around. Father Urbanek has been in touch with Father Bayer's sister. We are going to send her a list of his things, in case she should want anything. But I doubt she'll be interested in his books."

Casanova took several large breaths. I glanced over at him and raised a brow. He shook his head slightly.

"If you see anything you would like while you are there, take it," Dauer said. "The rest we'll either put in the library at the archbishop's palace or discard." He pulled a large ring from his cassock pocket and handed me a key. "Keep it if you would like, while you decide. There is no hurry."

"Are you all right?" I asked as Casanova and I crossed the side plaza.

"Yes, fine," he answered. "Because I'm so tall, low ceilings annoy me, that's all."

We entered Alois's office building and mounted the stairs to his office. I unlocked the door and stepped inside. The must of old books and the sharp scent of peppermint drops overwhelmed my nose. The muscles in my eyes tightened. I stumbled to the desk, pulled out Alois's chair, fell into it and began to weep. Casanova came and patted me gently on the back.

A few moments later, my grief for my dear friend spent, I took my handkerchief from my pocket, wiped my eyes, blew my nose and stood. "We can't look through all the books," I said to Casanova. "But let's search through his papers."

"You think there are messages containing Dante quotations from the killer?" Casanova asked.

I nodded.

Casanova began sorting through piles of notes Alois had kept on his shelf, while I rummaged through the desk. I found them in the small drawer where the old priest had kept his psalter and Bible. My hands shook as I pulled the papers from the drawer and unfolded the first. The paper appeared to be the same as that sent to Hennen—light-colored rag with an elaborate watermark. The lines had been copied out in the same neat, small handwriting: "Remember the evil doers formed from the clouds, who, drunken, battled Theseus with their double breasts."

"More Dante?" Casanova had come over and was reading over my shoulder.

I nodded. "It's about the legend of the Centaurs," I said. "Ixion was the ancient king of Thessaly, who lusted after Hera, Zeus's wife. To punish him, Zeus formed a cloud that looked like Hera and tricked Ixion into coupling with it. The Centaurs were half man, half horse, thus the double breasts."

Casanova was silent.

"Sinners in Purgatory are instructed about their sin and given the opportunity to correct themselves and proceed to Paradise," I explained. "There is one terrace on the mountain for each deadly sin—pride, gluttony, envy, lust, avarice, sloth, and wrath. As Dante and Virgil pass through the terraces, they see and hear examples of the sin and its corresponding virtue. These lines are about gluttony," I said. "The Centaurs were invited to a wedding, where they became drunk and tried to carry off all the women. Theseus defended the women, killing most of the Centaurs."

I picked up the second message. "Remember the Hebrews whose drinking showed their lack of care, so that Gideon did not allow them to accompany him when he descended the hills to Midian."

"I recognize that reference," Casanova said. "Gideon was leading the army of the Jews against Midian. God instructed him to choose his soldiers by leading them to a river and observing how they drank. The ones who ran into the river and gulped the water were rejected, while those who showed caution by merely scooping up the water and drinking slowly were chosen."

"Yes," I said. "It's another passage about the sin of gluttony."

"You believe he is choosing a victim for each of the seven sins?" Casanova asked.

"I did," I said. "But now I'm not so sure." As I folded the pages and tucked them into my satchel, disappointment washed over me. "My idea was that the killer was using the Dante excerpts to accuse his victims of sin. I can see that Hennen might be full of envy. He was a passionate supporter of the war, but could not serve with the emperor because he was crippled. But Alois a glutton? He led the life of an ascetic. He spent what little money he had on books, not on food or wine."

"We don't know what the killer is thinking," Casanova

said. "We don't even know if it is he who is sending these messages. Perhaps Hennen and Alois were involved in some reading club that was studying *Purgatory*."

I shook my head. "No, I'm sure Alois would have mentioned such a club to me, even invited me to join. He knew I loved the great Italian poets."

I closed the desk drawer. As we left the office, I paused at the door to take one last look around the tiny room, and then quietly pulled the door closed.

Eighteen

I spent the rest of the afternoon completing the new scene for Cavalieri, and it was seven o'clock when I finally left the theater. In the Michaelerplatz, workmen were lighting the street lamps. The Kohlmarkt and Graben were filled with people enjoying the summery weather. Near the spot where Hennen's body had been found, a vendor had set up a small tent and was dispensing lemonade and ices to the crowd.

No one was about when I arrived home. I climbed the stairs to my room. As I was about to enter it, a door at the end of the hall opened. Sophie, dressed in the same pink dress she had worn to the ball, her hair dressed in a fashionable chignon, tiptoed out of her room and closed the door quietly behind her. She paused to don her cloak, then turned and started when she saw me watching her. I opened my mouth to greet her, but she touched her finger to her lips, nodded toward her mother's door, turned and scampered down the stairs.

I crossed the hall and knocked on Marta's door. There was no answer. I knocked again, and called her name, then remembered she had dined with Christiane Albrechts this afternoon. Perhaps she was still at the palais.

Once in my own room, I hung my coat and waistcoat in the cupboard and carried my satchel to my desk. Sophie had left the window open when she had cleaned earlier. The bells in the neighborhood church rang eight o'clock. As I started to close the window, a fancy carriage turned into the street and came to a halt in front of the house. The lantern at the front of the house flickered while I watched as von Gerl's manservant, Teuber, helped Sophie into the carriage. He closed the door after her and climbed up to his seat. The carriage turned and headed down the dark street.

A moment later, a figure emerged from the linden trees. I leaned out the window and watched as it hurried to a modest stonemason's cart, climbed in, shouted an order to the horse, and drove off in the same direction.

I drew back into my room, closed the window, and lit a candle on my desk. I pulled the messages I had found in Alois's office out of my satchel and laid them side by side. I picked up one of the pages and studied it, squinting into the candlelight, trying to make out the form of the elaborate watermark. A ring about two inches in diameter had been embossed in the center of the page. Inside the ring, a sinuous serpent rose from the juncture of two long, clawlike leaves. An elaborate crown at the top of the ring hovered over the reptile's menacing head. I frowned. I had never seen such a mark before on any paper I had used. If it was a rare mark— My pulse raced. I would take the sheets to my bookseller, Krenner, the next day. Most bookshops in the city carried a stock of paper, and if Krenner did not sell these sheets himself, he might be able to steer me toward someone who did.

I tucked the sheets back into my satchel and went out into the hallway. I knocked on Marta's door once more. There was no answer. I went back to my own room, undressed, snuffed out the candle, and crawled into bed. It was not long before weariness overcame me, and I fell into a lonely, troubled sleep.

The heat had cleared out during the night, and as I walked to my office on Saturday morning, spring had returned to the city. The air was cool, the sun bright in the sky.

Once at my desk, I continued writing the scene for Cavalieri. But after several minutes, I threw down my pen. My thoughts and emotions were in a tangle. I had tapped gently at Marta's door before I left this morning, but she had not answered. Now my imagination considered unwelcome possibilities. The message she had been reading when I came to her room to take her to the theater—why had she hurried to hide it from me? Had it really been a note from Christiane Albrechts inviting her to dinner, or had it been from someone else? A stab of jealousy shot through me. Had von Gerl finally summoned her? Where had she been last night? Had she indeed dined with Christiane, or had she lied to me and instead gone to von Gerl?

A crash sounded in the hallway. I jumped up, hurried

around my desk, and threw open the door. Benda was crouched on the floor, attempting to straighten the pile of warrior's helmets he had knocked over.

"Benda?" I asked. "What are you doing here?"

I drew in a sharp breath as he stood to face me. His face was ashen, his hair disarranged, his eyes full of fatigue.

"Da Ponte, thank God I've found you," he rasped. "I've just been out to your lodgings." His hands shook.

"What is it?"

"He's struck again."

I drew him into my office and led him to the chair I keep for visitors. "Who is it? Where? Is it the same?"

He buried his face in his hands. "My God! I cannot believe it! Christiane—he's truly a demon!"

"He's killed Christiane? Tell me!"

He raised his head and gulped for breath. "No, no, not her. Out at the Belvedere—Christiane's summer palace. The watchman sent for me—I rushed out there—"

"Is it the same? The cut throat, the markings?"

Benda nodded dumbly. "Why there? Why him? I don't understand. What is this monster doing?"

"Who is the victim? Tell me, please!"

"Christiane's—her neighbor."

My heart grew heavy.

"Her neighbor, the baron. Valentin von Gerl."

PART III

Masquerade

Nineteen

Valentin von Gerl lay comfortably at the foot of a marble statue of Apollo and the nymph Daphne, his blood draining into the gravel of the Belvedere garden. His eyes were closed, and a slight smile played on his lips. His arms spread languorously from his sides. But for the bloody mess around his neck and on his forehead, he would have appeared to be a gentleman napping in the warm April sun.

Benda's carriage had sped through the streets of the city to the Karntner gate. Once out of the city, the driver had rushed by the Karlskirche and the Schwarzenberg Palace to the Rennweg, finally depositing us in a large courtyard.

"This is the back entrance," Benda had explained as we hurried into the palace. "The grand entrance is on the other side of the property, up the hill, behind the upper palace. He's outside, in the garden." We walked through a long hallway and out the other side of the palace to the gardens. A constable stood at attention at the door.

As we exited the palace into the garden, I looked about in wonderment. The Albrechts' property stretched up a long, rolling hill as far as the eye could see. Directly in front of us was a long allée. Lined with statues, it was bordered on both sides by a small forest of short trees, their branches beginning to leaf. The allée led to a low, expansive stone fountain flanked by wide steps. Behind the fountain, the formal gardens, dotted with fountains and statues, swept gracefully up the hill. On the horizon sat the grandest palace I had ever seen, the Prince of Savoy's party house.

As Benda led me down the allée, I saw that the trees formed four separate thickets, each with two narrow entrances from the wide path.

"They are called *bosquets*," Benda murmured. "When the trees have leafed out, they are like private rooms."

I nodded dumbly as we made our way past the thickets. These garden rooms must be larger than any apartment I had ever lived in. When we reached the end of the allée, Benda directed me to the left, where von Gerl had been found.

I kneeled to examine the baron's lifeless body. He wore breeches and a simple shirt that was soaked with blood. I looked around. His waistcoat, coat, cloak, and plumed hat were nowhere to be seen.

"The slashed throat looks the same as the others," Benda said.

I nodded. "But look at the cuts on the forehead," I said. "They are deeper and wider than those the killer made on Hennen."

"Richter knows we suspect him," Benda said. "He is in a hurry to finish his fiendish mission. He's in a frenzy."

"Or perhaps the killer was interrupted," I said. "Maybe he heard the watchman making his rounds."

Benda snorted. "The night watchman was in no condition to make rounds," he said. He gestured toward a middle-aged man who stood at the far side of the garden. "This fellow comes on at six in the morning. There's a small watch house up the hill, behind the upper palace. He found his colleague passed out on the floor in there, next to an empty bottle of apricot brandy. When he was making his rounds, he found the body. He sent for me immediately. I alerted Troger, and went to your lodgings to find you."

I returned my attention to von Gerl's body. I thrust my hand in each pocket of his breeches, but found nothing. I sighed. I had hoped to find a note like that both the general and Hennen had received before going to meet their killer.

"Look at his breeches," I said to Benda. "There are three buttons, but only the top one is fastened."

Benda stooped down to take a look. "He must have received the summons from the killer and dressed in a hurry."

A constable emerged from the nearest thicket holding a small leather pouch.

"Have you found anything of interest?" Benda asked.

"The usual things, sir, from the garden of a fancy house like this," the man said. "Various ribbons, feathers from ladies' bonnets, some pipe stems, pieces of broken glass. And this." He handed Benda a jeweled brooch encrusted with dirt.

"Where was this?" Benda asked.

"Under a pile of matted leaves, sir. Near one of the benches inside the thicket here."

"It must have been there all winter," Benda said. "Last

autumn seems so long ago now. The general always gave a large party before closing up the estate for the winter. There were hundreds of people here. Young couples always found their way into the privacy of the garden rooms. A lady must have lost it and never noticed." He handed the brooch to the constable, who put it in the pouch. "Continue searching," he ordered.

A moment later, Troger came around the corner. He nodded at us and stared down at the body. "That's four now," he said.

"Yes," Benda replied. "It's time to arrest Richter, before he strikes again."

I shook my head. "I don't believe—"

"Da Ponte has another theory," Benda told Troger. "But I'm certain Richter is our man. Another nobleman murdered—it fits into the pattern I've described."

Troger glanced at me. "I've heard Da Ponte's theories before," he sneered. "He has quite the imagination—better suited for the theater than for investigating crimes."

I bit off an angry retort. I should not waste my time arguing with these two. Benda had already made up his mind before reviewing any evidence; Troger despised me and would not welcome any ideas I had to offer. I stood and watched as the two of them walked back to the palace, their heads together, planning the unfortunate protester's arrest.

The constable approached me. "I think I've found everything I can, sir," he said, handing me the pouch.

"Was there anything else?" I asked.

"Not much, sir. Just more litter from that party, I guess. A few more ribbons, a lady's earring, and some shoe buckles."

Benda returned. "The hearse is on the way," he said. "Troger has sent a man over to guard von Gerl's house. We should go there now to interview his manservant. Then I'll have to report the news to Christiane." He clenched his fists. "The fiend! It will be a pleasure to see him hang. He murders her father and now he despoils her property. She's always loved coming here. She once told me it was her refuge."

I held out the pouch. "Do you want this?" I asked.

"No, I don't see that it's of much use."

I tucked the pouch into my cloak pocket and started to follow Benda. I hesitated, and then turned to take a last look at the scene. Atop the tall marble plinth, Apollo, the god of art, music, and light, leaned on his tambourin, wooing the beautiful nymph. Below it lay von Gerl, his bloody, handsome face in repose, as if dreaming of his own last lover.

Twenty

Benda's carriage rumbled through the city to the Freyung. When we reached von Gerl's palace, Benda instructed the driver to return to the Palais Albrechts and to avoid mentioning his errand to his mistress. Troger's constable stood outside the door.

"Is anyone home?" Benda asked him.

"The manservant, sir," the constable replied.

"What's the fellow's name?" Benda asked me as we stood in the empty, still foyer.

"Teuber," I replied.

"Hello! Teuber! Are you there?" Benda's shout echoed up the stairs.

A moment later, the manservant appeared on the landing and started down the stairs. The cocksure demeanor I had observed in my previous dealings with him had vanished. His face was lined with worry, his clothing was disheveled.

"Signor, is it true what the man out there told me? My master is dead?"

I nodded.

Teuber collapsed on the lowest step. "No, it is impossible! It can't be!" he moaned.

I stepped forward and put a comforting hand on his shoulder.

"Now what shall I do?" he cried. "Where will I go? How will I find another job without a reference?"

I pulled my hand back.

"And what about the wages he owes me?"

"Your master has been brutally murdered!" Benda snapped. "This is no time for such concerns."

The manservant looked up at us with guarded eyes.

"Murdered?" he asked.

"Yes. When did you see him last?" Benda asked.

"Last night. He went out at about seven o'clock. He was expecting a guest for supper. I was setting the table in the dining room and helping the cook."

"If he was expecting a guest, why did he leave?" I asked.

"A boy came with a message. My master read it and told me he had to go out for a few hours."

Benda and I exchanged glances.

"Do you know what the message said?" Benda asked.

"No."

"Where is this message now—in his chamber?" I asked, my excitement growing.

"No," Teuber said. "My master put it in his pocket and took it with him. He instructed me to make his guest comfortable, and told me that he would return before midnight.

He hurried off. He did not even put on a waistcoat and coat or take his cloak."

"Did he take the carriage, or just a horse?" I asked.

"Neither, sir. He walked."

"He must have hailed a cab in the street," Benda murmured to me.

"What happened to him, sir?" Teuber asked Benda. "Did this maniac who is roaming the streets get him? Where did you find him?"

"None of your concern," Benda said. "We must search the house. Come along. You can tell us if anything is out of place."

Teuber reluctantly shuffled behind us as we climbed the stairs.

"Had the baron received any other messages lately?" I asked him as we passed through the two large, empty salons on the first floor.

"I don't know what you mean, sir." The manservant sniffled. "He received many messages in the post—letters from people he had met in his travels, bills of sale and notices related to his collections, those sorts of things."

"No, I meant a message from someone here in the city, delivered by another boy, or by a lackey."

"I don't recall anything," Teuber said. "The master had held off hiring more staff. It is just me and the woman who comes in to cook. If someone had come to the door with a message, I would have known."

"What was the baron's attitude toward the war?" Benda asked as we approached the library.

Teuber frowned. "The war, sir? I don't know. He never mentioned it to me."

"Was he acquainted with that war protester, Michael Richter?"

"I don't recognize the name, sir."

"The young man who stands on the crate shouting against the war. He's all over the city. Surely you must have seen him."

Teuber shook his head. "I don't get out much, sir. I'm busy here seeing to my master's needs."

We entered the library. Except for a pile of papers on the desk and a rumpled blanket on the sofa, the room looked the same as when I had toured it a week ago. I went to the desk and riffled through the papers. There was a bill of sale for a painting, a catalog from an art dealer in Paris, a letter from a butterfly-collecting society in Prague, but no sheets with quotations from Dante. I looked around the library. The Dante excerpts could be anywhere, I thought.

We glanced at von Gerl's room of natural artifacts, and then retraced our steps to the staircase. "What's in there?" Benda asked Teuber, pointing toward von Gerl's art galleries.

"The baron's painting collection," the manservant replied.

"Let's search his chamber," Benda said. I led the way up the stairs and down the hallway to von Gerl's chamber.

Benda reached to open the door. "Why is this locked?" he asked Teuber.

Teuber's hand went to his mouth. "The master wanted it kept locked," he said.

"Open it," Benda said.

"I cannot, sir. I don't have the key." He shoved his hands into his trouser pockets. "The baron always kept it on his person."

"What's that in your pocket?" I asked.

He pulled out a key. "This key, sir? Uh . . . it is the key to the pantry."

"Give it to me," Benda said.

Teuber sighed and handed the key to Benda, who fitted it into the lock and turned the knob. The door opened.

The manservant raised his hands. "I don't know how—"

"Quiet!" Benda ordered.

Von Gerl's chamber looked as though a cataclysm had struck—the bedclothes disheveled, the baron's many suit coats strewn over the bed, the chairs, and the floors. The plumed hat lay askew on an armchair.

"What has happened here?" Benda asked.

"This is how it usually looks, sir, before I am allowed in to straighten it," Teuber said. Beads of sweat had formed above his lip. I crossed over to the small table by the bed, but found no papers on it. Swearing softly, I opened the drawer of a writing desk that sat under the large window. It was empty.

We walked through the half-empty closet into von Gerl's butterfly room, then into his private art salon. Both rooms appeared in the same state as they had when I had last seen them. I searched through the drawers of the wooden cabinet, but found nothing amiss. Closing the door behind me, I followed Benda and Teuber downstairs.

"Is there anything else, sirs?" the manservant asked.

"What did you do last night?" I asked.

"As I told you before, sir, I was here. When the master went out, I told the cook to put the dinner at the edge of the hearth, in case he should want it when he returned. I sent her home. I was here the rest of the night."

"What about the baron's guest?" Benda asked.

"No one arrived, sir. I guess my master must have run into the person on his way out, and decided to eat supper elsewhere."

"You didn't leave the palace at all?" I asked.

Teuber shook his head. "No, sir. I was here all night, I swear." He slumped onto the step and renewed moaning over his fate.

As Benda and I walked outside, I wondered why the manservant hadn't mentioned picking my landlady's daughter up last night at eight o'clock.

Twenty-one

I decided it best to speak with Sophie before telling Benda that Teuber had lied about his whereabouts. I did not want to involve her or her mother in this sordid mess if it wasn't necessary.

"I'd better go break the news to Christiane," Benda said as we walked toward the Freyung. "It will upset her. Not only did this fiend defile her home, but she was fond of von Gerl. He was a good neighbor to her."

"Marta must be informed also," I said. "She knew von Gerl in Venice. I should come with you and tell her."

"Marta?" Benda asked. "Oh, Miss Cavalli. I don't understand. Why should you come to Christiane's house to see her?"

"I was under the impression she had spent the night at the palais as a guest of Mademoiselle Albrechts."

Benda shook his head. "No. She was here yesterday, to dine with Christiane. But when I arrived home a bit before six, Christiane's maid told me that Miss Cavalli had left. Christiane was ill and had gone to her room. She had asked not to be disturbed, so I changed my clothes and left a half hour later for a dinner at the chancery."

I frowned.

We agreed to speak again the next day, and I walked back to my office, my mind filled with questions. Where had Marta been last night, while I was knocking on her door? Why had Teuber not told us that Sophie Lamm was the guest von Gerl had been planning to entertain before he was called away by the mysterious message?

I arrived at the theater and took the stairs down to my office. Workmen had removed the pile of props that had collapsed when Benda had fetched me this morning. I took off my cloak and hung it in the cupboard, fished the leather pouch out of the pocket, and placed it on my bookshelf. The message von Gerl had received—had the killer sent it? Three of the four victims had received messages the night they had been murdered. Yet no missives had been found on their bodies. The killer was clever, removing any evidence that could be traced to him.

But if my theory were correct, there would be some evidence—the pages containing the Dante excerpts. I shook my head, frustrated that I had been unable to find any such papers in von Gerl's palace. They must have been there, tucked away somewhere in the baron's vast collection. Troger and Benda would surely laugh if I asked them to assign the ten or more men it would take to search the palace from cellar to attic, in order to prove my theory. But by now I was certain the murderer had sent von Gerl quotations from

Dante, referring to one of the five remaining deadly sins—avarice, sloth, lust, wrath, or pride.

I worked for about an hour, until dinnertime, but found I had no appetite, so I decided to return to my lodgings. I did not look forward to breaking the news of von Gerl's death to Marta. I wanted very much to believe that she no longer loved him.

I walked through the Graben and the Stephansplatz, at each location averting my gaze from the scene of Hennen's and Alois's murder. I cut down the Schulerstrasse, a street lined with expensive apartment houses and the city's finest hotel. A block down the street, I saw a familiar figure standing in front of the entry to number 846.

"Constanze!" I bowed and kissed her hand. "Where's Wolfgang?"

"Hello, Lorenzo," Constanze Mozart said. "He's at home with the children. It is such a beautiful day, I decided I wanted a walk."

Her normally cheery face was tinged with gloom. I glanced at the entry of the building, where she and Mozart had lived two years ago in a spacious, luxurious apartment on the first floor. Her dark, almond-shaped eyes followed mine.

"How is the little one?" I asked.

She sighed. "She is still ill. But it appears that spring has finally arrived. We hope she'll recover soon."

I reached for her arm. "Come, I'll walk you home," I said.

"Oh, no, thank you, Lorenzo. It's out of your way," she protested. "And I'd like to stay out for a while longer." She studied my face. "You look tired. Are you getting enough rest?"

"I just have a lot of work," I lied. "Please don't be concerned about me. Just take care of your family."

She reached up and kissed me on the cheek, then started down the street. After a moment, she turned back to me. "Lorenzo, please," she said.

I raised a brow.

"When you see Wolfgang, please don't tell him you saw me over here."

I nodded, and we parted.

Marta was sitting in the garden, a small book in her hands, when I arrived at my lodgings. I took a deep breath and approached her.

"Marta," I said.

She looked up at me with eyes red from weeping. I dropped my satchel on the ground and sat on the bench next to her.

"You've heard the news," I said, offering her my handkerchief.

She shook her head. "What news, Lorenzo?"

"About von Gerl."

"Please, Lorenzo. Valentin is the last person I care to discuss right now." She dabbed at her eyes with the handkerchief. "I've been sitting out here for hours, thinking about what a fool he's made of me."

I frowned. "But—"

Her fists clenched in her lap. "I said I did not wish to discuss him," she said.

I reached over and unclasped her hands, taking one in mine. "Marta, you must prepare yourself for terrible news. Von Gerl is dead."

She snatched her hand away. "What! Are you playing with me also, Lorenzo? What do you mean, he is dead?"

"You must believe me. He was murdered. His body was found early this morning."

Her mouth dropped open. "Murdered? Valentin is dead?"

I nodded.

Her eyes squeezed shut as she shook her head back and forth. "No, no," she moaned. "Not Valentin. No, it cannot be." She grasped at my arm. "Please, Lorenzo, tell me it is not true."

"I cannot."

"What happened to him?" she whispered. Her eyes widened as I told her about the previous murders.

"My God!" she cried. "But why Valentin?"

"We don't understand the killer's motives yet," I said gently.

She began to weep. I reached to take her in my arms, but she pushed me away.

"Valentin!" she cried. She clutched her arms to her chest and rocked back and forth, tears streaming from her eyes. "My poor husband! My love!"

"Marta—"

She looked up at me. "Please, Lorenzo, please. Leave me."

"You shouldn't be alone," I said.

"Go away," she shrieked. "Leave me alone! Oh my God! Valentin, no, no!"

Misery flooded my heart as I stood. I looked down at her sobbing figure for a few moments and then I went into the house.

Twenty-two

I rose early the next morning and went to my office. Since it was a Sunday, the theater was empty. I poured my sorrows over Marta into a poem for a while, and then tore the paper into pieces and threw it away. I turned to my work, and was deep into editing a new libretto when Casanova came in at noon.

"Is it true what everyone is saying? There's been another murder?" he asked.

I sighed. Pergen, Troger, and Benda were foolish to believe they could hide these killings from the people of Vienna. A slip of the tongue from one of the constables, a speculation made by one of the victims' neighbors, an identification passed on by a gravedigger at the cemetery in St. Marx, and rumors would spread faster than the pox that plagued the city in very hot summers.

"Yes," I said. "The victim was Valentin von Gerl. You met him at the Redoutensaal ball."

"Did you find any Dante?" Casanova asked.

I threw down my pen. "No. But he was an avid collector. His palace is filled with objects from his travels. It was impossible for Benda and me to perform a thorough search."

"Benda is still fixed on the idea that the murders are related to the war?"

"Yes. I've tried to tell him my theory, but he dismisses my ideas. He is certain that protester, Michael Richter, is the killer. He and Troger were going to have him arrested yesterday."

"He's going to have to look elsewhere," Casanova said, his eyes gleaming.

"What do you mean?"

"Take your cloak and come with me," he said.

"What? I have a pile of librettos to edit."

He came over and pulled my arm. "You must come with me. I have someone I want you to meet."

I grumbled about my work as Casanova led me up the Herrengasse to a grand palace near the end of the street.

"Whose palace is this?" I asked.

"Wait a moment. You will see," my friend said. I followed him into the courtyard and was surprised when he opened the door and ushered me into the foyer. A lackey came to us, bowed to Casanova, and took our cloaks. My friend bounded up the stairs. I followed more slowly, baffled by the ease with which he had gained entry to the palace.

When we reached the second floor, Casanova led me down a long hallway to a wide set of double doors. He knocked twice on the door and opened it, beckoning me to follow. We were in a large, opulent bedchamber. A large bed draped in gold velvet, the bedclothes in a tangle, stood against one wall of the room. Across from it, a velvet chaise and two armchairs were grouped around a fireplace with a mantel elaborately festooned with garlands of marble laurel leaves. Paintings of well-dressed ladies frolicking in pastoral settings hung on every wall.

In the center of the room, a middle-aged woman in a white silk dressing gown sat at her toilette, applying spots of rouge to her sagging cheeks. When she saw us in her mirror, she turned and stood.

Casanova bowed over her hand and kissed it. He gestured to me. "Elisabeth, may I present the theater poet, Lorenzo Da Ponte. Lorenzo, this is my esteemed friend, the Countess Stoll."

"It is a pleasure, Excellency," I said, bowing. I squirmed as she assessed me from my head to my feet, as if I were a stallion she was considering as a mate for a mare on her country estate.

"Please call me Elisabeth," she said, motioning us to the armchairs. "All of my friends do." As she reclined on the chaise, her dressing gown dropped open, revealing a plump breast and brown nipple. I fixed my eyes on the painting hanging on the wall behind her.

"I owe you an apology, signore," she said. "I am sorry my boy alarmed you when he delivered Giacomo's messages."

Ah, this must be the absent diplomat's wife, Casanova's hostess.

"I understand you are investigating these terrible murders," she said.

I glared at Casanova, who merely shrugged.

"No, you must not blame Giacomo. The entire city knows about them. Giacomo and I were discussing them last night. He told me he knew someone involved in the investigation. You are working with Richard Benda, correct?"

I nodded.

She shook her head. The dressing gown opened further. "I don't know what Anton Pergen was thinking, choosing Benda to find this killer. I suppose it is because of his connection with Christiane Albrechts. The count is so upright, so dull, so unimaginative. I don't believe he possesses the qualities necessary to solve these murders."

I said nothing.

"It has come to my attention that Michael Richter has been arrested on suspicion of murdering General Albrechts, and perhaps the other victims, also."

I decided I might as well tell her. "Yes. He was heard arguing with the general and seen rushing from the Am Hof the night the general was killed."

To my surprise, she laughed and shook her head. "I cannot explain why Michael allowed the general to goad him into argument. I do not understand his passion against the war."

I raised my brow. "You are acquainted with Michael Richter, madame?"

"Of course. I can explain why he was rushing from the Am Hof that night. He was coming here to see me."

"He was coming here, madame? I don't understand."

"You silly man." She laughed again. "Must I spell it out for you? He is my lover." She glanced over at Casanova. "One of my lovers. He comes to me late at night. He is devoted to that old mother of his, so he cannot leave until she goes to bed."

I leaned forward eagerly. "Do you remember what time he arrived that night?"

"Of course I do. It was a little after one. He was late. He usually arrives between eleven and twelve, but he had sent me a message earlier in the day, telling me that he had a meeting that night and that he would be late."

"How did he seem when he arrived?"

"How did he seem? He seemed as he usually seemed— anxious to see me and eager to take me to bed." She smiled. "His passions expand to other activities besides opposition to the war, I'm happy to say."

I shook my head involuntarily. I could not imagine that unkempt, shabby young man being entertained by this woman in this elegant room. I racked my brain for further questions to ask.

"Was he out of breath when he arrived?"

"Yes, he was. He told me he had run all the way here." She arched an overplucked brow. "He realizes that if he keeps me waiting too long, I will have no more of him. Even with the war on, there are still many handsome young men in Vienna. A woman like me can take her pick."

A wave of sympathy for her husband flowed over me.

She gazed at me, a small smile on her painted lips. "Do you have any other questions? Is there anything else you want to know? You must have the police release Michael immediately."

"Was there anything else, anything out of the ordinary about him that night?" I asked.

"He wasn't soaked with blood, if that is what you want to hear. He was out of breath from running, and happy to see me. I gave him a brandy and let him rest for a few minutes. He told me he had encountered the general in the Am Hof. The old man had recognized him and shouted at him, calling him a traitor for opposing the war."

I chewed on my lip. She looked at me expectantly.

"Did Richter ever read anything by Dante, do you know?"

"Dante? The poet? I have no idea. I'm not interested in him for his mind. We don't discuss books when he is here. We don't discuss much at all."

"Richter is exonerated," I said to Casanova as we headed to a catering shop near the Minorite Church for dinner. "How could he possibly have killed the general and arrived at Countess Stoll's palace a few minutes later without any blood on him? These murders have been brutal. The killer must be soaked in blood afterward."

We arrived at the shop, were shown to a table, and placed our orders.

When the waiter had left, I put my head in my hands. "I've never felt so useless," I told my friend. "Two more men have died since I agreed to help Benda investigate this case. We've made no progress. We can't even agree on a possible motive for these murders."

"Well, Elisabeth's story weakens Benda's theory,"

Casanova said. "It is difficult to believe that there is another person in Vienna who speaks against the war as vociferously as Richter."

"I think there are many people who oppose the war," I agreed. "But Richter is the most visible. He was an easy choice for Benda."

"Let us put theories aside and consider what we know," Casanova said. "There have been four victims. Three of the four had strange markings—" He held up his hand to stop me from interrupting. "These markings may or may not be the *peccatum* from Dante's *Purgatory*. The fourth victim's lower torso was burned."

The waiter arrived with our dinners. Casanova hung his head over his plate and took a deep breath. "It smells delicious," he said. We ate in companionable silence for a few minutes.

"You've been told that three of the four victims—the general, Hennen, and von Gerl—received a mysterious note the evening of the murders."

"Yes. Alois may have received a note, also. But we couldn't find it in his office, and it appears the murderer is taking the note away with him after he slays his victim," I said.

"Finally, you've found lines from Dante's *Purgatory* in the possession of two of the victims, Hennen and Alois. We don't know if the general or von Gerl received similar messages."

"I couldn't find anything in von Gerl's palace," I said. "Although it's possible they might be there. He may have tucked them away somewhere in those vast collections of his. And Benda has been hostile to my theory, so I have no idea whether the general ever received any excerpts."

"Let us suppose that your theory is correct—that someone, for reasons known only to himself, is working through the list of the seven deadly sins. He chooses a victim, sends the unfortunate subject of his attention the passages from Dante."

"Yes," I said.

"But why does he do this?" Casanova asked. "The quotations Alois and Hennen received are full of arcane references. Did the killer expect his victim to understand them? Not everyone has read *Purgatory*. You had to explain one of the gluttony passages to me, and I consider myself a very well-read individual."

"I don't know," I admitted. "Most likely the passages mean something to the murderer. He's carrying out some sort of mission, some task his deranged mind has invented. He understands the passages, so perhaps it doesn't matter if the victim understands them."

"If we assume that the killer is the one sending the victims notes on the evenings of the murders, another questions arises. Why are the victims answering his summons? What could the notes possibly say that would lure these men to meetings in deserted city squares in the small hours of the morning?"

"I wish I knew," I answered. We returned to our food and finished eating in silence. The waiter removed the plates.

"There is one thing we are overlooking," Casanova said.

"Something—or I should say someone—at least three of the four victims have in common."

"Who?"

"The woman, Christiane Albrechts."

I thought a moment. "Of course!" I said excitedly. "The general was her father. She had been engaged to Hennen several years ago but broke it off when he was injured in the carriage accident. And Alois told me that he had been her confessor when she was young."

"Perhaps the killer is obliquely aiming at her in some way," Casanova said.

"Murdering all the men around her?" I asked. A thought niggled at the back of my brain. "You know, now that I think of it, it seemed that she and von Gerl had a relationship of some sort." I described the behavior I had observed the first day I had met the two of them—Christiane's nervousness in von Gerl's company, the pleading look she had directed toward him, his raised brow.

Casanova sat quietly for a moment. "Have you considered that Benda might be the killer?" he asked.

"Benda! You must be joking!"

"Listen to me, Lorenzo," Casanova said. "If Christiane Albrechts is the common factor in all the killings—"

"What are you saying?" I said. "You expect me to believe that Benda is killing every man who has been close to her? What is his motive—some perverted jealousy? Besides, I truly believe he was surprised to learn that Hennen had been engaged to Christiane." I shook my head. "No. I'll admit I don't like the man, but I don't think he's capable of these killings."

The waiter approached and Casanova ordered a milk ice for dessert. "You are probably right," he said after the waiter left. "And we have no proof that Christiane and von Gerl had any sort of relationship. The baron was an attractive man," Casanova said. "Many women must have reacted the same way in his presence. What you observed likely means nothing."

The waiter returned with the ice.

"Did you disapprove of Elisabeth?" Casanova asked me as he took large bites of the frozen concoction.

"No," I said. "Who am I to judge her? But I'll admit that she shocked me a bit. I'm of the old school, I suppose. I believe a woman should allow a man to be the pursuer."

Casanova raised a brow.

"All right." I laughed. "A woman should allow a man to believe that he is the pursuer."

"I've known Elisabeth for thirty years, since she was sixteen," Casanova said. "Like most marriages, hers was a business arrangement between families, not a love match. Her husband is away at his diplomatic posts. She won't agree to live in a rural outpost, so she remains in Vienna. They see each other once or twice a year." He scraped the remaining ice from the bowl with his spoon. "A woman like Elisabeth needs attention. She's very lonely."

I nodded, and signaled the waiter for the check.

"Things are changing, Lorenzo," Casanova said. "Women are different now. They are much more independent, much more concerned with their own needs. Just look at your Miss Cavalli, selling everything she owned to travel here to Vienna. In my day, it was the rare woman who would do that." His eyes twinkled. "But there were a few whom I met on my travels. Long days spent in a dark coach, our bodies thrown together whenever the wheels hit a rut . . ."

I did not want the discussion to lead to Marta, so I changed the subject.

"What about you? Will you go back to Dux?" I asked.

He sighed. "Yes. As I told you the other day, it is not a perfect situation for me. But I think that at this age, it is good for me to be settled somewhere. And of course the count pays for all of my expenses." A faraway look came to his eye. "I long to go home one last time before I die, though."

"To Venice?"

"Yes. Perhaps I still might, when I finish my work in the count's library."

I sighed. "You are lucky. You can return whenever you wish."

"How many more years on your sentence?" he asked.

"Seven," I said.

"You should do what I did," Casanova said. "Offer to spy for the Council of Three. You have access to some of the top people in government here. Your banishment could be reduced if you were able to relay Austrian state secrets to Venice. Once you've proved you are a changed man, they'd welcome you back. There's money to be had working for the Inquisition there. That's what I was doing when we first met."

My mouth dropped open.

"Don't give me that look," he said. "A man must do what he must do. If you want to return home, that's the way to get there. For God's sake, you're working for Pergen on these murders! He's becoming as oppressive as the Council of the Three. What's the difference?"

I just shook my head. The waiter brought the check and I placed enough coins to cover it on the table. I glanced over at my old friend. His shoulders sagged as he stared down at his hands. I hated to see him so unhappy. So I said the words that I knew would cheer him.

"I have a little more time," I said. "Tell me again about your escape from the doge's palace. I never tire of hearing the tale."

Twenty-three

I stayed for another half hour, listening to Casanova's account of his escapade: how he had been arrested for alleged crimes against religion and sentenced without trial by the Council of Three to five years in a low, small room in the Leads—the dreaded prison cells directly under the roof of the doge's palace, broiling hot in summer, freezing cold in winter; how after nine months he was allowed out to exercise in a vaulted area under the roof, where he found an iron spike which he eventually managed to smuggle to a fellow prisoner, who dug a hole in his own ceiling and one night escaped his cell and came for Casanova; how the two men waited until the moonlight would cast no shadows, and then climbed out onto the lead roof of the palace, where they found a skylight and slipped down a rope made of bedsheets into the locked offices of the Inquisition, where they convinced a night watchman that they were noblemen who had been mistakenly locked in overnight; how they strode out of the front door of the palace, hailed a gondola, and crossed the lagoon to Mestre, where they parted, Casanova riding a donkey toward the border near Brenta and then making his way to Paris, where he dined out on the story for years.

After I left my friend, I went to the Palais Albrechts, eager to inform Benda that Countess Stoll had vouched for Richter. A maid opened the door, took my cloak and satchel, and asked me to wait. She returned a moment later, telling me that Benda was not at home, but that her mistress had asked me to come upstairs. I followed her up to the salon.

Christiane sat in the large armchair, a piece of embroidery lying idly in her lap. Her skin was ashen, her eyes rimmed with red.

"Richard is not in, signore," she told me. "He received a message from Bohemia this morning. He hurried off to attend to matters at the chancery. Is your errand anything I can help with?"

The maid returned with a tray of coffee. Christiane told her she would pour and dismissed her.

"I've learned some important information about the murders," I said.

"Oh, please, I would be obliged if you would tell me," she said. Her hands trembled as she poured the coffee. I hurried over to take mine before it splashed all over the tray. I sat on the sofa near her chair and reported my encounter with Countess Stoll.

"Elisabeth Stoll. I am not acquainted with her. She is much older than me. She has a reputation as a very liberal person." She stared at a place somewhere to the left of me. The lone sound in the room was the ticking of the clock.

Finally she spoke again. "I feel as if I am in a nightmare. My beloved father, torn from me. Father Bayer. Now my neighbor has been taken. And you may not be aware, but I knew Walther Hennen when we were younger."

I nodded.

"I despair of my father's murderer ever being caught." She sighed. "Richard will be disappointed. That protester was the best suspect."

"Do not worry, mademoiselle. We will catch this monster. The last murder was different from the others. The killer is becoming more frenzied. He is beginning to make mistakes."

She closed her eyes.

"I wonder, mademoiselle, if you could tell me—" I paused, reluctant to increase her unhappiness.

"Yes, signore?"

"Do you know if your father received any strange messages in the days before his death?"

She frowned. "Messages? Are you speaking of letters? Strange in what way?"

"Sheets of paper with brief quotations from Dante written on them," I said. "Just a few lines on each page."

She pulled herself out of the chair. "Wait here," she said. "I'll be back in a moment."

I paced up and down the salon as I waited. If the general had indeed received messages from the killer, then surely I was on the right path.

Christiane returned a few minutes later and handed me two sheets of paper. "I found these in his library, a few days after—" Her voice faltered.

I scanned the lines on the first sheet. "Worldly fame is nothing but a puff of wind, that goes this way or that, and changes name when it changes direction." I drew a sharp breath and turned to the second sheet. "Your renown is the color of grass, it comes and goes, and that which fades it is the same as that which first drew it unripe from the earth," it read.

I recognized the lines. Before he had butchered him, the killer had accused General Albrechts of the deadly sin of pride.

Twenty-four

"Da Ponte." Benda entered the room. "Why are you here? What has happened?" He noticed Christiane sitting in the armchair and rushed to her side. "My love, what is wrong? You are so pale. Are you ill again?"

"I am merely tired, Richard. I will be fine," she said.

"You must rest. The last few weeks have been too much of a strain for you. I'll ring for Charlotte."

She placed her hand on his arm to stay him. "I'll go up myself," she said. "Signore, I hope I've been of help."

I thanked her and bowed. She left.

"What is happening?" Benda said.

I told him about my meeting with Countess Stoll.

He frowned. "Yet you believed her? Her reputation is such that—"

"I believed her," I interrupted. "You must send word to Troger to release Richter."

Benda sat on the sofa and put his head in his hands. "I

don't know what to think anymore. I don't know what to do. We haven't been able to stop this fiend from killing two more victims. Now you tell me that our best suspect is innocent. I was so sure it was him."

I cleared my throat.

He looked up at me. "You saw Christiane just now. Her grief for her father is eating her away. Yet she refuses to leave Vienna. I must solve these crimes and take her to my estates in Bohemia, or I feel she will die."

"She just gave me these," I said, handing him the messages I believed the killer had sent to the general. "Three of the four victims received such messages."

He grasped the sheets of paper and scanned them. "More quotations from Dante?"

I nodded. "Yes, from the second book of *The Divine Comedy, Purgatory*."

He stared dumbly at me. "I don't understand what these excerpts mean. They make no sense to me."

"Each passage is about the sin of pride," I explained.

"Pride?" Benda shook his head. "The killer accused the general of pride? Of course he was proud—he was a great war hero. He had a right to be proud."

"Dante is speaking of the seven deadly sins—avarice, pride, gluttony, lust, wrath, sloth, and envy," I explained. "Every person has some of these qualities to some degree. Most of us think about committing sins. But when a man gives in to temptation and commits sinful acts, when he lets his desires take over his life, then, according to Dante, he must either burn in Hell or atone in Purgatory instead of entering Paradise directly."

"So the killer believes the general had an excess of pride," Benda said. He took a deep breath. His eyes widened. "He has appointed himself the judge of his victims," he whispered.

"Yes," I said. "He has accused each victim of one of the deadly sins—the general of excessive pride, Hennen of envy, and Alois of gluttony."

"Gluttony?" Benda asked. "I saw the priest's body. He was as thin as a reed."

"The killer must believe Alois had an insatiable desire for something," I said. "The man is deranged. He does not think rationally, like we do. He believes what he wishes to believe about his victims.

"Yes, he is acting as a judge. In *Purgatory,* each sinner must be educated about his sin before he may be absolved of it." Excitement entered my voice. "I see now—he is sending the passages to teach his victim about the sin. Then he summons the victim to judgment."

"But we don't know that," Benda objected.

"The general, Hennen, and von Gerl all received a mysterious message the evening of the murder. These messages are nowhere to be found. The killer is taking them away. They must contain some sort of enticement, to ensure that the victim appears at his judgment."

"He thinks he is God," Benda said.

A chill traveled down my spine. "Yes. I understand now. When the victim appears at the appointed time and place, the killer offers him a chance to repent his sins. If the victim repents, the killer tells the poor soul he is bound for Purgatory, to serve time for his sins before he may enter Paradise.

He then slashes the man's throat and carves the *P* in his forehead.

Benda's face was ashen. "But the general—there were no markings on his forehead."

"No, but his lower torso was burned," I said, my mind racing. "Perhaps he refused to repent. A man in the general's position would be defiant to the end. So the killer resigned him to Hell. He slashed the general's throat and set the body on fire."

"To re-create burning in Hell," Benda whispered. "My God. This man is the devil incarnate."

I shook my head. "He is just a man, like you and me," I said. "Something has perverted his mind and soul to make him act this way. We must find him, quickly. He's already killed four times. There are still three more sins to go before he completes his mission."

I walked home slowly in the dusk, my thoughts on Marta. Her reaction to the news of von Gerl's death had left me disappointed and confused. I had hoped that she had realized that von Gerl had abandoned her, and that she had determined to make a fresh start with me. It was possible that her grief yesterday was merely the natural shock of someone who had just learned of the death of a friend. But part of me worried that her anguish was something more. I had to admit to myself that I was afraid to go to her. I should give her some time to grieve. And it was probably wise to refrain from demanding that she assess her feelings for me so soon. I might not be happy with the results of such an examination.

As I picked up my pace and hurried by the cathedral, I realized that I had not seen the man in the green cloak since I had confronted him Friday morning. Had I just imagined that he was following me? Had my glimpses of him throughout the city been mere coincidences? I smiled grimly. If so, he would avoid me in the future, steering clear of the crazy man who had accosted him in the university square. And if he were indeed trailing me for nefarious purposes, perhaps I had discouraged him by showing my anger.

I had just started down the Wollzeile, picking my way through the horse dung that littered the street, when a sharp cry made me look up. A woman leaned out the third-floor window of an apartment several doors down, calling a child to come indoors. The young boy climbed off his stick-horse and grudgingly carried it into the house.

The long street was empty except for a lone figure walking a block ahead of me. My eyes widened. *Was that . . . ? No! It couldn't be.* It was impossible. I was tired, and my eyes were playing tricks on me in the shadows. I was imagining things. *But then—who else in Vienna wore a hat like that?*

I ran down the street after him. "Von Gerl! Wait!" I shouted.

The man glanced back at me, hurried past the university plaza, and turned left. A moment later, I arrived at the corner. I stopped to catch my breath and looked around. No students stood chatting outside the long dormitories that lined the first block of the street. Up on the hill, the tall wooden doors of the Dominican Church were closed, the building silent. Von Gerl had vanished. The street was empty.

Twenty-five

The Hoher Market was Vienna's oldest marketplace, a long wide strip that connected the Bauernmarkt and the Tuchlauben at the southeastern edge of the city's Jewish quarter. Once famous for its fish vendors in the Middle Ages, the market was now lined with apartment buildings. At the center of the quadrangle stood the lofty Nuptial Fountain, built by the current emperor's great-grandfather to commemorate his heir's safe return from battle. Four tall, fluted columns held a highly ornamented marble canopy, under which a high priest blessed the betrothal of Joseph and Mary. A fountain stood in each of the two side niches in the base of the monument. It was at the base of one of these that Hieronymus Dauer lay staring upward, his heart-shaped mouth frozen open, his throat cut from ear to ear. His right arm was draped along the blood-splattered base of the monument; his left lay peacefully at his side. His forehead was clean.

Once again Troger's driver had come for me in the early hours of the morning, telling me that another murder had occurred. Now I stood with Troger, the driver, and a few constables, gagging as the pungent, sweet smell of burned flesh washed over me.

"Where is Benda?" I asked him. "Hasn't he been notified?"

"I don't know," Troger answered. "When the constable found the body and alerted me, I sent my carriage to the Palais Albrechts."

The driver stepped forward. "I went there first, sir," he said. "I knocked on the door several times. When a servant finally answered, he told me the count was not at home."

I frowned. "Did he say where the count had gone?"

The driver shook his head. "I asked, sir, but the man said he did not know. He did not want to disturb his mistress, so I came to fetch you."

That was odd, I thought. Benda had said nothing to me about leaving Vienna when I had spoken with him yesterday.

"Count Pergen will be in his office soon," Troger said. "I must report to him. I cannot wait for Benda to arrive."

"I'm sure we'll hear from him sometime this morning," I said. "I'll go over to the cathedral now and bring the priests the news." Troger nodded and climbed into his carriage. A hearse pulled into the plaza from the Tuchlauben end.

"Oh, by the way, Da Ponte," Troger called from the carriage. "When you see Benda, tell him that the protester, Richter, is still in prison. The paperwork to release him took longer than we expected. He'll be out this afternoon."

. . .

Except for a few of the faithful from the immediate neighborhood who waited in the chilly nave for the early mass to begin, the cathedral was quiet. When Maximilian Krause saw me enter through the front portico, he hurried toward me.

"Good morning, Lorenzo," he said. "Have you come for the mass? It's rare that we see you here."

"I'm afraid not, Maximilian," I said. His friendly face grew pale as I told him about Dauer's murder.

"Was it the same as the others?" he asked. "I've heard the rumors, that these killings are particularly gruesome."

"Yes," I said. "It seems to be the same killer."

"What is happening, Lorenzo? Do you have any idea?"

I shook my head. "I've been helping with the investigation, but we aren't getting anywhere."

"Why is this monster choosing these men? First Father Bayer, now Father Dauer—it's as if he has some sort of grievance against the cathedral."

"There have been three other victims who were not connected to the cathedral," I reminded him gently.

"Yes, I'd forgotten." He sighed. "It's too easy to simply think of the ones I knew myself." He signaled to a deacon, who came to us. Krause murmured in the young man's ear, and then the deacon went to the waiting worshipers and ushered them into one of the side chapels.

"Where was Father Dauer found?" Krause asked.

"In the Hoher Market. The hearse had just arrived when I left a few minutes ago."

"I must go there to attend the body," the priest said. He started toward the door.

"Before you go," I said, catching his arm, "will you tell me when you last saw Father Dauer?"

His brow creased in concentration. "Yesterday—yesterday afternoon. Yes, he had come over from the archbishop's palace to lead vespers."

"What do you know about him?" I asked.

"Not very much," he said. "As I told you a few weeks ago when I introduced you to him, he came here from the abbey at Melk." He sighed. "I haven't had much time to talk with him. He runs—ran—from one meeting to another."

"Had he made any enemies since he arrived?" I asked.

Krause shrugged. "I have no idea. He and I do not work at the same level. He was involved in all of the planning meetings regarding the cathedral. It's possible someone he met over at the archbishop's palace resented his arrival here. Or someone in the hierarchy might have opposed his ideas to modernize the church administration." He shook his head. "But to cut a man's throat, as if he were a farm animal? I cannot imagine such an act of anyone Father Dauer would have met here."

"Where is his office?" I asked.

"Upstairs." Krause motioned toward the steps off the north tower portico. "But he always kept it locked. I believe Felix is up there. He has keys to all the offices. He can direct you." He turned and hurried out the door.

I trudged up the worn stone stairs to a mezzanine, where a long corridor ran the length of the cathedral's nave. A waist-high balustrade lined the left side of the hall, closed office doors ran down the right. At the end of the hallway, a door stood open. I walked down to it and knocked.

Felix Urbanek looked up from his reading. "Signor Da Ponte," he said. "Good morning." He stood and smiled at me. "Have you changed your mind about the priesthood? Have you come to lead our morning mass?"

"I have terrible news," I said. "Father Dauer has been murdered."

Urbanek gasped and clutched the edge of his desk. "What? Are you sure? But where—I must go—"

"Please sit down, Father," I said. "There is nothing you can do for him now. Father Krause has gone to see to the body."

Urbanek collapsed into his chair and put his head in his hands. His lips moved in silent prayer. When he had finished, he looked over to where I stood near the door. "Was he killed the same way as Father Bayer?" he asked.

I nodded.

His face was gray. "Where did they find him?" he asked, his voice hoarse.

"Over at the Hoher Market," I answered.

"Who could have done such a thing?" he asked me.

"I don't know, Father," I said. "But I'm helping the police investigate the murders. Can you think of any enemies Father Dauer may have made in his short time here? Or any information that would be of use to us?"

"I don't know," he said. "I didn't know Father Dauer very well. He was involved in the political side of the cathedral." He thought for a minute and frowned. "He was found in the Hoher Market, you said? That doesn't make sense."

"What do you mean?"

"Father Dauer lives right here, in the archbishop's palace across the plaza. He has very wealthy patrons. Why would he be over on that side of the city? He has no need to go to the market to buy food. I've heard that the archbishop employs a very fine cook. I don't understand."

"It's possible that he went to meet the killer there," I said.

But Urbanek was not listening to me. "Perhaps he was visiting Father Krause," he mused. "He lives over there, in the Judengasse. Yes, that's the explanation. He must have been with Father Krause last night. The murderer came upon him when he was crossing the market on his way back to the archbishop's palace."

"We think that the victims—"

Urbanek shook his head. "No, that's not right," he muttered. "Why would he have been visiting Krause? Those two haven't been friendly, not since—"

I leaned forward. "Since when?"

"Oh, I shouldn't say. It's just an impression I had, that is all."

I took a deep breath. "Please. Anything you know might be helpful."

Urbanek sighed. "Many years ago, Father Bayer served as Christiane Albrechts's confessor. She is the daughter of the late general."

I nodded. "Yes. I am acquainted with her."

"After Father Bayer retired, the young lady could not make up her mind as to who would be her new confessor. She tried one priest, then another, but none made her happy."

He clucked with disapproval. "As if choosing a confessor is some sort of contest."

I clenched my teeth, willing him to get to the point. "But what—"

"After a few years of changing her mind again and again, she had finally settled on Father Krause. He had just begun to prepare her for her marriage to Count Benda when Dauer arrived. It did not take Dauer long to see that the Albrechts family would be valuable patrons. He courted the young lady and her father assiduously, almost as though he were planning to marry her himself." He gave a wry smile at his own joke. "But his efforts were fruitful, for she informed Father Krause that she had decided to choose Father Dauer."

"When was this?" I asked.

"Just a few weeks ago, two or three days before her father died," the priest answered.

I sighed inwardly. Surely this man did not believe that one priest would kill another over such a trivial matter.

He read my thoughts. "You think it is meaningless, I know. But a relationship with a powerful, wealthy family like the Albrechts can help a priest's career in many ways. Father Krause might seem a quiet scholar on the surface, but I can tell you he is as ambitious as the next man." He stood. "Is there anything else you wish to ask me? I must go down and pray for Father Dauer's soul. Will you come with me?"

"I cannot," I said. "I must search Father Dauer's office. Do you have a key?"

He crossed over to a cupboard and took out a ring of keys. He shuffled through them and chose one, and then handed it to me. "It's the first door after the stairwell," he said. "Just leave the key on my desk when you are finished. I never lock my door."

When I opened the door to Dauer's office and stepped inside, I understood why the priest had insisted on keeping it locked. The walls of the large room were hung with paintings and tapestries from the cathedral's cellar treasury. The small marble Pietà Dauer had been admiring the day Casanova and I had spoken to him sat on one of the bookcases. The desktop was clear except for a neat pile of documents. I riffled through them, but found no messages from the killer.

I opened the right-hand drawer of the desk. My pulse quickened as I saw a packet of letters neatly tied with a ribbon. I grabbed the packet, untied it, and scanned the letters. Most of them were from the dead priest's family. I swore in frustration and turned to the left-hand drawer. I pulled at the knob, but the drawer was stuck. I jiggled it, but it still did not open. I took Dauer's paper knife from the top of the desk and inserted the sharp blade into the space between the desk frame and the recalcitrant drawer, then moved it up and down and side to side. The drawer loosened, and I pulled it open.

It was empty except for two items—a pair of messages, written on light paper, embossed with a mark of a serpent and a crown.

Twenty-six

"Which sin did the killer believe Dauer committed?" Casanova asked.

I had taken the messages from the dead priest's office back to my own desk. An hour later, Casanova had arrived, full of questions about the latest murder.

"Avarice," I said. I showed him the messages. "We repeat the story of Pygmalion; how betrayal and thievery and parricide sprang from his insatiable wish for gold," read the first. The second continued the quotation about the deadly sin of greed. "And the misery of the greedy Midas; what followed from his unquenchable demand for gold; a result that always is cause for laughter."

"I understand the Midas reference," Casanova said. "The king of Phrygia, who wished everything he touched to turn to gold. But when his food turned to gold and he began to starve, he saw the error of his greedy ways."

"Yes," I said.

"But Pygmalion? The sculptor who fell in love with his own statue? I don't understand how that relates to avarice."

"Dante was writing about the other Pygmalion, the brother of Dido, who killed her husband so he could seize his wealth. Dido dreamt about the murder and fled, taking the riches with her, and eventually founding the city of Carthage."

We sat quietly for a moment.

"Was Dauer's forehead cut?" Casanova asked as he examined one of the messages.

"No. His lower torso had been set on fire." I took the messages from Casanova and placed them on my desk. "I think the killer was re-creating the fires of Hell. He's appointed himself God's representative on earth." I explained my theory that the killer was first educating his victims as to their sin, summoning them to a reckoning and giving them a chance to repent, then sending them to either Purgatory or Hell.

"So in his deranged mind, he believes he is dispensing justice," Casanova said. He placed the message on my desk. "How will you catch him?"

I shook my head. "I have no idea. And to make matters worse, Benda has disappeared. Troger's driver went to pick him up this morning and was told he was not at home. I should have heard from him by now."

"Should we worry about him?" Casanova asked. "Remember what I suggested about the killings being somehow connected with Christiane Albrechts? He is her fiancé. Perhaps he is in danger."

I chewed over this idea. "Christiane had recently chosen

Dauer as her new confessor," I said slowly. "So he fits into that pattern."

"So four of the five victims had an association with Mademoiselle Albrechts," Casanova murmured. "And you think von Gerl may have also been connected to her in some manner."

"But what could be the killer's motive? Is he in love with Christiane, and killing every man who is close to her out of jealousy? In that case, why hasn't he gone after Benda already? Or does he believe, in that disordered mind of his, that he is protecting her from these men he has killed?"

Casanova shrugged.

"If he is killing to protect her, what danger to her could the victims possibly represent?" I continued.

"Perhaps she is the clue to a dark secret the killer is trying to keep hidden," Casanova suggested.

I threw up my hands. "Perhaps. But it is impossible to solve the puzzle of this man's mind. And how do you explain the Dante messages, the carvings on the foreheads, the burned torsos? None of it makes any sense."

I picked up one of Dauer's messages. "There is one hope of catching him, though, Giacomo."

Casanova quirked a brow.

"Look at the watermark on this paper. The same mark has been on every one of the messages containing the Dante quotations. Let's take a page over to Krenner's bookshop to see if he can identify the watermark." I sighed. "I meant to do it on Saturday, but then we found von Gerl and I was distracted. Perhaps if I had gone, Dauer might still be alive."

"You cannot know that, Lorenzo," Casanova said. "Don't

torment yourself. You are not responsible for the actions of a lunatic."

I tucked one of the messages in my cloak pocket and followed Casanova upstairs and out into the Michaelerplatz. We walked down the Kohlmarkt and then down the Tuchlauben to the Kienmarkt, the narrow street where my favorite bookshop was situated. Franz Krenner, the proprietor, looked up from the book he was reading as Casanova and I entered the empty shop.

"Signor Da Ponte," he said. "How good to see you." He stuck a mark in his book, closed it, and stood. "I'm sorry we did not have the chance to talk at the memorial for Father Bayer."

"Good morning, Franz," I said. "Yes, I had some business to attend to and could not linger."

"Poor Father Bayer," Krenner said. "I will miss him. He used to come in several times a week, to see what I had acquired. I knew that if a volume of religious philosophy came my way, I could sell it to him." He looked curiously at Casanova, who had moved over to a shelf and was perusing the volumes.

"Franz, this is a friend of mine from Venice, Giacomo Casanova," I said.

The bookseller's eyes widened.

"Giacomo, my favorite bookseller, Franz Krenner."

Krenner hurried out from behind the counter and grabbed Casanova's hand. "Is it really you, sir? *The* Giacomo Casanova?"

Casanova bowed. "At your service," he said.

Krenner went over to a shelf near the front door of the

store and pulled out a few books. "I keep a few copies of your translation of the *Iliad* for my Italian customers, signore," he said. "I have also been able to obtain the philosophy essays you published two years ago, and of course, your recounting of your escape from Venice."

Casanova beamed.

"Have you written anything new I should be aware of?" Krenner asked.

"Yes, a novel is being published in Prague in a few months. It's the story of a young couple who live in a utopian underground world. And I've been working on some mathematical essays, also."

Krenner pulled out a logbook and wrote a note. "I'll seek these out, signore. I have several customers who enjoy avant-garde works." He closed the logbook and replaced it on a shelf. "If I might be so bold as to suggest, signore—" he said, turning back to Casanova.

"Yes?" Casanova asked. "Please, I'm interested to hear your thoughts. I seldom speak with anyone these days who is familiar with my work."

"Well, signore, I am wondering—have you ever considered writing a memoir? You have led a fascinating life. You've traveled everywhere, and have met everyone. A retelling of your life—just a small volume, it wouldn't take long to write—would sell well, I believe. Your name has been on the lips of people in every fine house in every city of Europe."

My friend flushed with pleasure. He puffed out his chest, and looked like the Casanova I had met years before in Venice. "I'll give that some thought," he said.

Krenner turned to me. "Was there something in particular I can assist you with, Signor Da Ponte?"

I pulled the sheet from my pocket and unfolded it on the
counter. "Yes, Franz. Could you tell me if you recognize the
watermark on this paper? I am trying to trace the man who
wrote these lines. I know you sell a lot of paper."

Krenner put on a pair of spectacles and examined the
page. "Oh, Dante's *Purgatory*," he said. "Is this from a study
group you belong to, signore?"

I shook my head.

"I sell a steady supply of *The Divine Comedy,* in Italian,
French, and German." He studied the watermark. "It appears to be a serpent, signore. A serpent wearing some sort
of crown." He shook his head. "I'm sorry, I do not recognize
it. I don't sell paper with this watermark."

"Would you have any idea how to find a shop that sells
it?" I asked.

He thought for a moment. "It is probably a special order,
signore. There are a few watermarks that are popular here in
Vienna. The post horn is the most common. If you are looking for paper for everyday use, that is what you usually will
get. A lot of people are not particular about the watermark,
so they just take the post horn. Many of the ladies in the
fine houses like the fleur-de-lis. I order large quantities of
that paper from Paris. And the members of the Masonic
lodges often request paper with a star watermark—it is some
meaningful symbol to them, I suspect.

"Some members of the old noble families have arrange-
ments with a papermaking company to use their coats of
arms as watermarks," he continued. "I help them procure

the paper. It's probable that this paper was obtained in that manner."

"How hard would it be to find the shop that ordered the paper?" Casanova asked.

"Oh, it would be difficult, signore," Krenner replied. "There are so many shops that sell paper here in the city, and of course, there are also shops in the suburbs. And as you probably know, other establishments also sell it, not just bookshops. It's also possible that the paper doesn't even come from a shop here in Vienna. Many people order their paper directly from shops in other cities. They might buy large quantities while they are abroad, or request friends who are coming to Vienna from other cities to bring them the paper they like."

I tried to keep the disappointment from my face as we thanked Krenner and walked toward the door.

"Good luck, Signor Da Ponte, Signor Casanova," the bookseller called after us.

"We need it," Casanova muttered.

We ate dinner in a catering shop outside the Judenplatz and then I returned to my office. I had just settled in to work when Thorwart, the assistant theater manager, knocked on my door and handed me two new librettos to edit.

"I've heard a disturbing rumor, Da Ponte," he said. "Is it true that you are assisting the Ministry of Police in the investigation of these murders?"

I sighed. Nothing was secret in Vienna. "Yes," I said. "I am working with Count Benda to solve the case for Count Pergen. A good friend of mine was one of the victims."

"Ah, the old priest," Thorwart said.

"Yes."

"Is it true what people are saying on the streets—that General Albrechts was the first victim?"

"I shouldn't discuss the case," I said.

He frowned. "These murders are bad for business, Da Ponte. You know that we just escaped being closed under the budget cuts the emperor ordered last fall. Attendance at performances has started to decline because of the war. If people are afraid to come out in the dark for a night at the theater, I fear the company cannot survive."

"I know."

"Please, at least tell me that the lunatic who is committing these crimes will be caught soon!"

I didn't want to tell him that we were no closer to solving the murders than when we had first begun the investigation. "Count Pergen has ordered all of the resources of the empire to be used in finding the killer," I assured him.

After a few feeble attempts to get me to reveal some details of the killings, Thorwart left. I closed my office door after him. The assistant theater manager was the nervous sort, always fretting over costs and revenues. But his warnings struck a chord in me. How would I be able to remain in Vienna if the theater closed and I lost my job? What kind of work could I do? Times were changing, and few aristocrats patronized musicians anymore, let alone poets. Would I have to follow Giacomo's example, and find some boring post in a rural backwater?

I looked at the librettos Thorwart had left me and shook my head. I couldn't worry about the future right now. I would deal with whatever happened when it happened. I reached for the libretto I had been editing. For now, I just had to go on working. It was all I knew how to do.

I worked for an hour on the libretto and then quickly looked over the scene I had written for Caterina Cavalieri. It was not as long as she would have liked, I was sure, but I was pleased with it. I took it up to the lobby of the theater and gave a boy a coin to deliver it to Mozart. I had just turned to go back downstairs to my office when a young woman dressed in a simple black dress entered the theater. She looked around as if she had never been in the building before. "May I help you, miss?" I asked.

"Oh, thank you, sir. I'm looking for the theater poet, Lorenzo Da Ponte."

"I am Lorenzo Da Ponte."

"Oh! Good afternoon, signore. Would you be so kind as to come outside with me?"

I glanced at the steps leading to my office.

"My errand will take but a few moments, signore. Please, it is important."

"What is this all about? What is your name?"

"I am Charlotte, signore, lady's maid to Mademoiselle Albrechts."

"Is it Count Benda? What has happened?" I asked.

"Please, signore. I cannot say. I was told only to bring you."

I followed her out the door and across the Michaelerplatz toward the Spanish Riding School stables. "Where are we going?" I asked. "You said it would take only a few moments."

She turned down the short street that led to the rear of the stables. A familiar carriage was parked halfway down the street. Charlotte knocked on the door of the carriage and opened it. "Please, signore," she said, motioning me to enter.

I climbed into the carriage and the door closed behind me. The interior was dark after the bright sunlight of the afternoon, and all the shades at the windows were drawn.

"Please, Signor Da Ponte, have a seat." Christiane Albrechts's soft voice came from the gloom. As my eyes became adjusted to the dimness, I saw her sitting on the right-side bench, bundled in a cloak. A heavy fur more suitable for Vienna's winters than this cool spring day sat on her lap. I took the bench across from her.

"Mademoiselle Albrechts?" I asked. "What is the meaning of this summons? Has something happened?"

"I apologize for the drama and mystery, signore. I had to speak with you, and I did not want you to come to the house."

"Is it about Benda? Where is he?"

She sighed. "He was called away late last night. The manager of his estate sent for him. There has been a riot—the peasants are angry about the price of food. He is probably halfway to Bohemia by now." She twisted her hands in her lap. "No, it is not about Richard." She stared at the floor of the carriage. "No, it is about me—I cannot live with myself anymore. I must confess to someone."

"I do not practice as a priest, mademoiselle," I said gently.

She waved her hand at me. "No, no, you misunderstand me. I do not seek absolution. I come to you in your role as investigator of the murder of my father." She hesitated.

I leaned forward in my seat. "What is it you wish to tell me, mademoiselle?"

She stared at her hands in her lap and then looked up at me in the faint light. "I am the killer you and Richard seek," she said.

Twenty-seven

My jaw dropped. "*You* killed your father, mademoiselle?"

She nodded. "Yes. I confessed it all to Father Dauer before he died. Valentin—"

"Please start from the beginning."

"It was Valentin—Baron von Gerl. Richard has been away at his estate many times since Valentin arrived back here in Vienna. My father was writing his memoirs, and was busy with work." Her voice was a monotone. "I suppose I was lonely. Valentin visited me often for coffee. Once he took me to the Prater for a stroll."

She ran her fingers along the fur blanket.

"He flirted with me outrageously. Of course, he understood that I was loyal to Richard. But I enjoyed Valentin's attentions, I will admit that. He was an attractive man." She pushed the fur aside. "But as the days went by and Richard did not return, my resistance began to waver."

I nodded.

"The afternoon before my father was murdered, Valentin sent me a note." She stared at the carriage wall behind me. "He wanted to make love to me. He asked if I would receive him in my chamber after my father retired for the evening."

I remained silent.

"I knew that I should refuse him, but I could no longer help myself. I sent a reply allowing him to come."

She took a deep breath. "After my father went to bed, I waited until after twelve-thirty, when I knew the steward would be asleep, and then I crept downstairs and unlocked the door. Valentin was waiting in the shadows of the court-yard. I led him to my chamber."

She twisted the soft fur on her lap.

"Once Valentin and I were alone in my chamber, I lost control of myself. We—"

Her cheeks burned in the dim light.

"I understand," I said. "Please go on."

"I must have cried out just when I was about to surrender to him. There was a noise in the hallway—footsteps—my father's footsteps. He must have heard me and was coming to investigate. I pushed Valentin away and told him to climb out the window. He wanted to stay and hide, but I was fran-tic. He went out the window and climbed down the vines."

She swallowed hard. "Then the nightmare began."

"I don't understand," I prompted her. "You said you killed your father."

"Yes, yes I did. You see, my father must have seen Valen-tin in the courtyard. He must have rushed downstairs to confront him."

"But von Gerl did not kill your father," I said. "He is one

of the murderer's victims himself. No, mademoiselle. You have it wrong. Those pages you gave me yesterday—the killer sent them to your father. He accused him of excess pride—"

"Don't you see?" she cried. "That is how the killer found him. If my father had not gone out to follow Valentin, to protect my honor, he would have remained safely in his bed. He would be alive today." She buried her face in her hands and wept.

I moved over to the bench next to her and put my arm around her. "No, no. You are not to blame," I said. "Your father was leaving the house at that hour to keep an appointment with his killer, not because he heard you and von Gerl. He left the house and went to the Am Hof. A witness saw him there just before one. If he had been chasing von Gerl, he would have gone the other way."

I offered her my handkerchief. She took it and dabbed at her eyes. "Are you certain about this?" she whispered.

"Yes," I said. "Two witnesses saw the general that night. Both said he was walking with purpose, toward some sort of meeting."

"But I understood that—"

"Is that why you said you were the killer?" I asked. "That was all?"

She sighed. "I was certain I was to blame. I knew my father's body was found in the Am Hof, but I assumed the killer found him in the street outside the palais and dragged him there."

"You should have asked Benda for more information," I said. "He would have been able to reassure you."

Her eyes widened. "No! No! Richard must not know

anything of this!" She clutched my arm. "Promise me you will not repeat to him what I've told you! Please, you must promise me!"

"You have my word," I said.

I mulled over Christiane's admission as I walked back to my office. Casanova had been right—all five of the killer's victims were involved with her in some way. Alois and Dauer had been her confessors; Hennen her former fiancé and von Gerl a potential lover; and of course, the general was her father. A pang of worry shot through me. I could not think of a reason why someone would kill every male connected with Christiane Albrechts, but I was glad that Benda was off in Bohemia, safe from the killer's dagger.

Back in the office, I completed work on the libretto I had been editing earlier in the day, then took my cloak and satchel and headed for home. Thorwart's fears that the murders would keep the people of Vienna indoors appeared to be justified this evening, for the streets were empty of the usual crowds of people going to suppers and soirees. Or perhaps it was just the weather. The chilly air of mid-April had returned, and showers threatened.

I hurried down the deserted Wollzeile, past the university, my eyes alert for any sign of von Gerl's plumed hat. But I reached the Stuben gate without incident. Fatigue must have caused my eyes to play tricks on me the other night. A guard waved me through the Stuben gate. As I reached the end of the wooden bridge that spanned the *glacis*, I heard steady footsteps behind me. I quickened my pace and walked across the broad pathway and over the river bridge. The footfalls continued behind me. I walked even faster. Within a few moments, I arrived at my street. I turned the corner, concealed myself in the dark archway of the first house, and stretched my neck so that I could see the street corner. Within a minute, my pursuer arrived. He stopped and peered down the street. I drew in a sharp breath as I recognized the young man in the forest-green cloak.

I held my breath as he stood looking down the street. After a minute or two, he turned and went back in the direction of the city. I waited several moments more to make certain he was gone, and then ran down the street to the safety of my lodgings.

Twenty-eight

I stayed home and worked in my room on Tuesday morning. I knew that I had put off speaking to Marta for too long, and I was determined to see her before I left for the rehearsal that was scheduled for the afternoon.

I was packing up my satchel and planning what to say to Marta when the door opened and Sophie entered. She carried a pitcher of fresh water; a clean towel was tucked under her arm. She started when she saw me standing at the desk.

"Oh, Signor Da Ponte, I am sorry," she said. "I thought you had already left for the theater."

"Come in, Sophie," I said.

"No, signore, I don't want to disturb you. I'll leave these and come back later." She took the water and towel over to my basin.

"Please, Sophie, do what you would do if I were not here," I said.

She nodded. "Thank you, signore. I'll be quick about it."

She opened the window, then carried the basin over to it and threw the dirty water out. She wiped the basin dry with the soiled towel, replaced the basin on the washstand next to the fresh water. Crossing over to my bed, she took the coverlet off, shook it, plumped the mattress and the pillow, then replaced the coverlet.

"There you are, signore," she said. "I will sweep later this afternoon, while you are out."

"Thank you, Sophie." I hesitated. Now that I had made up my mind to approach Marta, I was eager to go across and knock on her door. But since Sophie was here, I ought to ask her about what had occurred the evening von Gerl was killed.

"Sophie, have you heard the news about Baron von Gerl?" I asked.

"You mean about the murder, signore?"

"Yes," I said.

"Stefan told me the baron had had his throat cut at the Belvedere," she said. "He told me that it wasn't the first time this had happened—that there's a monster roaming the streets late at night, killing people."

She looked at me curiously. "Stefan also said he heard that you were working with the police to find the killer, signore."

"Yes, that is true. So I must ask you a few questions, Sophie."

"Me, signore? I know nothing about murder. And I haven't seen the baron since the night of the ball."

She stared at me, her eyes defiant.

"Come, Sophie," I said. "You know I saw you sneak out of the house last Friday night."

Her cheeks reddened.

"Where were you going?" I asked.

She stared at the floor. "I don't want to say, signore."

"I saw you get into von Gerl's carriage, Sophie. I saw Teuber drive you away." I did not tell her that I had also watched as Stefan followed her.

"Then you already know what there is to be known, signore."

"I'd like to hear it from you. Where did Teuber take you? To von Gerl's palace?"

She blew air from her cheeks. "You must promise not to tell Mother," she said.

I nodded.

"After I met Valentin—the baron—at the ball at the Redoutensaal, he began to send me gifts. The first day it was a posy of flowers. The next day, a pair of gloves; the next, a jeweled pin for my hair. Please, signore, do not tell my mother. She knows nothing about this. If she knew that I had accepted the baron's gifts, she would be furious with me."

"I won't tell her," I said.

"Each day I received a note from him, telling me how soft my hands were, how much he wanted to hold one of them again, how beautiful I was." Her eyes grew dreamy.

"You don't have to give me the details," I said. "I've written many such notes myself."

She smiled. "On Friday morning, he sent another note, inviting me to come to the palace for supper that evening.

He mentioned that he wished to discuss our future. He told me to expect his carriage at eight o'clock."

"Did Teuber take you directly to the palace?" I asked.

"Yes. Oh, signore, what a grand place it was! I've never been in any of the fancy houses in the city."

"Tell me what happened next," I said.

"When I arrived, Valentin was not there. The manservant told me that he had been called out on some business, and would return as soon as possible. He said his master had told him to serve me dinner and give me anything I wanted."

"And then?"

"He showed me to a beautiful chamber and told me I could freshen my rouge. Then he led me to the dining room." Her eyes widened at the memory. "It was so elegant, signore. I've never been in such a large room. I sat at the table by myself, and the manservant brought me dinner. There must have been ten courses. And there was music! Three musicians were there, on a little stage, playing just for me. It was wonderful. I felt as though I were a countess."

"Was anyone else in the house?"

"I have no idea. I didn't hear anyone. The musicians were playing the whole time."

"When did you finish eating?" I asked.

She pressed her hand to her lips. "Oh, about ten, I would say. Yes, I remember I heard the clock in the dining room chime. The servant, Teuber, you said his name was, cleared all the dishes and dismissed the musicians. He then brought me the most beautiful dessert—a small silver tray with three tiny cakes on it. He told me Valentin had ordered it especially for me." Her eyes gleamed. "One was a meringue, I think it is called. It had been baked in the shape of a swan and filled with cream. Then there was a chocolate ball. That one was especially delicious. It had a crust on it, and when I broke into it, melted chocolate oozed out of it. The third one—"

"What happened when you finished these cakes?" I asked.

"When Teuber came for the plate, he apologized, telling me he had just had a message from Valentin. He was still in his meeting and could not see me that evening after all. Teuber brought me my cloak and then took me home in the carriage. I slipped back into the house. My mother never knew I had been gone."

Her pretty face paled. "Oh! You don't suppose Valentin was being murdered while I was eating my dessert, do you?"

"I don't believe so, Sophie. The killer attacks his victims much later in the night."

She let out a breath. "Good. I would hate to think that Valentin was lying dead while I was enjoying his delicious gift. I wouldn't be able to think of it with such pleasure if that were so. Will what I just told you help you find the killer, signore?"

"I don't know, Sophie. But I am glad you told me."

She started toward the door, and then turned back to me. "I hope you don't have a bad opinion of me, signore, because I am not mourning for Valentin. I was angry with him that night, because I had agreed to come to him and he went off. But I've given my situation a lot of thought over the last few days, and I now see that I love Stefan." She smiled. "Now I just have to convince him of it."

I laughed. "I'm sure you'll have no problem doing that," I said.

"You are really working for the police, signore?" she asked.

"Yes."

She hesitated. "There is something I— No, it is probably nothing."

"You should tell me anything you know, Sophie. I can decide if it is important."

"Well, it is the other lodger, Professor Strasser."

"What about him?"

"Lately, when I've cleaned his room, I've been finding something strange."

"What?"

"Blood, signore. His towels are sometimes stained with blood. And once I found his bedclothes were stained with blood. I had to scrub and scrub to get it out."

My pulse quickened. "When did you find the blood?" I asked.

"I think the first time was several weeks ago. I haven't cleaned in there yet today, signore. The professor teaches a class on Tuesday mornings. His room is not locked. I could show you."

I hesitated. I did not believe for a moment that Erich Strasser was the killer. Could I in good conscience search his room? I would not like my own privacy invaded because of the imagination of a cleaning girl. But I had agreed to investigate the murders, so I was obligated to pursue every possible clue. Sighing, I followed Sophie into the hallway.

She knocked at the door opposite mine and, when there was no answer, opened it. Strasser's room was the same size as mine and furnished in a similar manner. I went to the wash-stand and examined the towel, but saw no bloodstains. Sophie unfurled the bedclothes. There were no stains.

"He puts his laundry in here, signore," she said, going over to the cupboard and pulling out a linen bag. "Here!" She handed me a handkerchief. A large splotch of dried blood covered the center of the cloth. "And here is another."

My heart sank. "Thank you, Sophie," I said. "I'll close the door when I go." She hesitated, perhaps hoping I would change my mind and invite her to stay and join my search, but then went to the door.

"Oh, Sophie," I called. "Don't mention this to anyone else, please. Not to your mother, nor to Stefan." She nodded and left.

I pulled a clean handkerchief from the cupboard and wrapped it around the soiled ones. I looked through the rest of the cupboard. Strasser's clothes were what one would ex-pect from a professor at the university—two woolen suits of lower quality than the ones I purchased to wear to the the-ater, a pair of plain brown trousers, and two linen shirts. A candlestick sat on the small table by the bed. I glanced out the window. Marta stood in the garden below. I crossed to the desk. On top were a bottle of ink, a few pens, and a miniature portrait of a woman with dark hair and brows the same ebon color as Strasser's. I pulled open the single desk drawer. I took a sheet from the stack of light-colored paper inside and held it up to the light streaming in the window. The familiar serpent gazed at me from underneath his crown. I folded the paper and put it with the bound handkerchiefs, then went to a small bookcase by the door. Most of the titles were in Turkish, possibly histories related to Strasser's research. The rest of the volumes were by various French *philosophes*, including Voltaire and Rousseau. And at the very bottom of the shelf was a single volume of Dante—*Purgatory*.

Twenty-nine

Marta sat on the garden bench, a small volume in her hands. She looked up from her reading as I approached.

"How are you?" I asked.

"Oh, Lorenzo. I don't know. I'm still in shock, I think." She gestured for me to sit next to her. I longed to take her in my arms, but I was unsure of her reaction, so I took her hand. To my relief, she did not pull it away.

"Has there been any news about Valentin's killer?" she asked.

"No, nothing yet. And the killer has struck again. Early yesterday morning, he murdered another priest from the cathedral."

She shuddered. "Who is doing these horrible things?" she asked. "Why would anyone wish to kill Valentin? It makes no sense. I just don't understand."

"Neither do I," I said. "But I am certain that in the killer's mind, what he is doing makes perfect sense."

She said nothing. I glanced at the book she was holding.

"Ah, you are reading Shakespeare," I said. "I've read that one."

She put the book by her side. "I hoped a comedy might cheer me," she said. "But even the tinkers and the fairies cannot take my mind off Valentin."

We sat quietly for a few long moments.

"Have you given any thought to what you will do next?" I asked.

She sighed. "I spent all of my money to travel here to be with Valentin," she said. "I know now that was foolish of me. I just don't know what I will do."

"Stay here," I said. "Stay with me."

"Are you proposing to marry me, Lorenzo?" she asked softly.

Was I? I didn't know if I would ever be able to free myself from the bonds of the church and marry. I simply knew that I wanted her by my side, forever. "I've been ordained as a priest," I said. "Marriage in the church might be impossible for us. But I want to take care of you, for as long as you'll have me. We could find a small apartment, perhaps out here, or even in the city if you would like. I send a lot of money to my father to help him educate my stepbrothers, but I could cut that back. Lately I've been turning down commissions, so I'd have time to write poetry, but I can take on more work."

She put a finger on my lip. "Please, Lorenzo. I don't know. Perhaps I should go home to Venice."

"I want to be with you, Marta," I said.

"I don't know, Lorenzo. I need to think. Have you considered returning to Venice?"

I shook my head. "I cannot return. I was banished eight years ago for my political writings. If I go back before my fifteen-year sentence elapses, I will be thrown in prison."

She made no reply.

"But I could be happy here in Vienna with you," I said. "And I would do everything in my power to make you happy."

"I must think," she said. "I need time, Lorenzo. Time to grieve for Valentin, and for my dreams of living out my life here in Vienna as his wife."

"I understand," I said stiffly. I made a show of pulling out my watch and checking the time. "I did not realize it was so late," I said. "I must go. I have a rehearsal at the theater." I stood and started toward the door of the house.

"Lorenzo, please," Marta cried after me. "Do not let us part like this."

I turned back to her. "When you are ready, you know where to find me, Marta," I said. I hurried in the door and upstairs to retrieve my satchel.

"'There's no pity for the likes of you!'" Luisa Laschi, dressed in the costume of a peasant girl, screamed as she pulled Francesco Benucci onto the stage by his hair. She waved a foot-long razor in her other hand.

The baritone, playing the role of Don Giovanni's man-servant, who had just been caught trying to seduce a young woman while disguised as his master, held up quivering hands. "'Then you mean to cut off—'"

"'Yes!'" Laschi cried. "'I'll cut off your hair, then your head, and then I'll carve out your heart and your eyes!'"

"Good, signora," I called from my seat on the main floor of the theater. This was the first time the three of us had worked through the new material. Because it was a burlesque, we were concentrating on gestures, acting, and stage marks, rather than the music. We would rehearse with Mozart, and then again with the orchestra, in a few days.

The heavily pregnant soprano looked frantically around the stage. "'Where is everyone?'" she called. "'Who will help me punish this villain?'" She pulled her victim toward an empty chair, which sat a few feet away from a window that had been built into a prop wall on the stage. "'Sit down!'" she ordered.

Benucci fell into the seat. "'But I'm not tired.'" He looked at the razor in Laschi's hands. "'Do you mean to shave me?'" he asked.

"'I'm going to shave you,'" she said. "'But without soap.'" She pulled a handkerchief from her dress. "'Give me your hands!'" As she tied Benucci's hands together, the two singers launched into the new duet Mozart and I had prepared.

"'Let these little hands of yours have pity on me,'" Benucci sang.

"'I have no pity for you,'" Laschi replied. "'I am a raging tigress.'" She took out a cord, bound Benucci onto the chair with it, then crossed to the prop window and fastened the other end of the cord to the window.

The two continued through the duet, Benucci pleading for release, Laschi exulting in her power over him, and wishing it could extend to all men. As they sang, repeating several refrains, my mind wandered back to the morning. I pushed thoughts of Marta from my mind. I would just have to wait for her to make a decision. I sighed inwardly as I recalled my search of Strasser's room. Try as I might, I could not imagine my fellow lodger as the murderer, despite the presence of the bloody handkerchiefs, the paper, and a copy of Dante's *Purgatory*. There must be some innocent explanation for his possession of all of these items. Still, I knew I had to confront him about them, and I dreaded doing so.

"Signor?" Luisa Laschi called to me from the stage. "Are you all right?"

"Oh, forgive me, signora," I said. "My mind was somewhere else."

"That doesn't say much for your writing, Da Ponte," Benucci said, smiling. "If even the poet falls asleep during the scene—"

We all laughed.

"Do I exit at this point?" Laschi asked.

"Yes," I said. "Then you, Signor Benucci, will go through the recitative. At the end, stand up, with the chair still attached, and jerk the cord. The window will fall out. Then hop off, dragging the window with you."

Laschi came and sat next to me. We watched as Benucci practiced jerking and hopping, a stagehand replacing the window into the fake wall each time, until the baritone had the moves mastered.

"Bravo, Signor Benucci!" Laschi and I cried.

I turned to her. "After he leaves the stage, you will return with Signor Bussani and Madame Cavalieri. We'll work on that scene with Mozart next time."

. . .

I spent the rest of the day in my office then dragged myself home at six. As I walked into the courtyard of my lodgings, I looked over at the small garden. I was relieved to see the bench empty. Marta and I could talk and talk, but would never find a resolution until she rid herself of her feelings for von Gerl. And unluckily for me, those feelings seemed to have strengthened since she had learned of his murder.

I went into the house and slowly climbed the stairs to my room. Once inside, I put my satchel on the floor, hung my cloak and coat in my cupboard, then crossed to the desk and lit a candle. A message sat on the desk—a light-colored, single sheet which had been folded in thirds and left unsealed. There was no address on it. I picked it up with trembling hands and unfolded it, and then stared at the distinctive watermark in the middle of the page—a large serpent rising from clawlike leaves set in the middle of a ring, an elaborate crown hovering over its head. Written across the page, in handwriting that was now all too familiar to me, were a few lines of poetry. I did not need to read them to know that they were from Dante.

PART IV

The Wrath of Heaven

Thirty

I dropped the paper onto the desk and rushed down to the kitchen, where I found my landlady putting away the remnants of supper.

"Signor Da Ponte, what is it?" she asked. "Has something happened?"

"Madame, I found a message on my desk when I came in a few minutes ago. Did you put it there?"

She frowned. "No, signore. I've been working down here all afternoon. As far as I know, nothing was delivered for you."

"Perhaps Sophie took it in," I said.

"That's possible, signore. She was out at the dress shop earlier, but came home an hour or so ago. She must have taken the message up to your room."

"Is she at home? I must speak with her," I said.

My landlady's eyes were full of concern and questions.

"I'm sorry, signore, but she is not here. Stefan came by about twenty minutes ago. They've gone off for a ride in his cart."

I let out an exasperated sigh.

"Signor, what is it? Is there something I can help you with?"

I shook my head. "Please forgive my impatience, Madame Lamm. I've been discomposed ever since the death of my friend."

"I understand, signore. Have you eaten? I can put together supper for you in a few minutes."

"Thank you, madame, but no. I haven't much appetite tonight. Please do not worry. I am fine."

"Then I'll say good night, signore."

I climbed the stairs back to my room. I picked up the message from the killer and read the passage. "Remember that those for whom the sea opened died before Jordan saw their heirs." The quotation was from the part of *Purgatory* where Dante and Virgil encounter the slothful. It referred to the Book of Numbers, where God ordains that of all the men who came out of Egypt, only Joshua and Caleb should see the Promised Land. The others were doomed to die in the wilderness, because they muttered against Moses, and did not follow God assiduously.

The innocent words of one of my most treasured poets sent a chill down my spine. The killer knew me, and had judged me guilty of the deadly sin of sloth, of neglecting what is most important in life, of carrying out my responsibilities in an indolent manner. I lay on my bed and racked my brain, trying to identify someone in my professional life who also knew the other five victims. I could think of no one. Soon anger overcame my reasoning, and I thought of everyone I had encountered in my time here in Vienna, remembering every criticism and slight, every arched brow, every instance of quickness to anger, searching for signs that someone I knew was a madman hiding behind a cultured façade.

I washed and changed into my nightshirt, and then went to bed. I tossed and turned for an hour longer, fear a cold pit in my stomach, but no answers came to me. I had no idea who the killer was. But I was about to find out.

After a sleepless night of worry, I rose early and attempted to work a bit in my room. But the words that usually flowed so easily when I was working on an opera with Mozart failed to appear, and after a while I laid down my pen.

I took the blank piece of paper I had found in Strasser's room from my drawer and laid it side by side with my message from the killer. The two sheets were exactly the same color, and both had the strange watermark of the crowned serpent.

A knock sounded at the door. It was probably Sophie looking to clean the room. Perhaps she could tell me how the sinister message had arrived at my desk. I shoved the blank sheet back into my drawer and pushed the libretto pages I had been working on over the killer's missive.

"Come in," I called.

"Good morning, Lorenzo." Erich Strasser entered.

I nodded and motioned him toward my bed. My neighbor's skin was pale, and large dark circles hung under his eyes. His hands quivered as he came over to my desk.

"I wanted to speak to you before I approached Madame Lamm," he said. "I was sorting my laundry for the washerwoman. I seem to have lost some items. Have you noticed anything missing from your room?"

My nose began to itch. I rubbed it. "I haven't," I said. "What sort of things are you missing?"

"A few handkerchiefs," he said. "I was certain that I had put them in my bag for the wash, but they are nowhere to be found. I've looked everywhere in my room. I believe that Sophie has taken them while she was cleaning."

I shook my head. "I haven't noticed anything missing."

He looked over at the libretto pages on my desk. "Is this for your current work?" he asked. He picked up the sheets. "May I have a look?"

"Please," I said. I tried to push the letter from the killer under another pile of papers on my desk, but I did not act quickly enough.

"Is this yours?" he asked, reaching for the light-colored page. "I thought I was the only person in the city who used this paper."

"This?" I picked up the message and took a deep breath. "It isn't mine. It was sent to me by the person who has been killing men in the city the last few weeks."

He started and peered over my shoulder at the letter. "What a strange message. Isn't that an excerpt from Dante's *Purgatory*? I've just been reading it, so I recognize it. It's about sloth, correct?"

I nodded.

"Who sent this, Lorenzo?" Strasser asked.

I took a deep breath. "Are you certain you don't know, Erich?"

His brow furrowed. "I should know? What are you talking about, Lorenzo?" Comprehension appeared on his face. "You believe that I—you think—oh my God." He stumbled over to my bed and collapsed on it. "You think I am this murderer?"

I crossed over to my cupboard and pulled out the bundle of blood-soaked handkerchiefs I had taken from his room yesterday.

He frowned. "You have them? How did you get them? I don't understand."

"Why did you hide these bloody linens in your room, Erich?" I asked.

He stared at me openmouthed.

"I'm afraid I need an explanation," I said.

"You searched my room? What right did you have to go through my personal belongings?"

"I am working with the police to solve these murders. I was told that your wash bag was often filled with blood-stained items."

"Sophie told you this?"

I nodded.

"You searched my room, you suspect me of murdering five people, all on the fancies of a silly young girl?" He shook his head. "I believed I knew you, Lorenzo. I had the impression that we shared the same sentiments and ideas. You! Working for the Ministry of Police! What ridiculous ideas do you have about me? That I am part Turk, so I must therefore be a bloodthirsty monster?"

"No, no, you misunderstand me, Erich. I cannot believe that you would murder these people. I am not accusing you. But you possess a stack of the same type of paper the murderer used to send messages to his victims—a paper that is not common in the city. And Sophie was right to tell me about the blood. What is your explanation for it?"

Strasser took a handkerchief from his pocket and wiped his face. "I have the blood disease," he said softly. "If I am cut, the bleeding does not stop. Those soiled handkerchiefs are from violent nosebleeds. I try to hide my condition. You've seen yourself how I am harassed in the street, because I am part Turk. There are many people in Vienna who would love to see me dismissed from my position at the Oriental Academy because they hate my political views. If word got out that I was some sort of freak, who hemorrhaged blood—"

I waved him silent. "I understand," I said.

"And as for the paper—the proprietor of a shop near the Stephansdom orders it for me. I like the watermark—it is exotic. It is a small conceit of mine to use the paper. I have no idea how your killer got hold of some of it. Perhaps he is someone who works in the academy with me, who stole the paper from my office."

"Where is the shop?" I asked.

"In the Grünangergasse, at the end near the Franciscan Church."

I did not know what to say. He stood. I handed him the bundle of soiled linens.

"I'm sorry, Erich," I said. "I—"

He lifted his hand to silence me. "Never mind, Lorenzo. I suppose you were doing what you thought you had to. This is my fault. I am too naïve. I was a fool to think that I could continue to live in this city during this war, with my background and political views. It's obvious I do not belong here, if even men like yourself are so eager to blame me for whatever dreadful events occur."

I watched, my tongue tied with embarrassment, as he walked out the door, closing it behind him.

I slipped my work and the paper I had taken from Strasser into my satchel, took my cloak, and went out into the bright morning. I trudged toward the city, chastising myself for my clumsiness in confronting Strasser. What was happening to me? I hated having to treat my friends this way, and I cringed at the thought that people equated me with Pergen and Troger. And I was disturbed at my reaction to the latest murder. I had approached and examined Dauer's body as if I were an anatomist, not a human witnessing the destruction of another person. I was becoming inured to the sight of violent death. Perhaps that's what the crime of murder does—it not only kills its victim, but extinguishes a part of those left behind.

After I had crossed through the Stuben gate, I turned left and walked along the narrow street that hugged the wall of the city, then turned down the winding street that led to the Franciscan Church. At the end of the next block, I turned into the Grünangergasse. I found Strasser's bookshop several doors down on the left.

The shop was dark and cramped, not at all like Krenner's airy shop in the Kienmarkt. I glanced through the collection of books on offer as I waited for the proprietor. Many of the volumes were in Hungarian; the rest were tomes about religious history and philosophy, a subject that interested me little.

"May I help you, sir?" A small man with a heavy Hungarian accent came from the back room.

I pulled the paper from my satchel and put it on the counter. "I'm trying to find anyone who uses this paper, with this watermark," I said. "I was told you sell it."

He looked at the sheet. "Oh, yes. I order this for Professor Strasser over at the Oriental Academy. He likes the watermark. He has a standing order for fifty sheets a month."

"Would you know if any other shop in the city sells this same paper?"

"Oh, no, sir. I am the only one who can obtain it. It is made in Buda, my hometown. The papermaker's and my families go a long way back. I can assure you that you can buy this paper exclusively from me."

I had hoped that the paper would easily lead me to the killer. Perhaps Strasser had been right. The killer worked at the academy and had stolen the sheets from Strasser's office there. I would have to ask Troger to investigate the backgrounds of everyone who worked at the school.

I handed the bookseller a coin. "Thank you for your time," I said. I put the paper back into my satchel and turned to leave.

"But wait, sir. Don't you want to know about the other man?"

"What other man?"

"The other man who buys this paper through me. I place orders for two customers."

"Who is the other?"

"That priest over at the cathedral."

"Which priest? Father Dauer, the new one?"

"No, no sir. Not him. I heard he was murdered by that Turk who is loose on the streets." He shook his head. "What is happening to this city? When I came here, it was very safe. You could walk around at night. But now—"

"Which priest?" I asked, my voice loud with excitement.

"The scholar. I order thirty sheets a month for him. I have no idea where he gets the money to pay for it. It is expensive paper. Perhaps he has money from his family. I'm sure the archbishop doesn't buy it for him. If you ask me, sir, now there's a man who loves money more than God."

I frowned. "The scholar? Do you mean Alois Bayer, the old priest? He is dead."

"No. The younger intellectual. Krause, his name is. Father Maximilian Krause."

Thirty-one

"'In what excesses, oh gods! In what horrible, dreadful misdeeds is the wretch ensnarled!'"

Caterina Cavalieri stood on the stage of the theater, her back toward the seats. Mozart sat at the fortepiano at one side of the stage. Two violinists from the court orchestra sat at the other side. I had raised my brow at the presence of the other musicians, which was unusual for the first working through of a new scene. Mozart had merely gestured toward the man now seated beside me, and I had immediately understood. Salieri sat quietly, his attention focused on his former student and longtime mistress.

Cavalieri turned slowly toward the empty seats of the theater. "'Ah, no, it is not possible to delay the wrath of heaven, or its justice!'" She was the classic woman scorned come to life, angry at both the man who had rejected her and at herself for continuing to love him. She clenched her fist and thrust her hand toward the heavens. "'Already I feel the fatal lightning bolt that is aimed at his head!'" she cried. Her shoulders slumped and she closed her eyes as her voice lowered. "'I foresee the opening of the deadly abyss—'"

"Brava!" Salieri shouted.

"'Miserable Elvira!'" Cavalieri continued. She looked down at her dress, her expression conveying her character's disgust at her emotional weakness. "'What contrasting emotions are borne in your breast!'" The violinists interspersed sighing strings as the soprano clasped her hands as if in prayer. "'Why these sighs, why this anguish?'" she asked herself. The violins sighed again. Cavalieri sank to her knees and began the aria.

"'That ingrate betrayed me and left me unhappy, oh God,'" she sang. She clutched a velvet cloak around her. "'But betrayed and abandoned, still I have pity for him.'" Her trademark vocal fireworks began, as she trilled the words "still I have pity" again and again. "'When I feel my torment my heart favors vengeance, but when I see the danger he faces, my heart hesitates.

"'I still have pity for him,'" she sang, manipulating the syllables of the word "pity" for full dramatic effect. A few moments later, the scene came to an end. The rejected woman slumped on the stage, her emotions spent.

"Brava! Brava!" Salieri leapt to his feet. I joined Mozart and the musicians in applauding Cavalieri. I had to admit, Mozart had taken my simple words and, using his knowledge of the aging soprano's voice, written a masterpiece that showed both her talents and her character's feelings toward her former lover at their best.

Cavalieri curtsied. "Do you think I am ready?" she asked in a girlish voice.

"It was perfect," Salieri called up to her.

She turned to Mozart. "Wolfgang?"

"It was perfect, Caterina," Mozart replied. "You will stop the show at the premiere." He and the musicians gathered up their scores.

Cavalieri beamed as she climbed down the steps at the side of the stage. "That is, if we are all not dead before the premiere," she said as she joined me and Salieri. She grasped his arm. "These murders. I am so frightened." Her shoulders shook in the practiced shudder of a seasoned thespian.

"There is no need to be frightened," Salieri said. "All of the victims have been men. I'm sure you are perfectly safe in your lodgings."

She glared at him and pulled her hand away. "Yes. That is easy for you to say, Antonio, isn't it? I'm sure your wife is glad that you are home in bed with her when she hears a strange sound at the door. A butcher is on the loose, and I am left all alone!"

"*Cara,* you know what I mean," Salieri said. "If I feared for your safety for one moment, I would—" He took her hand.

She arched a brow. "You would hold your wife tighter, is that what you mean, Antonio?" She snatched her hand away. "Perhaps I should just pack up and go to Paris or London, where I would feel safer. Why, I could be on the coach for Paris tonight."

"Now, *cara,*" Salieri said. She glared at him.

I decided to intervene before Salieri said more and ruined our whole production. "Madame, there is nothing to fear," I said. "I've been helping the police with their inquiries, and I can assure you that the killer is not choosing victims at random. And as the music director said, he is only killing men. You are safe here in Vienna." Her face softened as I gave her a reassuring smile. "And the production needs you," I added. "It was a brilliant idea you had to add this scene for Elvira. You will steal the show next week."

She turned away from Salieri and put a hand on my arm. "If you believe so, Signor Poet, then I will stay. A woman just needs some reassurance, that is all." She tucked a stray curl behind her ear. I bowed to her and excused myself, leaving Salieri to his fate. As I approached Mozart, I saw her sweep down the aisle of the theater, the music director trotting after her like a lady's lapdog.

"She was good," Mozart said. "With that scene and the new burlesque scene, I think we've enough to please Viennese ears."

"The second act is a bit too long," I said. "Is there anything you think we can cut?"

He thought for a moment. "Benucci's aria, where he pleads for mercy from the rest of the cast. He can just sing a few lines instead."

"Shall I tell him?" I asked. I hated informing a singer that his role had been diminished.

"I'll do it," Mozart said. "He'll be fine with the change. He already has the catalog aria in the first act to show off his talents. And he is really the star of the burlesque scene, even though he spends most of it tied to a chair!"

We headed into the lobby. At the door, Mozart hesitated.

"Is what you told Cavalieri true, Lorenzo," he asked, "that you are helping the police?" I was relieved to see no judgment in my young friend's eyes.

"Yes," I said.

"Because of your friend Alois?" Mozart asked.

I nodded. "He was like a father to me," I said softly. "I don't like what the ministry has become, but I feel I must find Alois's killer. If I'm not involved, he'll be forgotten."

After Mozart departed, I headed downstairs to collect my cloak and satchel. As I started down the hallway to my office, I drew a sharp breath. My door stood ajar. I always take care to close it when I leave. I shook my head. I must have absently forgotten to close it in my hurry to meet Mozart, Cavalieri, and Salieri.

But as soon as I entered the room, I knew he had been there. An eerie sensation that I was in the presence of evil gripped me. I forced my eyes to look over to my desk. My papers had been shoved to the floor, leaving a clear surface for the single piece of folded paper that sat in the center. I swallowed hard, and then picked it up, unfolded it, and flattened it on the desk. The serpent glowered at me as I read the lines inked across the page. "Those who would not endure to the end with Anchises' son, who instead gave themselves up to a life without glory."

My hands were cold and damp as I folded the message and put it into my satchel. Once again, the killer had sent me a passage from *Purgatory* in which Dante and Virgil encounter the slothful. This time, Dante had referenced the *Aeneid*, Virgil's epic about the founding of Rome, reminding the sinners of the followers of Aeneas, who instead of choosing to continue the journey with the hero to the site of the new city, were content to remain in the comfort of Sicily. Virgil had called these men *animos nil magnae laudis egentes*— souls who needed no great fame.

I picked my papers off the floor and put them into my satchel, took my cloak, closed the door tightly behind me, and slowly climbed the stairs to the lobby.

Dusk was falling as I walked through the Michaelerplatz, passed the Spanish Riding School stables, and then cut down a short street to the Neuer Market. I continued down the Kärntnerstrasse and then turned into the Himmelpfortgasse. The street was deserted. Hennen's house was shuttered, dark and lonely. His housekeeper must have found a new position already, or had gone to stay with relatives.

I sighed. It seemed so long ago that Benda and I had been here, Benda so certain that the killings were politically motivated and eager to suspect Richter, the war protester. But Countess Stoll had vouched for Richter, and the protester had still been in Troger's prison cell when Father Dauer had been killed.

Casanova had noted the connections between the victims and Christiane Albrechts. I had laughed when he had suggested that Benda might be the killer. But it was odd that the count had left Vienna in the middle of the investigation. Perhaps I had been too hasty to dismiss him as a suspect. Could he have told Christiane that he was leaving, then stayed in the city to continue his crimes? Had he been motivated by extreme jealousy to kill any man close to his fiancée? I shook my head. He had been as surprised as I when Hennen's housekeeper revealed that the baron had been engaged to Christiane. And I just could not believe him to be capable of committing these brutal crimes.

The paper the killer was using to send his infernal messages had to be the key, I thought. The bookseller supplied it to just two men in the city. I was sure that Strasser was innocent. What motive could he possibly have to murder five men, and to come after me next? He barely knew any of the victims.

No, the killer must be Maximilian Krause. But I could not fathom his reasons for judging and sentencing his victims to death. I recalled my conversations with the gentle, friendly priest. Had he been born a monster, and murdered many times before, but never been caught? Or had something happened to him lately, some traumatic event, one that had injured his brain and led him to begin killing? Perhaps the devilish urges to commit murder had crept up on him slowly, changing his perspective on life in small increments, until the desire to murder had taken over his life.

If Krause was the killer, why had he chosen me as a victim? Why had he accused me of sloth? What was it that I had failed to do in my life that rose to the level of a sin in his estimation? He must know that I was helping the police with the investigation. Did he choose me as his next victim because he wished to be caught? Perhaps he was appalled at his actions, and, knowing that he could not control his murderous impulses, was begging me to stop him.

I turned into the street that ran parallel to the city walls, and walked in the direction of the Stuben gate. Ahead of me, several doors down the quiet street, a man exited a small apartment building. I stopped and gaped as he adjusted his cloak, donned a hat with a large plume, and sauntered down the narrow way toward the city gate.

I followed von Gerl as he suddenly turned left onto the Weihburggasse. He must have heard me behind him, because although he did not turn to look at me, he quickened his pace. I matched my pace to his.

Horses' hooves sounded behind me. "Watch out!" a voice called. I pressed myself against the side wall of the Franciscan Church and waited as a fancy carriage rushed by me and continued up the street. I looked ahead. Von Gerl had disappeared.

I ran into the small plaza that fronted the entrance portico to the Baroque church. Above me, Saint Jerome stood at the apex of the portico arch, his simple wide-brimmed hat and staff cast in gold, the devoted lion at his feet. Shouts and laughter came from a small tavern across the plaza. The candles in its windows were the sole lights in the square.

"Von Gerl! Where are you? It is me, Da Ponte!" I shouted. I peered down the Weihburggasse, but saw no one. I started down the Ballgasse, on my right. A moment later I saw him, a few yards ahead of me, about to turn into the Suninger-strasse. I ran after him.

"Von Gerl?" I grabbed his arm. "Is it you? How is it possible?" I pulled at him to turn him so I could see his face.

He grunted and yanked himself out of my grasp. The air went out of my chest as he pushed me, hard. I stumbled and fell to the ground, dropping my cloak and satchel. He wrapped his own cloak around his body and ran.

"Von Gerl, come back!" I shouted. "I mean you no harm!"

He turned to look at me, and as he did, he tripped over a loose stone in the street and fell flat on his face. The plumed hat tumbled off his head. I pulled myself up on all fours, then stood and ran to him. He scrambled to right himself. I lunged and grabbed him around the waist with both hands.

"Let me go!" he cried as he tried to pull away. I started as I recognized the voice. He clawed at my hands and writhed in my grasp. I let go of him and pushed him onto the ground. As he twisted his body to pull himself up, I kicked his leg. He howled with pain, sat up straight, and grabbed his shin.

"What did you do that for?" he cried. "You've hurt me!"

I looked down into his face. "How could I have hurt you?" I asked. "You are dead, are you not?"

He clamped his mouth shut.

It was von Gerl's manservant, Teuber.

Thirty-two

"Why are you wearing your master's clothes?" I demanded.

He cowered as I looked down at him. "Please, signore, please have mercy on me," he said. "I was just having some fun."

"Fun? These things don't belong to you. Get up!"

He struggled to his feet and pushed his hands out in front of him as if to ward off a blow. Did the idiot actually believe I was going to hit him? "Tell me what you were doing," I said.

"Well, signore, the ladies—one in particular, who lives in that house around the corner—I've found they respond better to my wooing if they believe I am Baron von Gerl, not his lowly manservant."

"You've been seducing noblewomen by claiming to be your dead master?"

"Oh, no, signore, not noblewomen—their maids." He glanced at me, a conspiratorial gleam in his eye. "I've been around my master long enough to pick up a few of his techniques with women. Those get me an audience with a lady's maid, and if I am particularly persuasive, perhaps a kiss or two. But when I tell them I am Baron von Gerl, they let me do anything I wish."

I shook my head in disgust.

"What are you going to do, signore? Turn me in to the police? Please take pity on me. I am a poor servant. My master left me with nothing. I meant no harm."

I paused for a moment, and then shook my head again. "No, I'm not going to report you to the police. They have too many other things to deal with besides a fraudulent manservant. No, I won't turn you in this time. But if I see you out here again, wearing those clothes and that hat, I will take you before Count Pergen himself and have you charged with impersonating a nobleman."

He made an exaggerated bow to me. "Thank you, signore, thank you," he said. "I promise, I will mend my ways."

"And you must move out of von Gerl's palace," I said. "Try to find a new master."

"I will, signore, I will." He backed away from me, bowing again. "There's a tavern back by the church. I'll stop in there right now and see if anyone is looking for a manservant. Thank you, signore, thank you."

"Go along, then," I said. He took a few steps back, scraping to me as though I were royalty, and then turned and ran.

Back at my lodgings, I ate a solitary cold supper in the cellar kitchen, and then climbed the stairs to my room. I lit a can-

dle and sat at my desk, idly turning the pages of my copy of
The Divine Comedy. A shiver ran down my back as I reached
the canto in *Purgatory* where the poet and Virgil meet the
slothful. I imagined Krause sitting at a small desk similar to
mine, reading these same words, but instead of seeing them
as instructions to mankind about how to live a good life and
achieve Paradise, interpreting them as messages he could
send to the people he had determined to judge. My stomach
churned as I thought about my impending confrontation
with him. I took a deep breath and tried to relax, but when
I closed my eyes, I pictured myself laid carefully at the foot
of one of the city's monuments, my head nearly severed from
my body, the dress shirt I had mended so many times soaked
with my own blood.

I jumped as a knock sounded at the door. "Who is there?"
I called.

"Lorenzo? It is Marta."

I closed the book, slipped it back onto my bookshelf,
took a deep breath, and went to the door. She stood as she
had the first time she had come to me, clad in a white dressing gown, her hair curled about her shoulders.

"Are you all right, Lorenzo?" she asked. "You look so
tired and pale."

A pang of longing stabbed me. I wanted to take her in
my arms, bury myself in her return embrace, and pour out
my fears to her. But I could not.

"May I come in?" she asked.

I nodded dumbly and motioned her toward the bed. I
came and sat next to her. The scent of her perfume tortured
my nose.

"I wanted to apologize for my words this morning," she said. "I was not fair to you."

"There is no need for you to apologize," I said. "You have lost someone you loved. I understand that."

She looked into my eyes. "I must be honest with you," she said. "I don't know if I am able to give you the love you deserve."

She took my hand.

"But you have been kind to me, and I've enjoyed our times together." She blushed. "Perhaps I have been too quick to succumb to my emotions in the past," she continued. "I met Valentin and fell in love with him rapidly, without thinking about the consequences. A man like you might be what I need to make me happy. May we start over, Lorenzo?"

I took my hand away, rose, and went over to lock the door. When I returned to the bed, she stood. I took her in my arms. "I love you," I murmured as I buried my lips in her soft hair. She pulled me down to the bed. Our lovemaking was impassioned and unbridled, as if we both were seeking a release from our separate disquietudes: she seeking to banish her memories of von Gerl; I thirsting for the moments of sheer pleasure that would supplant my fear of the ordeal ahead of me.

When it was over, she fell asleep in my arms. I lay awake in the narrow bed, staring first at shadows the dying candle cast on the ceiling of the room, then at the flickering tallow itself, trying to quiet the Dante passages that echoed through my brain, wondering what the next day would bring.

. . .

When I woke the next morning, Marta was gone. I hurriedly washed and dressed, took my cloak and satchel, and went to Pergen's office, where I demanded to see Troger. After a wait of half an hour, I was ushered into his office. He looked up from a pile of papers on his desk as I entered.

"What is so important, Da Ponte?" he asked. "Have you found the killer?"

"I believe I know who he is," I said. "And he is after me."

He raised a brow and gestured for me to sit. "What are you talking about? Who is it?"

I pulled the messages from my satchel and laid them on Troger's desk. "The killer sent similar messages to the general, to Alois Bayer, to Hennen, and to Father Dauer," I explained. "These are quotations from Dante's *Purgatory*. The killer accused each victim of one of the seven deadly sins, lured him to a confrontation, and then passed judgment on the poor soul by cutting his throat."

Troger pulled the sheets toward him and studied them.

"You see the watermark on the page?" I asked. "All of the notes I've found were written on the same type of paper. The watermark is rare. I've traced it to a small shop behind the cathedral. The proprietor told me he orders it from Buda for two people in Vienna." I related my interview with Erich Strasser, leaving out the details of his blood disease. "The other purchaser is Maximilian Krause, a priest at the cathedral. I believe he's our killer."

Troger dropped the sheets on his desk and leaned back. "What is the sin he's accused you of, Signor Poet?" he asked, smirking. "Excessive imagination?"

"You don't believe me? Look at those notes! I am Krause's next victim! You must arrest him immediately!"

"I see the notes," he said slowly. "But I'm not convinced that they are linked to the murders. You have no evidence that the killer sent them. For all you know, someone might be playing a joke, and it might be coincidence that four of the five dead men received these messages."

I opened my mouth to speak, but he held up his hand to stop me. "And even if the messages are from the killer, it is a leap to believe that Father Krause is the murderer."

"But I told you, the paper is sold only in one shop in the city, and is ordered for just two customers," I said, my voice shaking with anger.

"Yes, that may be true, but the murderer could be any number of people—your friend Strasser, or someone who works with him at the Oriental Academy, or someone who knows Father Krause. He could even be the bookseller, or someone who stole the paper from the bookshop."

"I'm convinced it is the priest," I snapped. "The person writing these notes is well-read and educated, like Krause." I clenched my teeth. How could I convince this dolt to listen to me?

Troger shook his head. "You need to bring me more proof before I can lock up Krause," he said.

"What more proof can I give you? My dead body? I tell you, I am the next victim!"

His lip curled as he gazed at me.

"I'm tired of dealing with you, Troger," I shouted. "Let me talk to Pergen, right now! He'll agree with me, I am sure. You must arrest Krause."

Troger smiled. "I'm afraid I cannot do that, Signor Poet. The count is upstairs in Prince Kaunitz's office. The troubles in the Netherlands have reached a crisis point. He's left me in charge of this case. So you'll have to do more to convince me."

I slumped in my seat. "I don't know what else I can do," I said.

He gave a tight, sardonic smile. "Let us play out your theory, signore. You say that these notes are from the killer? He accuses you of one of the deadly sins? Which one?"

"Sloth," I said. "Wasting my energies on meaningless activities."

Troger raised a brow. "So our man is not an opera fan, then?" He laughed aloud at his joke.

I glared at him.

"He sends each victim two notes, you believe?"

I nodded. "Yes. But Benda and I have learned that the general and Baron Hennen also received a third note, which arrived right before their murders. Each man left his house late at night, to keep an appointment. The others must have received similar messages. We just weren't able to find witnesses."

Troger sat silently, staring at the messages on his desk.

"So according to your theory, you should be getting a third message sometime soon?"

I nodded. "Yes, the timeline I've been able to work out with the others suggests that it could come at any moment."

Troger turned his head and stared out the window. My heart sank as I realized what he must be thinking. He turned back to me.

"If your theory is correct, our course of action is clear," he said.

"No—"

"If you are indeed summoned to an appointment, you must keep it," he said.

"Oh, no," I said, shaking my head vehemently. "I won't be your bait again, Troger. I barely survived the last time you and Pergen used me as a pawn."

Troger smiled again. "But you must, Da Ponte," he said softly. "Don't you see? The killer has chosen you. If you fail to keep the appointment, it is unlikely he will move on to someone else. He has accused you, and he will judge you. You cannot escape him. At least if you answer his summons, we can have men there to catch him. Do you want to spend the rest of your days on earth looking over your shoulder, never knowing when you will feel his dagger at your neck?"

My heart sank. What Troger said made sense. I could not avoid an encounter with the killer. Perhaps I had been on a journey toward our meeting from the first moment I determined to seek justice for Alois's death.

Troger tried to smile at me, but managed only a grimace. "This is our chance to catch him in the act, Da Ponte," he said. "You'll be doing the emperor a great service, and you'll avenge the death of your friend."

I nodded dumbly.

"Notify me as soon as you receive the next message," he instructed. "I'll send men to the meeting place. They are well trained. The killer will never know they are there waiting for him. And just in case you are correct and it is indeed Krause, I'll assign a man to follow him."

. . .

I stumbled down the stairs to the Hofburg courtyard, my stomach churning with worry. I could not bear the thought that my life was in the hands of that churl Troger, who had always treated me with contempt and scorn. Could I trust him to protect me? I stopped in the lobby of the building and took a deep breath, trying to calm myself. Troger might have little respect for me, I assured myself, but in the end he was responsible for my safety. Count Pergen had promised that I would come to no harm. If anything happened to me, Troger would answer to Pergen for it, and perhaps even the emperor. I could only hope that I would still be alive to witness his punishment.

The sun shone brightly in the courtyard, which was full of soldiers and bureaucrats milling about. As I started toward the main gate, which would take me to the theater and the solace of work, a blur of dark green appeared at the corner of my eye. I glanced over to the other side of the yard. The young dark-haired man who had been following me lounged against the wall, staring at me with mocking eyes.

I pulled my cloak tightly around me to melt the ice that ran down my spine, and hurried as fast as I could to the theater door.

I was relieved to see no third message waiting on my desk when I entered my office. I shed my cloak, hung it in the cupboard, and sat down. I pulled a libretto from my editing pile and took out the first page, hoping that work would calm my jangling nerves. But try as I might, the words swam before my eyes, and after a half hour of effort I gave up, gathered up the pages, tied them together, and returned them to the pile. I laid my head down on the desk and closed my eyes.

"Lorenzo!" Casanova's voice boomed at my door.

I lifted my head. "Come in, Giacomo," I said.

"Were you sleeping?" he asked as he entered.

"Just thinking," I said.

"What is happening?" He peered at me. "What is it, my friend? Your face is ashen. Are you ill?"

"No," I whispered. "It's the killer. He's coming for me, Giacomo. I am to be his next victim."

"What! What are you talking about? Have you received the Dante passages?"

I nodded. "Yes, two of them."

"Were they on the same paper, with that watermark?"

"Yes, they were the same. They are from him, I am sure. He's accused me of sloth."

"We must find the distributor of that paper," Casanova exclaimed. "It's our only hope of catching him."

"I've found the source of the paper," I said. I explained about Sophie's suspicions of Strasser, and my finding the paper in his room, then told him about my visit to the Hungarian bookshop.

"Krause! I don't think I've ever met him. A priest, committing these crimes!" He shook his head.

"He is a quiet man, a scholar, very friendly. If you met him, you would never believe he harbored such evil urges in his heart."

"What will you do next?"

"I've just been to see Troger. I'm to act as bait for a trap. When the third message comes, telling me the place of assignation, I am to alert Troger. He'll send men to wait there. They'll catch the killer before he harms me."

We sat silently for a moment.

"You don't seem too confident of that," Casanova said softly.

"Chances are I'm just letting my imagination run wild," I said. "But nothing in my dealings with Troger has led me to believe I can trust him with my life."

"Don't go," Casanova said.

"I must. If I fail to answer his summons, the murderer won't let me go. He'll come after me."

"Let me help you, then. I have a pistol. Let me go with you to the meeting place. I'll shoot him as soon as he appears."

I smiled at my friend's earnestness. "He will likely hide himself until I come, to make sure I am alone," I said.

"Then I will go beforehand, and stay hidden in the shadows. When he accosts you, I'll be there, listening. When he attacks you, I'll reveal myself and shoot him."

"Are you a good shot?" I asked.

"I've used my pistol many times to extract myself from unsavory circumstances," Casanova said. "And as you say, the police will also be there. If I shoot and miss, at least I'll startle him enough to stop him from harming you. Troger's men can take it from there."

I had to admit Casanova's plan reassured me. If Troger let me down, at least I would have a chance against the killer. "All right," I said. "Thank you, Giacomo."

"Signor Da Ponte?" The theater porter stuck his head in the open door. "A message was just delivered for you."

My stomach lurched. My hands began to shake.

Casanova took the small packet, and then closed the door behind the porter. He looked down at the message and then at me. "Shall I open it?" he asked.

"Yes." My voice was a croak.

He broke the seal on the missive, unfolded the page, and read it aloud. "Da Ponte, you seek me, so find me. Tonight at one, in the Neuer Market, by the fountain. Bring this message with you."

I buried my face in my hands. Casanova came around the desk and put a hand on my shoulder. "It will be all right, my friend," he said. "I promise I won't let anything happen to you."

I raised my head. "I must send a message to Troger," I said.

"Tell me what to say. I'll write it for you, and send a boy to bring it to him," Casanova said.

I quickly dictated the details of the killer's summons. Casanova wrote it all down, and then presented it for my signature. My hands still shook as I signed my name.

"I'll deliver this myself, on my way out," he said. He squeezed my shoulder. "Do not worry, Lorenzo. I will be at the Neuer Market by a quarter to one. Troger's men will be there. You will be protected."

I stood and embraced him.

After he left, I closed the door, sat back in my chair, and stared at the killer's missive. Despite Troger's arguments to the contrary, I was convinced that Krause had murdered the five victims. I struggled to remember my most recent encounters with the engaging priest. Had he said anything to me that was a harbinger of his indictment of me for the deadly sin of sloth? I could think of nothing. I had been a bystander that day in the cathedral as he and Alois had engaged in friendly banter about church philosophy, and I remembered nothing from Alois's memorial service that indicated that Krause had judged me and found me wanting. Something niggled at the back of my mind. *What about when—no, but—*

There was a knock. I opened the door to a young boy, who handed me a message with the Ministry of Police's seal. I dug in my pocket, gave a coin to the boy, returned to my desk, and tore open the message. Troger reported that he would station men in the Neuer Market before one tonight, and that he had assigned two men to trail Maximilian Krause. I slumped in my chair in relief. As long as Krause adhered to his usual practice and accosted me at the designated time and place, I would be safe. If he deviated from his evil ritual, however, only God could help me.

Thirty-three

I left my lodgings a little past midnight, taking a small lantern I had borrowed from my landlady to light my way through the dark city. I walked slowly across the bridge that spanned the Vienna River, crossed the deserted pathway that ringed the city, and made my way onto the bridge that crossed the *glacis*. Everything was silent; my own footsteps were all I could hear. In front of me, no lights rose from inside the walls of the slumbering city. The Stuben gate had been closed hours before, its great wooden doors protecting the citizens of the capital from enemies without the walls, but not from the terrors that concealed themselves within the bastions.

When I rang the bell to gain entry, the sound echoed around the gate. I waited a few minutes, but no guard came to answer. I frowned. I did not usually go about late at night, but everyone in Vienna knew that a full complement of guards were stationed at each gate to the city throughout the night. I rang the bell again and waited. Again there was no answer. My mind began to entertain possibilities. If I were unable to enter the city and meet Krause at the appointed hour, perhaps Troger's men would arrest him and he would confess everything, saving me from the confrontation. I should just turn around and return to my lodgings, and wait until I received word from Troger that the killer had been caught.

I had just convinced myself to go home when the wooden doors creaked open and a guard looked out.

"Who's there?" the guard called. "You there, what do you want? It is past curfew. No one may be admitted to the city."

"I am Lorenzo Da Ponte," I said. "The theater poet. I am on an important errand for the minister of police, Count Pergen."

"Stay there, sir," he said. "Let me see if your name is on the list." He retreated into the gatehouse and closed the doors.

I considered an alternative scenario should I not arrive at Krause's meeting place on time. What if the deranged priest hid himself, and when I did not arrive by one, watched as the police came out from the shadows? Would he be so angered that he came to my lodgings to butcher me?

The wooden doors scraped open once more and the guard beckoned to me. "Come in, sir," he said. "There is a message here from Inspector Troger of the ministry telling us to allow you passage."

I walked through the doors.

"You are lucky I wasn't making rounds along the bastions, sir," the guard said. "I'm alone here tonight."

"I don't understand," I said. "I was under the impression that there were several guards at each gate at this hour."

"That's right, sir," he said. "There were four of us here when curfew began. But just an hour ago the others were summoned into the city. Apparently there is some disturbance going on near the Am Hof. Someone reported a break-in at the basement of the fire station where some of the smaller arms destined for the troops are stored. The constable who came by told us that it might be some Turkish sympathizers trying to steal the weapons. The constabulary was trying to get enough men to search the city between the Am Hof and the canal."

I nodded.

"Go about your business for the minister, sir," the man said. "But be careful if you are headed in that direction."

"I'm going to the Neuer Market," I said.

"Then you should have no trouble, sir. As far as I know, that area is quiet tonight."

He bade me good night. I drew my cloak around me and walked into the dark city.

Thirty-four

I turned down the Suningerstrasse, straining to hear any noise behind me, but all was quiet. I passed the spot where I had tussled with Teuber. A few steps later I was at the corner of the Grünangergasse, where Krause had bought the paper on which he wrote his sinister messages. My heart pounded as I walked by the Church of the Teutonic Order. My destination was a few blocks away. I wondered if Casanova had already arrived and secreted himself in the shadows.

The Stephansdom loomed on my right as I skirted the edge of the Stephansplatz and turned down the Kärntnerstrasse. The broad market street was empty, the vendors' carts shuttered, the shops bolted against the evils of the night. My knees shook as I made my way down the street, my ears straining to hear if anyone else was about. Perhaps Krause was nearby, on his way to our assignation from the cathedral. He could be standing in any of the dark entryways, watching me go by. I shook my head. No, that was nonsense. Urbanek had told me that Krause lived in the Judenplatz. He would be approaching the Neuer Market from the opposite direction.

I walked two blocks down the street. As I was about to turn right into the side street that led into the Neuer Market, my ears perked. Were those footsteps sounding behind me? A stab of fear shot through me. Was it Krause? Did he guess that he was walking into a trap? Had he decided to confront me here? I quickened my pace, hurrying toward the Neuer Market, where Troger's men and Casanova waited to protect me. The footsteps sounded behind me again, louder this time, my pursuer picking up his pace to match mine. I reached the entrance to the Neuer Market. Stopping to catch my breath, I strained to hear any sound behind me. Everything was quiet. I took a deep breath to calm myself. Just as I turned into the market square, the candle in my lantern went dark.

The marketplace was lit by a sliver of moon. Vendors' carts lay scattered along the long expanse, empty and abandoned. Directly opposite me, at the other end of the plaza, Prince Schwarzenberg's city palace sat dark. The windows of the smaller palaces that lined the plaza stared blindly down at me. The buildings were unoccupied, their owners having decamped to their country estates either to stamp out uprisings like Benda, or to situate themselves in a place of safety should the emperor's military mission fail and the Turks descend upon Vienna. The Mehlgrube was closed up, its dwindling crowd of patrons having left for home hours before. Across from it, the Capuchin Church was closed and still. Between the two buildings stood the fountain where Krause had instructed me to await him.

I walked down to the other end of the marketplace, staying at the center of the plaza, so as to avoid any sudden grabbing of my cloak by the killer lurking in an entryway to a building. My eyes darted back and forth, peering through the gloom for a sign of Troger's men or Casanova, but they were well hidden, for I saw nothing.

My legs were shaking violently by the time I reached the fountain. I climbed the short set of steps that surrounded the basin and looked around me. What was that movement, there, under the portico of the Mehlgrube? A cloak moving? I squinted into the dark, but saw no other motion.

The large basin had been drained before winter and had not yet been refilled. Patches of mud and damp leaves were strewn over its stone interior. I sat on the edge and waited. It was too dark to examine my watch, but I was certain that it was near one o'clock. I took a deep breath, trying to dampen my fear so that I would be prepared for Krause when he arrived. I sat in the silence, occasionally peering at the tenebrous buildings around me.

I sat there for what seemed ten or more minutes. Nothing stirred. I shivered and pulled my cloak around me. Where was Krause? Had he noticed Troger's men following him, and decided to postpone my day of judgment? Or had the police already arrested him? I wanted to call to Casanova, but did not want to reveal his whereabouts should Krause be lurking somewhere nearby.

A rustling noise, like a cloak brushing past a wall, came

from beneath the wide portico of the Mehlgrube. I leapt to my feet. I had had enough of waiting. I started down the steps of the fountain.

"Krause!" I shouted. "Are you there?"

There was no reply. I squinted to see into the portico, but no one was standing in the shadows, as far as I could tell.

"Krause!" I tried to keep my voice from wavering. "Damn you! Where are you?"

All at once, a heavy weight girded my neck. My body was jerked backward. A hissing noise filled my ears. "He's probably at home, snug in his bed," a familiar voice said.

Thirty-five

I reached up and struggled to pull my captor's hands from my neck. He released me and shoved me forward. I stumbled on a step and fell prostrate on the hard stone, my chin hitting a sharp edge. I curled my body and rolled over. I looked up into the sneering face of Felix Urbanek. In his right hand was a small dagger.

I drew in a sharp breath. "You!"

He knelt beside me.

"Yes, I had you fooled, didn't I, Da Ponte? You think you are so smart, with your education and your poetry. You fell right into my little traps."

He held the dagger a few inches in front of my neck.

"After I killed Dauer, I told you Krause and Dauer were competitors, and you immediately suspected him." He laughed. "I thought it was a nice touch, killing Dauer over in the Hoher Market, near Krause's lodgings."

My stomach clenched as he moved the dagger closer. A salty liquid filled my mouth.

"And the paper," Urbanek said. "Krause was so fond of that paper, with that silly serpent and crown. He never locked his office. It was so easy for me to steal a few sheets as I needed them."

I stiffened as the cold steel touched my neck. "Why did you kill Dauer?" I hoped that if I kept him talking, Troger's men would have all the evidence they would need.

Urbanek's eyes widened. "Why, to protect the mother church, of course. She is no longer pure. There are sinners everywhere, even within her holy walls." His lip curled. "Dauer—he called himself a priest, but he came to the cathedral to chase after money and glory. He did nothing to succor the poor souls who came to us for care and guidance."

His laugh sent ice down my spine.

"I sent him a message, saying I was a wealthy noble who wished to make a donation to the church coffers. I told him that I wished to remain anonymous, but that I would see that he received credit from the archbishop for bringing in the money." He chuckled. "He came to the Hoher Market eagerly that night.

"And the general—always so proud of his war record and his glory. He attended church only when he was being honored in some way. He never came to honor God."

The sharp edge of the dagger grazed my neck. I bit my lip to avoid crying out as tears filled my eyes.

"I sent him a note telling him that I was an old soldier who had fought under him, and that I was about to reveal his cowardice on the battlefield to the world," Urbanek continued. "Of course, I knew of no such incident, but I knew he would come to me anyway, to prevent me from besmirching his name."

I struggled to pull my head away from the dagger. "Hennen—what had he done to offend you?"

"To offend me? No, no, Da Ponte. You misunderstand me. I did not kill these men because they offended me. I killed them because they had offended God and His church. Hennen? His envy for the whole, healthy bodies of others consumed him. All he wanted was the use of his legs back, so he could go off to war. But he didn't understand that his injury was God's will. How many times did I reach out to him, to bring him into the church, so that he could receive solace? He rejected me every time. He preferred to wallow in his envy."

He stared down at me and moved the dagger closer to my neck. My bladder began to fail me as he lightly swayed the blade against my skin.

"Hennen came willingly to me the night I killed him. I had mentioned in the note I sent that I possessed an elixir that cured lameness. The fool believed me."

"But what about Alois?" I rasped. "He loved the church. He was one of the pure."

Urbanek's froglike eyes gleamed above me. "No, he was not. Why, you heard it yourself, Da Ponte. I asked him to chair a committee for me, for war orphans. He told me he was too busy with his research. He was a glutton with those books of his. He preferred the delights of his study above the church's needs. So I used his sin against him. I sent him a message, telling him I was a visitor to the city, and that I had heard he bought rare religious treatises. He came running over to the chancel that night, to see what I had for him."

I clenched my teeth. I wanted to grab Urbanek's neck, but feared that if I moved, he would slice my neck open. Where were Troger's men? Surely they had heard enough by now. I looked up into Urbanek's deranged eyes. "And von Gerl? What did he do to the church that angered you enough to kill him?"

Urbanek squinted at me. "Who?"

"Valentin von Gerl, the nobleman."

Urbanek frowned. His grasp on the dagger loosened. I pulled my neck back.

"You killed him at the general's summer home, the Belvedere," I said, raising my voice so that the police could hear me. "You carved the *peccatum* into his forehead, as you did with the others."

Urbanek stared at me for a moment. He threw down the dagger and put his hands under my arms, jerking me upward. His strength seemed inhuman. "No! You are trying to distract me!" He shoved me hard against the basin of the fountain.

I groaned as my back hit the stone. I thrust my arms out to push him, but I was too late. He bent me over the edge of the basin and pressed the blade to my neck. A sharp stinging pain shot down my chest. I closed my eyes, waiting for the death blow.

Thirty-six

"I gave the others an opportunity to repent their sin," Urbanek hissed loudly in my ear. "Now it is your turn, Da Ponte. Do you admit you have committed the sin of sloth?"

Pain shot through my back as he pressed me backward across the lip of the basin. The dagger blade remained at my neck. Cold surged through my body.

"I don't understand the charge. What have I done?"

"You have wasted your life, Da Ponte, on unimportant matters. You were ordained a priest, yet you chose to reject the church and fritter away your talents on that ungodly theater."

"You would kill me for that?" I cried. "Who appointed you the judge of your fellow man?"

He drew close to me and pressed the blade into my neck. I winced, willing myself not to give him the satisfaction of hearing me cry out in pain. "God has called me. He is angry about the way you have treated His church. He has instructed me to convince you to repent."

My mind was racing. Where were Troger's men? And where was Casanova? I struggled to lift my head. "Giacomo!" I shouted as loudly as I could.

Urbanek started for just a moment and then tightened his grip on me. He laughed in my ear. "That old libertine cannot help you now."

Tears filled my eyes. The fiend had discovered my friend and had already killed him. Troger's men were not going to help me. I was experiencing my last moments on this earth. I allowed myself to go limp in Urbanek's grasp. Pain shot through my back. My legs felt like lead stumps.

"You've heard the charge, Da Ponte," he murmured in my ear. "Do you repent?"

I closed my eyes.

He shook me. "Answer me!" he shouted. "Do you repent?"

I said nothing.

Urbanek grunted in frustration. I felt the dagger leave my neck. I opened my eyes to see him pulling back his arm, readying to administer the deadly slash. Anger surged through me. As a roaring sounded in my ears, I bent my right leg and thrust my knee into Urbanek's groin as hard as I could.

He screamed and doubled over in pain. The dagger clattered to the ground. I rolled out from under him. The dagger was a foot in front of me, on the fountain step. My body throbbed with pain as I grabbed it and used my other hand to pull myself up on the edge of the basin. Urbanek righted himself and lunged for the dagger. I pulled my hand back just in time, but the weapon fell into the empty basin.

I pushed at Urbanek. He grabbed my arm and pulled me. I howled with rage as I twisted away from him and rolled into the basin. I groped for the dagger. He climbed onto the edge and jumped on top of me. We rolled around in the damp, each of us trying to grab the other's neck.

"Repent!" he screamed as he grabbed me and thrust himself on top of me. His hands went around my neck. I grappled to pull them off, but his grasp seemed almost superhuman. I pulled my arm up and poked him in the eye with my finger. He screamed again. I pushed him off me. As he rolled to the side, I pulled myself on top of him, grabbed his neck with both hands, and pressed as hard as I could.

He flailed underneath me. "Do you surrender?" I cried.

He grunted.

"Surrender!" I pressed my hands harder.

Then a shot rang out behind me.

Thirty-seven

"Giacomo! Thank God you're here!"

"Give up, Urbanek!" a strange voice called. "Signor Poet, I have him covered. You can let go."

I turned my head in the direction of the voice. "Giacomo? Where are you?"

Another shot rang out. Urbanek pushed me off him, thrusting me against the basin wall. My head banged into a jutting stone. He groped for the dagger, grabbed it, climbed out the opposite end of the basin, and ran in the direction of the Capuchin Church.

"Are you injured, Signor Poet?" I looked up to see the young man in the green cloak leaning over me. I frowned. Where was Casanova?

"Get him! He'll escape!" I cried.

Green Cloak ran after Urbanek. I pulled myself up, climbed out of the basin, and hobbled after him. My legs felt like aspic. Green Cloak passed the entrance to the church and turned the corner.

When I arrived at the far side of the old building, I found Green Cloak standing by a large wooden door, which stood ajar. He gestured for me to join him.

"He's gone down there, into the crypt," he whispered, pointing to a stairway that was shrouded in darkness. I shuddered. The wooden door groaned as Green Cloak pulled it open and gestured for me to follow him down the stairs. "Keep quiet," he whispered. "Stay right behind me." I nodded. We plunged into the darkness, Green Cloak feeling his way down the stairs, I keeping close behind him. When we finally reached flat ground, Green Cloak fumbled for the handle of another door. The hinges creaked loudly as he pulled the door open and we entered the crypt.

A lonely torch burned in a sconce inside the door. Green Cloak took it down. "Are you all right, signore?" he asked under his breath.

"Yes," I whispered. "But who are you? Why are you here?"

He placed a finger on his lips. "Later," he said.

We stood silently in the torchlight. The low space was filled with the tombs of the Habsburg family. I could just make out the nearest sarcophagi, which were large bronze monuments. I strained to hear an indication that Urbanek was here in the crypt. The scurrying of tiny feet came from somewhere ahead of us.

"Just rats," Green Cloak said. "Stay behind me, signore." He waved the torch in a broad arc. To our left, marble nymphs sat weeping at the base of a large monument, which was faintly lit by moonlight pouring in a window behind it.

"The old empress's tomb," Green Cloak whispered. A faint humming sound came from our right. Green Cloak swung the torch in that direction. "Follow me, signore," he murmured.

To my left, just beyond the circle of light, I saw several more large tombs. I followed Green Cloak for a few steps, past a large monument on my right. The humming sound grew louder.

I gulped for breath as I followed Green Cloak, keeping my eyes on the ground so I would not trip over any of the old stones that lined the floor of the crypt. As we passed a large monument, I looked up, and came face-to-face with the head of a skeleton wearing a jeweled, golden crown. He grinned at me, his bronze mouth frozen in a rictus of death. I stifled a cry.

We passed into a larger room of the crypt. In the flickering of the torchlight, I made out over a dozen sarcophagi, many of them small. Ahead of us, off to the right, a voice began to chant.

"'Oh, queen! Why in your anger did you choose to end your life?'"

"Urbanek!" Green Cloak called. "Come out. Surrender yourself!"

The chanting stopped. All was silent, except for the scrabbling noise of the rats. Green Cloak inched forward, motioning me to follow.

"'A figure, crucified—his face stained with disdain and fury as he died!'" Urbanek cried.

"Do you understand what he is saying?" Green Cloak asked me in a low voice.

"It's from Dante," I whispered. "It's about the sin of wrath." We moved down the line of coffins. The torch illuminated a narrow doorway a few feet ahead of us on the right.

"'Below him the great Ahasuerus, and Esther!'" the deranged priest shouted from inside the doorway.

Green Cloak gestured for me to wait, and then inched over to the door. He held the torch up and peered inside. He turned to me and motioned me over.

An eerie sensation gripped me as I walked toward him. The doorway led to a tiny room, only large enough to hold two ancient caskets side by side. They bore small bronze carvings of lions' heads, and sat on legs shaped to resemble the legs of that noble beast. Urbanek had wedged himself into the narrow area between the rightmost casket and the wall. He was hunched in the corner, holding the dagger to his own throat. His wild eyes looked at us.

"Repent!" he shrieked. "Change your life!"

"Urbanek, come out!" Green Cloak called.

The priest did not answer him. He seemed in his own world, holding a court where he was both judge and the judged. "The ultimate hour is here!" he cried. He pushed the dagger closer to his throat. "No!" he screamed.

"Urbanek, drop the dagger," Green Cloak said.

"Repent!" the priest screamed again.

His face was white in the torchlight. "Who tears at my spirit? Who roils my bowels?" he said softly.

My stomach heaved as I watched him. I willed myself to look away, but I could not.

"Come, there is a worse fate for you," he said. He pulled the dagger away from his throat. Green Cloak exhaled loudly.

"The terrors of the inferno," Urbanek said in a loud whisper. He raised his head and stared directly at me. My legs shook violently. The priest raised the dagger, screamed, and drew the blade across his neck in one rapid motion.

A gurgling noise filled the small room. Stars danced before my eyes.

"Christ!" Green Cloak shouted.

My legs melted beneath me, and I fell into darkness.

Thirty-eight

I opened my eyes to bright light and a familiar voice.

"Ah, there you are, Lorenzo." Casanova leaned over me. "I was worried about you. You've stirred a few times over the past hours, but then fell back to sleep."

"Where am I?" I asked. My voice was hoarse, my throat tight and dry.

"In the Hofburg," Casanova said. "You are safe. Urbanek is dead."

I reached up to find bandages around my throat.

"Your wounds will heal in a few weeks, the surgeon said." Green Cloak moved into my range of vision. "You were very brave, Signor Poet."

"Who are you?" I rasped.

He gave a small bow. "Thomas Zack, signore. Special agent to Count Pergen."

I frowned. "I don't understand."

"I work on special security matters for the count, signore. Apparently the emperor was very angry that you had been placed in danger during your investigation of the murders at the Palais Gabler. So as soon as you agreed to investigate this case, the count assigned me to follow you."

"But when I accosted you in the street—why didn't you tell me who you were?"

"My instructions were to let you go about your business. Also, I could not be everywhere, at all times. I wanted you to believe that you were being menaced, so you would remain alert."

I mulled this over for a moment. "I am grateful to you," I told Zack. "You saved my life."

He smiled. "I wouldn't say that, signore. You seemed to be defending yourself well before I intervened. I shot my pistol because I thought you were going to kill Urbanek."

I looked over at Casanova. "What happened to you, Giacomo?"

"I arrived at the Neuer Market early, as we had arranged. The fiend must have already been there, waiting. He sneaked up behind me and hit me on the head. I came to when I heard you and Urbanek fighting. I was trussed up like a roasted pigeon, but after a few moments, I escaped my binds." He glanced over at Zack. "I saw you and Urbanek rolling around inside the fountain. I was about to come to your aid when this fellow showed up and shot his pistol."

Zack winked at me. "Yes, that's how I remember it."

"Where were Troger's men?" I asked.

"There was an incident in the Am Hof earlier in the evening. There were reports that someone, possibly Turkish spies, tried to break into the armory. Men were called from every service to search the northwest part of the city. It was a waste of time and men—some overly imaginative residents in the Am Hof saw some workmen and raised a false alarm. Troger sent his men out there, and kept one back to follow Father Krause."

"He assumed you would be at the Neuer Market to protect me," I murmured.

"Yes, he thought that between me and the man following Krause, we could subdue and capture him."

A knock sounded at the door. Zack went to answer it.

I looked at Casanova. "Urbanek! I just don't understand. I never suspected him. How could his mind have become so twisted?"

Casanova patted my hand. "He was a madman, Lorenzo. There was nothing you could have done differently."

Zack returned to us, a message in his hands. "I've been called to a meeting. I must leave you now. Please stay and rest as long as you like, Signor Poet. If you would like something to eat or drink, simply ring the bell."

I shook his hand. "Thank you."

"We will meet again soon, signore, I am sure," he said.

After Zack left, I lay back on the pillows.

"Would you like to eat, Lorenzo?" Casanova asked.

"What time is it?"

"Past two."

"I've been sleeping for twelve hours?"

"Yes. You woke a few times, but after a few minutes went back to sleep. You must be hungry now."

"No, I have no appetite. But if you want something, ring the bell," I told him.

I lay quietly, straining to recall everything Urbanek had told me about his crimes. Some question floated at the back of my brain. What had he said? I sighed. I was too tired and dazed to think of it.

I leaned back and closed my eyes, trying to slow down the thoughts that tumbled through my mind. Then it came to me. I sat up straight. "Giacomo! Where are my clothes?"

Casanova jumped. "What is it, Lorenzo?"

"My clothes. Give them to me. We must go to my office, right now!"

I dressed quickly and the two of us found our way out of the Hofburg. We hurried into the Michaelerplatz.

"What is it, Lorenzo?" Casanova asked.

"Von Gerl. While you were unconscious, Urbanek explained to me how and why he killed each victim. He gloated about the messages he used to lure them to their deaths. But when I asked about von Gerl, he reacted strangely. It was as though he didn't know who I was talking about. He grew enraged and attacked me."

I opened the front door of the theater.

"I believed I just couldn't find the Dante passages because von Gerl had hidden them somewhere in his vast collections," I murmured. "But maybe there never were any."

"What are you saying?" Casanova followed me down the stairs. "That Urbanek did not kill von Gerl?"

"Yes." We entered my office.

"But you told me his forehead was carved, like some of the others," Casanova said.

"They were, but they were different, deeper," I said. "I noticed that, but Benda said it was likely that the killer was just becoming more frenzied."

I crossed over to my bookshelf and took down the small leather pouch the constable had given me at the Belvedere.

"But who else could have killed him?" Casanova asked.

I brought the bag over to my desk and sat down. "I don't know. Perhaps someone with a personal grudge against von Gerl, who took the opportunity to kill him and make it look like Urbanek's handiwork." I recalled Teuber's mumbled threat against his master, and Stefan standing in the shadows watching Sophie ride off in the baron's carriage. I dumped the contents of the bag on the desk. "Maybe there is something here that will give us a clue."

Casanova pulled the other chair opposite me and sat. I sifted through the various ribbons, feathers, pieces of broken glass and pipe stems, shoe buckles, and jewelry. Out of the corner of my eye, I saw Casanova pick an object from the pile.

"There's nothing here that will tell us who murdered von Gerl," I said, slapping my hand against the desk in frustration.

Casanova was staring at me.

"What is it?" I asked.

He opened his large hand to show an earring.

I gestured toward the pile. "There are other pieces of jewelry in there," I said. "Benda told me the general gave a large party at the end of the season. Wooing couples found their way into the *bosquets*. Some of the ladies lost their jewels."

Casanova's eyes were filled with pity. "Don't you recognize this, Lorenzo?" he asked softly.

I stared at the large clear teardrop. "No. What's so important about it?"

My friend sighed. "You must have been paying all your attention to the wearer, not the jewel. She was wearing it the night we went to the ball at the Redoutensaal."

My ordeal with Urbanek must have affected my brain somehow, because all I could do was stare at the earring. I had no idea what Casanova was talking about. "Who was?" I finally asked.

"Your lady, Lorenzo. Miss Cavalli."

Thirty-nine

"No, there must be some other explanation," I stammered as I took the earring from Casanova's palm. "It is a common design. Many women in Vienna must own a pair. Someone lost it last fall. I'm sure of it."

Casanova picked up the brooch the constable had shown Benda and me at the Belvedere that awful morning. "Look, Lorenzo. This brooch is covered with dirt. The earring is clean. It was lost recently." He sighed and took the earring from me. "I know my jewels. This is not from a common pair. It is expensive, made to order for a wealthy lady."

I said nothing. My thoughts were in a muddle. Casanova took the leather pouch and started to put the items in the pile back into it. "What are you doing?" I asked.

"Let me take the bag, my friend. I'll throw it in the river. Let us agree that Felix Urbanek killed von Gerl."

I shook my head. "But—"

Casanova held up his hand. "Yes, I know. No Dante

excerpts were sent to von Gerl. Very well. There's a simple explanation for that—they were in the palace somewhere. You weren't able to find them, that is all."

"But Urbanek didn't seem to know who I was talking about when I mentioned von Gerl," I said.

Casanova was silent. He rolled the earring back and forth between his large fingers. "Why would Marta kill von Gerl?" he asked.

A sudden weariness swept over me. "He seduced her back in Venice. She believed they were married, so she traveled here to be with him. He rejected her."

Casanova exhaled loudly. We sat quietly for a moment. My stomach churned.

"But how would Marta know to carve the forehead?" he asked. He set the earring on the desk in front of him. "Did you tell her anything about the previous murders?"

"No, not until after von Gerl was killed. But she's been about in the city. Rumors are everywhere. She could easily have heard that the killer was carving the foreheads."

Casanova put the last items into the pouch and drew the string closed. He placed it gently on the desk next to the earring. "What will you do?" he asked.

"I don't know."

He stood. "Listen to me, Lorenzo. Don't be a fool. It is obvious that you love this woman."

I opened my mouth to speak, but my friend continued.

"How old are you?" he asked.

"Thirty-nine last month," I answered.

"Learn from my experience, my friend. A man's attractiveness to women begins to fade as he ages. I am loath to admit it, and I confide in you only because you are one of my dearest friends. It happened to me just when I was your age. Suddenly the young beauties no longer responded to my charms." He drew on his cloak. "Urbanek is dead, Lorenzo. He is facing God's judgment now. It matters little whether he killed four men or five. Take my advice. Seize your chance for happiness."

Forty

After Casanova left I sat at my desk for what seemed like hours.

Marta had murdered von Gerl. She had been distraught about his rejection of her. She had heard rumors about the killings, and had somehow lured him out to Christiane Albrechts's summer palace. What better place to kill her former lover? She knew Christiane's household had not yet moved out to the palace, and that the grounds would be empty. What message had she sent von Gerl to summon him to the gardens that balmy night?

Now that I thought about it, it was probable that she had considered killing him all along, even before she left Venice, when it was apparent that he would not send for her. She must have taken a dagger from her uncle's collection and carried it with her. I lifted my head. She had certainly played me for a fool. Sensing my attraction to her, she had pretended to return my feelings, made love with me—no, I should admit it, whored with me—to deflect attention from her own motives for von Gerl's murder. Her tears when she told me she felt abandoned, her happiness the night we attended the theater together, her cries of passion during our lovemaking—all had been an act.

I reached over and picked up the earring. Casanova was right. I had been so wrapped up in Marta—in her silken, gold-flecked hair; her soft green eyes; her full lips—that I had never really looked at the jewels Christiane had loaned her. To me, her beauty needed no adornment. A pang of longing stabbed me. Despite what I now thought about her, I still wanted to rush back to my lodgings, take her in my arms, and make love to her again.

I tossed the jewel on the desk. Maybe I should heed Casanova's advice. After all, perhaps Marta had felt herself justified in killing von Gerl. He had seduced her, made promises to her, and then thrown her away. I was not a woman. I had no idea how desperate she may have felt. I should just return the earring to the pouch and let everything be.

I buried my head in my hands. I did not know what to do. Should I confront her with the earring? Or should I lie to myself and convince myself that Urbanek killed von Gerl? The horrible memory of Alois's mutilated body lying at the base of the Capistran Chancel filled my mind. I had found my friend's killer. His soul could now rest in peace. But what about von Gerl's soul? Shouldn't his true killer be punished? And what about my own peace of mind? Could I go home to Marta, make love to her, and live with her the rest of my life, knowing she was a murderer?

Forty-one

I found Marta sitting on the garden bench. She jumped up when she saw me.

"Lorenzo! What happened to you? Your neck—you look terrible!" She gingerly reached out to touch the bandages.

I brushed her hand away. "Where were you the night von Gerl was murdered, Marta?" I asked.

Her eyes widened as she hesitated. "I don't remember, Lorenzo. Is it important?"

"Think. You spent the day with Christiane Albrechts. Benda told me you had left the palais before he arrived home at six. But when I knocked on your door at eight, you were not here."

She sat back down on the bench.

"Why are you asking me this, Lorenzo?"

"Please, Marta. Answer me."

She chewed on her lip and looked away from me. "I

heard you knock," she said in a small voice. "I just didn't wish to speak to you that night."

I sat down next to her and grabbed her arm.

"Where were you?"

She jerked away from my grasp. "I just told you! I was in bed, asleep." She rubbed her arm. "You hurt me, Lorenzo."

"Don't lie to me," I said.

"I don't understand!" she cried. "What is this all about?" She peered into my face. "Why are you looking at me like that? What is it you think I have done?"

"Were you with von Gerl?"

"No!"

I remembered what had seemed odd about von Gerl's body when Benda and I examined it. Only the top button of his breeches had been fastened.

Jealousy surged through me. "You were at the Belvedere with him, weren't you?"

"No! I don't know what you are talking about! What is the Belvedere?"

"The Albrechts summer palace. You must know of it. Surely in your conversations with Christiane she mentioned it to you. The household has been preparing to move out there." I stared into her frightened eyes. "You were with von Gerl in the gardens, making love to him, weren't you?"

She rose to her feet. "I don't know what you are talking about, Lorenzo," she said. "You are mad!"

My voice turned to ice. "Did you moan with pleasure at his touch the same way you did with me? Tell me!"

She turned away from me, buried her face in her hands,

and wept. "No, no! You don't understand! You have everything wrong."

I pulled the earring from my coat pocket. "Look at this, Marta! It was found near von Gerl's body. Tell me how it got there!"

She raised her head and stared at the earring. She shook her head violently. "No, no! You cannot think—no, how can you think that? I swear to you, Lorenzo! I didn't see Valentin that night. I swear!"

"I don't believe you. You are hiding something from me."

Her body crumpled onto the bench. "I was not with Valentin that night," she murmured. "But I had planned to be."

"What do you mean?"

She sighed. "The night you and I went to the theater— the night before Valentin was killed—he had sent me a message that afternoon. He wanted to see me again. He apologized for ignoring me. He told me he wished to make amends for his behavior and resume our relationship." Her voice faltered. "He asked me to come to his palace the next night. He said he wanted to make love to me again."

I sat silently.

"I went to Christiane's the next day. When I returned here, I washed and changed my clothes, then took a cab to Valentin's house. I arrived a little after seven. That beast Teuber let me in. He told me Valentin was dressing, and had asked me to wait in the library for him. Teuber took me there. I waited for almost an hour. Finally, when I had had enough, I went to the door to call for Teuber, to demand that he take me to Valentin's chamber. But the door had been locked, the key taken away."

She twisted her hands together in her lap. "I waited there for hours, but Valentin never came. It was obvious that he was playing with me, that he never intended to resume our marriage. He had summoned me there to humiliate me once again. I cried myself to sleep on the sofa. I don't know how long I slept. Later, Teuber came and shook me awake. He told me his master would not be able to see me. He took me downstairs and called a cab for me."

"What time was it?" I asked in a strangled voice.

"Very late. I heard the clock in the dining room strike as I was leaving. It was one o'clock."

My heart was numb.

She looked up at me. "You think I murdered Valentin, don't you, Lorenzo? How can you think that? It shows how little you know of me. I loved him. He was the only man I ever truly loved."

My mouth was dry. I said nothing. Finally, I held out the earring. "But how do you explain this? How did it get to the Belvedere if you were locked in von Gerl's library, as you say?"

She stared at the jewel. "I don't know. But I swear to you, I did not kill Valentin. And I no longer had the earrings that night, anyway. I returned them to Christiane when I went to dinner that afternoon."

Forty-two

I tossed and turned in my lonely bed most of the night, my mind turning over possibilities and theories, working to avoid dwelling on Marta's confession that she still loved von Gerl. I must have slept a bit, for when I awoke, mid-morning light was streaming through my window. I groaned at the thought of the encounter ahead of me.

I washed and dressed, then took my cloak and satchel and left the house. My landlady was in the garden, tending the beds. She looked up when she saw me. "Good morning, signore," she called.

I waved at her and turned to go out into the street. She rose from her work and hurried after me. "Is everything all right, signore?" she asked, catching my arm.

"What do you mean, Madame Lamm? I am just in a hurry to get to work," I lied.

She flushed. "I know it should not be my concern, signore, but Miss Cavalli was down in the kitchen for breakfast an hour ago. She asked me to send a boy to inquire about the coach to Trieste. She told me she has decided to return to Venice."

She paused, waiting for my response. I said nothing.

"She's upstairs now, signore, packing her things."

I hesitated for a moment and then set my jaw. "I must go into the city, madame," I said. "Would you do something for me while I am gone?"

She nodded.

"Please, if you could, try to stall Miss Cavalli's departure. I must speak to her, but there is something I must do first."

My landlady's eyes gleamed. "I'll do my best, signore."

"Thank you, Madame Lamm! Do not let her leave!" I hurried out of the courtyard and into the street.

The courtyard of the Palais Albrechts was deserted. I hammered on the door. A minute later, the steward opened the door.

"Signor Da Ponte?" he said. "Can I help you? Count Benda is not at home."

"I must speak with your mistress right away," I said. I pushed by him and stepped into the foyer.

"Please, signore," the steward said. "My mistress is very ill. I am sorry, but I cannot allow you to bother her."

A faint voice floated down the stairs. "Who is it, Altmann?"

I glanced at the steward, then bounded up the stairs and turned into the salon. Christiane, her skin gray as ash, her cheeks hollow, huddled in the large armchair.

"Oh, Signor Da Ponte," she said. "It is you. Are you looking for Richard? He has not yet returned from his estate in Bohemia."

"I am here to speak with you, mademoiselle," I said.

The steward bustled in. "Shall I remove this man, mademoiselle?" he asked.

She looked from him to me, and took a deep breath. "No. I will speak with Signor Da Ponte. Please leave us and shut the door."

The steward frowned at me as he left us.

"Please, signore. Come sit down."

I took a seat on the sofa, my back to the door. "You must know why I am here," I said.

She sat in silence, staring down at her hands. Across from me, the large clock ticked loudly.

"Yes," she finally said.

I handed her the earring.

"Where did you find it? Near his body?" she asked.

I nodded. "Yes, in the nearby *bosquet*."

Her hands trembled. "I sent a message to Valentin that morning," she said. Her voice was so low I had to lean forward to hear. "I told him that I was anxious to see him, to finish what had been interrupted the night my father was murdered."

"Mademoiselle—"

She held up her hand. "Please, let me tell you. I cannot keep it to myself any longer." She took a deep breath. "I asked him to meet me at the summer estate, in the garden, at eight that evening. I ordered the servants to tell Richard that I was ill and did not wish to be disturbed. I went to my room and put on a simple dress. Marta had returned my earrings that afternoon. I put them on. I was so tired of wearing this drab mourning garb."

She swallowed. "After Richard had come home and then gone out again, I made sure the servants were not about. I left the house, went to the stables, and saddled my riding horse."

The clopping of horses' hooves sounded in the courtyard below. Christiane paid them no attention. She stared down at a spot at the edge of the chair and continued.

"I arrived at the Belvedere a half hour before I expected Valentin. There is only one staff member out there now, the watchman. I've known him all my life, enough to know that he is overly fond of drink. While he was walking about the buildings making his rounds, I went to the wine cellar, took a bottle of apricot brandy, and brought it over to the watch house."

I heard voices in the courtyard. The salon had grown warm. Sweat trickled down my side. The clock ticked.

"Valentin arrived just as it was getting dark." She stood and went to the window, her back to me. "I met him at the door to the lower palace and led him out to the gardens. We went into the *bosquet*. He began to kiss me. I must have lost the earring then."

I stared at her back. She lifted her head and straightened her slim shoulders. Her voice rose. "I pulled him out of the *bosquet* and over to the statue. He undressed me."

A soft click sounded at the door behind me. My eyes remained transfixed on Christiane's back.

"When we had finished, he fell asleep. I had hidden my

father's hunting dagger behind the shrubs near the statue. I cut his throat while he slept. Then I carved the letter into his forehead, so it would appear that my father's killer had attacked again."

I must have gasped involuntarily, for she hesitated for a moment.

"I took my clothes and the dagger into the house," she continued. "I washed and dressed, then buried the dagger in the garden scrap heap. I rode home. Richard was still out. No one saw me come in and return to my room."

"But why did you kill him?" I asked. "Because he raped you?"

She turned around and looked at me, her violet eyes wide. She gave a short, mirthless laugh. "No, no. He didn't rape me. I let him do what he wanted to me. I even begged him at times."

"I don't understand."

"Of course you don't. You are a man. You all think we women are no more than vessels for your desire—that we have no yearnings of our own." She sank back into the chair. "Ever since Valentin arrived back in Vienna, I have wanted him. I've been obsessed with him since the day we met. I tried so hard to banish him from my thoughts, but I could not. When Richard kissed me, I imagined Valentin's lips on mine. I wanted to know what it was like to be with him."

A groan came from near the door.

"I still don't understand," I said. "Why did you kill him?"

"Don't you see?" she cried. "I couldn't have him there, next door, while I lived here as Richard's wife. I knew I wouldn't be able to see Valentin all the time and not long to touch him, to have him touch me. But I love Richard. He will be my husband. He is such a good man. He foolishly believes that I am as good as he. I must make him happy. But as long as Valentin was alive, I knew I could not."

She buried her face in her hands. I sat rooted to my chair, shocked.

"But now I realize I was wrong," she said, raising her pale face to me. "We can never be happy, Richard and I." She stared with loathing at her quivering hands. "Look at me. I am dying. It is what I deserve."

"No! No!" I started as Benda rushed from his place by the door and fell at her feet. She leaned forward and put her arms around him. He clutched her skirts. Together they began to weep.

Forty-three

I closed the door behind me and hurried down the stairs, through the courtyard, and into the Freyung. There were no cabs about. I cut behind the palais and ran down the Herrengasse toward the Michaelerplatz. The large plaza was filled with people strolling in the fine morning. I pushed my way through a crowd of chatting soldiers and hurried past the theater door. Ahead of me I saw a driver leaning against the door of a cab outside St. Michael's Church. I waved at him and started toward it.

"Da Ponte!" A voice called from behind me. It was Salieri. I stopped and turned.

"Where are you scurrying to?" he asked.

"I must get home," I said, gasping.

"What is wrong with you?" Salieri gestured toward the theater. "Come inside. I'd like to discuss an idea for a new opera. It just came to me as my friseur was powdering my wig this morning."

I shook my head, trying to catch my breath. "I cannot, signore. I must get home right away. It is an emergency. Please, can we speak about this tomorrow?"

He stared at me, confusion in his eyes. "Yes, well, I suppose so. Come by at—"

But I did not stay to hear his words. "Thank you, signore!" I called as I rushed toward the cab. A finely dressed merchant waddled toward it from the direction of the pastry shop. I quickened my pace, shouted my address to the driver, and jumped into the cab. He clambered up to his seat. "Please hurry!" I shouted from the window. As the vehicle lurched forward, I saw the startled expression of the merchant. I sat back and tried to steady my breathing, and then prayed that I would arrive at my lodgings before it was too late.

The cab wended through the archway, around the back of the Spanish Riding School stables, and into the thick crowds in the Neuer Market, where cooks from nearby houses sampled the vendors' wares. I turned my head away from the sight of the fountain where I had almost lost my life. A moment later, we entered the Himmelpfortgasse. I sat back in the seat and closed my eyes. Please, God, do not let her leave, I prayed.

I held on to the seat with both hands as the driver made a rapid left turn toward the Stuben gate. A moment later the cab halted. I poked my head through the window. "What is it?" I shouted to the driver.

"They're moving some cannon through the gate, sir," he called back. "It looks like we'll be stuck here for a while."

I dug in my coat pocket for some coins and jumped out of the cab. "I'll walk," I said. I tossed the coins to the driver. "As you wish, sir," he said.

Ahead of me, teams of oxen were pulling wide, long carts through the city gate. I ran over and looked through. There was a two-foot-wide space between the edge of the cart and the stones of the gatehouse. A guard approached. "You'll have to wait, sir," he said. "No one can go through until the last cart comes in."

I hurled myself into the narrow space. "Wait!" the guard called. I bolted through the gate. I pounded over the wooden span and the pathway, and then over the river bridge and down the street. When I reached the corner near my lodgings, I stopped and bent over, resting my hands on my knees, gasping for breath. I looked down the street to the house. I exhaled. She was there.

Forty-four

She was dressed as she had been the first time I laid eyes upon her, in her simple traveling cloak, her soft hair neatly tucked up inside her little hat. Her valise sat at her feet.

She looked up as I approached.

"Oh, Lorenzo, I am glad you are here," she said. "I did not want to leave without saying good-bye."

"Where are you going?" I asked.

"I'm taking the mail coach to Trieste. When I reach there, I'll send word to my uncle. I hope he will send me funds to return to Venice."

"And what will you do there? Return to your uncle's house?"

"No. I will join one of the convents. I think that would be best."

I took her hand. She did not pull it away. "Marta, please," I begged. "Everything I said—I am so sorry. Please stay with me."

She looked into my eyes. "Oh, Lorenzo, I cannot."

"But why not?"

She chewed on her lip. "I was lying to myself, Lorenzo, when I decided that I no longer cared for Valentin. Although he betrayed me and deserted me, I still felt something for him."

"But—"

"Pity? Love? I don't know." She looked away. "Even now, when he is dead, he still is in my heart."

A wave of weariness washed over me.

"I must go home," she said.

"Then let me come with you. Please, I need you."

She placed a finger on my lips. "Hush, Lorenzo. You know you cannot return."

"I'll do anything—I'll talk to Casanova, see if he can give me an introduction to someone in the government. I'll do anything they ask of me. I'll become a spy."

"No, Lorenzo, I cannot let you do that. You are a good man. I cannot let you go against everything you believe in for me."

A cab turned into the street.

"But I love you."

She shook her head. "I am sorry, Lorenzo. I cannot stay."

The cab pulled up and the driver descended. He tipped his cap. Marta pointed to her valise. He opened the door and placed it inside, then held the door open for her.

"You would spend your life chanting faint hymns to the cold fruitless moon?" I asked, grasping her hand.

She smiled ruefully, pulled her hand from mine, and then reached up and touched her dry lips to my cheek. She turned to the driver. He helped her up into the cab and closed the door. He climbed up to his seat and shouted to the horse. The cab pulled away. It turned and made its way slowly down the street and around the corner.

I stood looking after it, my heart flooded with misery, abandoned.

Epilogue

The audience sat quietly as a loud banging sounded at the door at the back of the stage. Francesco Albertarelli, playing the role of Don Giovanni, threw the door open, while Benucci, as the manservant, huddled under a table. Francesco Bussani, dressed as a statue of the old man Giovanni had killed at the beginning of the opera, slowly made his entrance.

"'Don Giovanni,'" he sang. "'You invited me to dine with you. I have come.'"

The intrepid libertine nodded a welcome, and ordered his servant to fetch another plate for the stone guest. Unearthly trombones accompanied Bussani as he explained in his deep bass voice that having dined at the table of heaven, he had no need for mortal food.

I sat alone in the box reserved for the composer and librettist. This was the fourth performance of *Don Giovanni*. Mozart had begged off attending tonight, citing a lodge meeting. The opera had not been received as enthusiastically as he and I had hoped. Although the applause at each performance had been polite, I had already heard mutterings around the city that the music was too complex for the singers. But I was determined to ensure that our work be heard often, so that audiences would become accustomed to it, and I was pleased that more performances were scheduled for the upcoming weeks.

My life had slowly returned to normal over the last two weeks. A few days after I had had my terrifying encounter with Urbanek, I had reported all my findings to Troger. A few days later, I had received a note from him, informing me that Benda and Christiane had left Vienna for the count's estates in Bohemia. Christiane was very ill and not expected to recover, so Pergen had decided not to charge her with the murder of Valentin von Gerl.

The emperor and his troops remained outside Belgrade, waiting to invade. Michael Richter continued to protest the war. Just this afternoon I had noticed that he had moved his crate into the Michaelerplatz, where he could shout his opinions directly into the windows of the Hofburg.

At my lodging house, Strasser was cool toward me. Last week I had invited him out for a glass of wine, hoping to make amends for my suspicions, but had been rebuffed. Sophie and Stefan had announced their engagement a few days ago, much to the relief of Madame Lamm. Here at the theater, I had thrown myself into my next project, *Il talismano,* a libretto for Salieri. Yet all the hours of work could not assuage my yearnings for Marta. Although I tried to turn my thoughts away from her, she often crept into my mind, and I was left wondering where she was and what she was doing.

Down on the stage, the stone guest had invited Don Giovanni to come dine with him, and had offered the libertine his cold marble hand. As he demanded that Giovanni repent for his sins, I slipped from the box. I had had enough applause over the last three performances, and could do without it tonight.

A tall figure loitered in the almost empty lobby. I approached him.

"Ah, Lorenzo, I hoped you would be here," Casanova said as he embraced me. "I wanted to say good-bye. I'm headed back to Dux tomorrow at first light. I don't know why the count cannot wait until a more civilized hour." He peered into my face. "How are you?"

"I suppose I'm all right," I said.

"Come for one last drink."

I shook my head. "I should go home. I've been working too hard the last few weeks. I'm tired."

He stood looking down at me, concern on his face.

"You've been through an ordeal, my friend," he said. "But trust me, things will be better. And in the meantime, you can find solace in knowing that you've avenged Alois's death. He will rest in peace now."

I nodded. "Yes, I know that." But I felt no satisfaction.

"Have you had any word from Miss Cavalli?" he asked.

"No."

Inside the theater, the audience began to applaud.

Casanova pulled on his cloak. "There will be another woman for you," he said.

"I want that one."

We moved outside as the crowds poured out of the theater. Casanova gave me a final embrace. "I hope we will meet again soon," he said. "Perhaps in Venice!"

"Perhaps," I said, although I knew it wasn't likely.

Casanova turned and walked toward the Herrengasse. I followed the throng down the Kohlmarkt into the Graben. The night was warm, and people were standing about the large plaza chatting gaily with friends, as they used to do before the war started. I cut through the Stephansplatz. As I passed by the north side of the Stephansdom, I forced myself to look at the spot where Alois had died. I missed him so much. And I longed for Marta.

I took a short street down to the Wollzeile, and joined the crowd of people headed toward the Stuben gate. Perhaps Casanova was right. Life would be better. Soon I might look back at my experiences and feel content. But for now, I just felt numb and empty, all alone in a dark place.

AUTHOR'S NOTE

By 1788, when *Don Giovanni* premiered in Vienna, Emperor Joseph II and his supporters had grown disillusioned with the results of his aggressive program of enlightened reform. They had believed that allowing a free press, breaking down class barriers, modernizing education, and eliminating medieval superstitions from religious practice would create a new kind of society, one in which reasoned debate was the common currency and in which individuals took action only after considering the public good. Instead, a materialistic culture arose, in which everyone pursued their own interests and desires.

Joseph reacted to this turn of events by reasserting his autocratic authority. He reinstated censorship of the press and revoked many of his reforms. As dissent and unrest continued to grow both in Austria and its far-flung territories, he created a secret police force to protect the state from threats.

Into this political setting came Mozart and Da Ponte's *Don Giovanni*, full of ambiguities about morality, judgment, religion, and societal control of the individual. Is Giovanni a hero or villain? After he accepts the stone guest's invitation, the rest of the cast sings that those who do evil always come to an evil end. But what exactly are the crimes he has committed? Opera lovers, writers, and analysts are still debating these questions today.

The embodiment of the libertine in the eighteenth century was Giacomo Casanova—writer, adventurer, entrepreneur, spy—who was famous throughout Europe for his escape from the prison in the doge's palace in Venice in 1756. He became friends with Lorenzo Da Ponte in 1777, when the two met at the Venetian home of Count Pietro Zaguri, for whom Da Ponte worked as secretary. The two men corresponded with one another and met several times during their twenty-one-year friendship.

My decision to use Casanova as Da Ponte's confidant in this book was prompted by a historical mystery surrounding him and the composition of *Don Giovanni*. In the early twentieth century, draft verses of a replacement scene for the opera were found among Casanova's papers in Dux. It is not known whether he wrote the scene for his own amusement, or at Mozart's request (Da Ponte having been recalled to Vienna before the Prague premiere). In fact, we do not know if Casanova was even acquainted with Mozart. But many scholars believe that he attended at least one of the performances of *Don Giovanni* in Prague in the fall of 1787. He was not, however, present in Vienna in the spring of 1788; I placed him there for my own purposes.

As Da Ponte mentions in the epilogue, *Don Giovanni* enjoyed a modest success in Vienna. It was repeated fourteen times during 1788, and then was not produced there again in its original Italian until 1798. It became popular among writers in the nineteenth century, who seized upon the don as a romantic hero rebelling against an oppressive society. Today, of course, it is a staple of theaters around the world, most of which perform a pastiche of the Prague and Vienna versions, including *both* tenor arias and the *scena* Da Ponte and Mozart created for Caterina Cavalieri. The burlesque scene Da Ponte and Mozart wrote for Vienna is seldom performed today, but can be found on some recordings, most notably John Eliot Gardiner's 1994 Archiv production.

Many of the settings in the novel may be visited by a traveler to Vienna. Ludwig Dehne's pastry shop continued in business on the Michaelerplatz until 1857, when the founder's grandson sold it to his assistant, Christoph Demel, who changed the name of the shop to his own. In 1888, when the court theater was torn down, his sons moved the shop around the corner to the Kohlmarkt, where it remains today as a popular destination for tourists and locals.

The Belvedere palaces were built for Prince Eugene of Savoy, the great military hero of the war against the Turks in 1683. Empress Maria Theresa acquired the property from his heirs in 1752. In 1781, the palaces were used to house the Imperial Picture Gallery, which was open to the public, as were the expansive gardens. Both palaces remain art museums today; the upper palace contains the world's largest collection of paintings by Gustav Klimt.

The Habsburg imperial crypt in the Capuchin Church on the Neuer Market has been expanded substantially since the eighteenth century. The crypt contains both beautiful and spooky examples of funerary art. Joseph II's tomb there says more about his character than any biography—a simple casket resting at the foot of the grandiose monument his mother, Maria Theresa, had ordered designed for herself and her husband.

Historians are not certain where Da Ponte lived while writing *Don Giovanni*. It is likely that he resided within the city walls, as he did when working on *The Marriage of Figaro*. I moved him out to the suburbs.

Mozart and Constanze, on the other hand, did live in the cramped apartment on the Tuchlauben in the spring of 1788. On June 17, they moved out to the Alsergrund suburb, where they rented a large apartment with a garden. Mozart assumed the war would be brief, and looked forward to spending the summer writing in expectation of a larger role as court composer once the emperor returned. It was here that he wrote the first of his series of letters to his fellow lodge member Michael Puchberg, asking for a large loan to defray his expenses until his fortunes improved. It was also here that baby Theresa died on June 29.

Valentin von Gerl's art collection contains several important eighteenth-century paintings, links to which can be seen at my Web site: www.lauralebowbooks.com. The watermark that plays such a large role in Da Ponte's investigation comes from a letter written by Thomas Jefferson in 1787. The document now resides at the Library of Congress. A link to it can also be found on my Web site, as can a list of sources I consulted while writing this book.

I am indebted to the following people for their guidance, encouragement, and support: my agent, John Talbot; Keith Kahla and Hannah Braaten at Minotaur Books; and Bill Lebow, my tireless champion and cheerleader.

4/16